She opened the box. Inside was an ornate pistol and kit.

"Go ahead," ola Vivar said, and went to stand by the left wing. "The rest of you, watch her carefully."

Nin poured the powder, rodded and tamped the bullet, primed the pan and cocked the piece. "And shall I—"

"You know what to do," ola Vivar said.

Nin put the case on the floor. She stood up, aimed the gun squarely at ola Vivar's chest, pulled the trigger.

The pan flared. The muzzle blazed. The pistol jerked upward. Ola Vivar's white shirt blossomed red and he was thrown backward into the dark. There was a clatter of cans and wood.

Wirrel stared. Lisel screamed. Baren tilted his head, took a step toward the wing.

Ola Vivar walked back onto the stage. His chest looked like raw ground beef. "Thank you, Nin," he said. "Perfectly done. And by you, Chitaru."

The Tichenese wizard walked on from the right wing. He snapped his fingers, and the splatter disappeared from ola Vivar's shirt.

D1571757

Tor Books by John M. Ford

Casting Fortune
The Scholars of Night

CASTING FORTUNE

JOHN M. FORD

TOR
fantasy

A TOM DOHERTY ASSOCIATES BOOK
NEW YORK

This is a work of fiction. All the characters and events portrayed in
this book are fictitious, and any resemblance to real people or events
is purely coincidental.

CASTING FORTUNE

Copyright © 1986, 1987, 1989 by John M. Ford

All rights reserved, including the right to reproduce this book or
portions thereof in any form.

A TOR Book
Published by Tom Doherty Associates, Inc.
49 West 24 Street
New York, NY 10010

Cover art by N. Taylor Blanchard

ISBN: 0-812-53815-3   Can. ISBN: 0-812-53816-1

Library of Congress Catalog Card Number: 88-51640

First edition: June 1989

Printed in the United States of America

0 9 8 7 6 5 4 3 2 1

A Cup of Worrynot Tea

THE OBJECT ON the roadside looked like a bed, as much as it looked like anything. Two young people, a dark and muscular boy and a slim fair-haired girl, were climbing over it with a sort of exhausted good will. The girl, whose everyday name was Reed, said, "It's no use at all, Kory. The spring's broken and the hub is bent."

The boy, Kory, crouched next to the wheel of the light wooden landsailer and looked across the Saltmarsh in the direction of Liavek. It was no-longer-early afternoon in late Wine, the breeze off the marsh already turning chilly, and they had been no more than halfway from Hrothvek to Liavek when a gust sent the spidery windcar off the road. If they started walking now, it would be very late when Reed got home. Very, very late. Unconscionably late.

And you were no doubt thinking—oh, *shame* on you.

A two-horse coach appeared from the south. Kory said, "Look, there's someone. Maybe they'll give you a ride to the city. I'll walk the 'sailer back."

"You'll never get it back before night."

"Then I'll tent the sail over it and sleep inside. I've done that before, hunting dawn spooks. I've got all the stuff for an overnight."

"You do, huh? You didn't tell *me* that."

"Aw, Reed—"

"And what about me? What if I don't choose to risk

my life with the first stranger to come along the Hroth-vek road?''

''*Reed,*'' Kory said desperately, and then she laughed and hugged him. ''I'd better, uh, stop that coach. Before they decide we don't want to be rescued.''

''You said it, I didn't,'' Reed said, and kissed Kory on the nose.

The coach pulled rather suddenly to a stop. It was painted a dark maroon color, with polished brasswork; well-made and well-kept without being flashy. The driver was a big man in a long coat of blue leather. Kory looked up at him and blinked. The driver's face and hands were a shade of blue only a little paler than his coat. He was bald except for a line of bushy white hair around his temples, like fur trim on a collar. ''Good day,'' he said, in an accent unlike any Kory—who had grown up on Bazaar Street—had ever heard, flat and unmusical.

The side window opened and another man leaned out. This one looked like a Liavekan, with sun-bleached hair above an ordinarily dark face with bright blue eyes; he wore a black quilted gown with a high wing collar. He was smiling.

''Are you in need of assistance?'' the passenger said, in perfectly proper Liavekan. He looked past Kory to the car on the roadside. ''Mechanical difficulties?''

''Yes, master. I'll get the car home all right, but my . . . friend must be back in Liavek before dark. We were wondering if you could—''

''I'll ride on top of the coach, sir,'' Reed said, stepping in front of Kory. She looked up at the driver, who had not moved at all. ''Or on the back will be fine,'' she said, in a less certain tone.

''There's room for both of you inside,'' the passenger said. ''And for your vehicle on top, I should think, if you and Jagg can lift it without doing it any more damage. Jagg?''

The driver looked over the landsailer and said, ''The car folds?''

"Yes," Kory said, surprised. "I built her jointed, to carry and store."

"Plenty of room, then," the driver said. He climbed down. Kory glanced at the passenger, who was looking at Reed. There was something Kory didn't like about the way the man looked at her—but he supposed he was just annoyed. If the travelers had anything bad in mind, they were going to a lot of effort for it. Kory went to the landsailer and began pulling the hingepins that held it rigid. It folded up tightly, the side spars bracketing the pedal-drive cables. Jagg began folding the linen sail expertly.

In very short order Kory and Jagg had the car folded down to a square bundle of spars and a stack of wheels. They began to lift it onto the coach roof, when another hard gust came in off the Saltmarsh. The coach rocked slightly. Kory's grip slipped.

The bundle did not fall. Kory looked through the coach window. The passenger was smiling at him. *A wizard*, Kory thought. *So what kind of luck has this been?* He got the covered bucket with his and Reed's catch and handed it up to Jagg. "Please see that doesn't turn over," he said, and Jagg fastened a strap over it.

The coach got under way. Kory and Reed sat on red cloth cushions, facing the light-haired wizard. He seemed to be in early middle age, whatever that meant. "My name is Ciellon," he said. "My friend is called Jagg."

"Is he a Farlander?" Reed said.

"From a far land, yes. And whom have I rescued from the Saltmarsh?"

"I'm Korik Li. I'm . . . I trade and transport. People call me Kory."

"I am Cadie ais Ariom, called Reed. My father is Dyelam ais Ariom, of the Liavek Society of Merchants, and the Levar's Council."

"Korik Free-Fortune and Ariom's White Heron," Ciellon said. "Kory and Reed. Happy to meet you both." He paused, then said, "Ais Ariom is a Hrothvekan name. But you are both Liavekan?"

"Kory is," Reed said. "I was born in Hrothvek, but we moved to the great city when I was four. My father's trading business was prospering, and he needed to be near the centers of commerce."

And society and politics, Kory thought without saying.

Ciellon nodded. "I know your father's name, though I regret I do not know the man himself. I am Hrothvekan by birth as well, you see, but that was—oh, a long time ago."

After a brief silence, Reed said, "Have you returned for the celebration, then? The End of Wine?"

Ciellon said nothing for a moment, as if considering his answer. "Yes. I have come for the End of Wine." He reached inside his black tunic, took out a small silver flask, sipped from it. "Forgive me, an indulgence. I have juice of apples and apricots if you are thirsty, and I think a little cold milk left."

Reed accepted a glass cup of apple juice. Kory said, "I'm not thirsty, thank you," which was not true.

Ciellon poured himself a cup of apricot nectar, adding to it a little golden liquid from his flask. "May I ask why you were on the road? Visiting friends in Hrothvek?"

"We were hunting marsh crabs," Kory said. "The small ones, with the red patterning, called clawfires. I . . . trade in them, with Thomorin Wiln the apothecary."

Ciellon nodded. "Is it profitable?" he said, in the tone of any serious business discussion.

Kory relaxed a little. "Worth one day a week," he said casually. "It really depends on the size of the crabs, you see. Thomorin Wiln uses a small fluid sac from inside the crab, and the rest goes for animal fodder— or to a couple of inns in Old Town, which I can name for you."

Ciellon laughed. "My arrangements are made, thank you. So the apothecary pays more for big crabs, then?"

"That's what you'd think," Kory said, pleased with the question, "but it's just the other way around. He wants them tiny. He's said that if I can find one no bigger than my thumb, he'll pay me . . ." Kory thought, then doubled the figure for effect, ". . . half a levar."

"Extraordinary," Ciellon said. "But why is this?"

"I believe," Kory said, and gave his best guess, "the fluid in the sacs becomes less potent as the crab grows."

"That is logical," Ciellon said, nodding. "Though it is also a possibility that what the apothecary desires is not the fluid but the sac itself, and the skin of the sac must not be too stretched."

Kory felt himself flush. Reed grinned. Kory said, "Excuse me, sir. I did not know you were an apothecary."

"Excuse me for embarrassing you," Ciellon said. "And I am not an apothecary . . . though I do require the services of one. Do you recommend this Thomorin Wiln?" He added gently, "In your informed opinion."

"Very highly, sir. He does business on his boat, *The Vessel of Dreams*, which is anchored at Canalgate. I'd be pleased to introduce you."

"That would be most satisfactory!" Ciellon said. "It is true what they say, that a kindness is always returned with profit." He pointed out the window. "And look, you can see the city wall already." He took another sip from his silver flask, then put it away. "I am staying at the Sea Eagle; we'll be passing it very shortly. Would you have a cup of tea with me before going on?" Ciellon looked at Reed, and once again Kory found something to dislike in the wizard's expression.

Reed said, "I am expected at home."

"By dark, you said, and there's plenty of light left. And look, you're both all over salt and sand; you'll look better for homegoing after some water and a towel.

And you will have tea?'' Kory was not sure it was a
question.

"Yes, certainly we will, sir," Reed said finally, and
Ciellon nodded. Kory noted something in Ciellon's look
like . . . well, disappointment, though that made no
sense.

The Sea Eagle Inn was built on the seashore at the
farthest southwestern reach of Liavek, beyond Minnow
Island in the quarter sometimes called "Nearer Hrothvek," almost against the city wall. Despite its location,
it was not a new inn but a very old one, with an ancient
reputation as a smugglers' landing and place of unre-
fined pleasure. Then the city had rolled, like an incom-
ing tide of respectability, up to its doorstep; now the
Sea Eagle was considered a Quite Proper Place with a
Colorful Past.

The innkeeper, a former captain named Zal najhi Zal
who still shaved the right side of her head, came out
on the portico to meet the coach. Kory saw her stiffen
at the sight of Jagg helping Ciellon to the ground. Her
lips moved in the First Prayer to Bree Amal, Goddess
of Keepers of Disorderly Houses: *May These Events
Not Involve Thy Servant.* Kory looked at the blue-gray
driver and knew what the innkeeper was thinking: her
guest really was ridden by a troll.

Ciellon leaned on a black-ash walking stick and said,
"Blessings on this house you keep, my friend. I am
Ciellon; you received my message?"

"Of course, master. The room you requested is
ready."

"With a view of the Saltmarsh? I do insist on that."

"A splendid view, master, from the topmost floor."

Ciellon leaned heavily on his stick. "Everything has
its price, I suppose. No matter."

"Your baggage, master . . . and your message mentioned only two persons—there *is* a surcharge—"

"My man will carry the baggage." Kory thought he
heard the hint of a threat in that. "And my friends are

pausing only briefly. You will, please, have hot water sent up? And tea, for four.''

"The Sea Eagle," the innkeeper said with formal pride, "has hot water in all rooms, heated by the sun in our roof cisterns, which also provide safety from fire."

"Lovely idea," Ciellon said, smiling.

"And the master's tea . . . what blend would be preferred?"

Ciellon said innocently, "Do you have Worrynot?"

Zal blinked, startled at the sudden mention of the contraceptive leaf. Kory chuckled to himself. It was not the sort of thing that ought to startle an innkeeper. "Why, of *course*, master . . . but the *tea* . . .''

"Just what I meant," Ciellon said. "No matter. We'll take Tichenese Gunpowder. Unless you've got Prince Fyun's Folly.''

"I'll . . . see, master."

"Good, good." Ciellon turned to Kory and Reed. "Shall we?" As they went up the stairs, Kory noticed that Ciellon bore down on his cane as if an enormous weight rode his shoulders.

Whatever sorts of things were in the wizard's mind, Kory thought as Ciellon poured tea, he had been right about washing up. He and Reed looked a hundred times more presentable now, as if they had just been feeding doves in the Levar's Park. Not, of course, that Reed's father would believe that. Dyelam ais Ariom seemed to suspect Kory of everything short of treason with his daughter. More than once Kory had wanted to demand that ais Ariom accuse him directly—though if he proved his case to the merchant, what would he do? Challenge ais Ariom to a duel over Kory's wounded honor? Not very likely. He sometimes wished that Reed had some other suitor. One chosen by her father, one that Reed detested, and she wept on Kory's shoulder for horror of marrying. One he *could* challenge, and settle things once and for—

"I was just thinking," Ciellon said, pouring more

tea into Kory's cup, "how admirable was your concern for your friend, there on the marsh. It would have been a cold night for Wine, and very lonely."

"I . . ." Kory said, "that is, we . . ." He wondered if the wizard had been reading his mind.

Reed said, "We met when Kory was employed as a courier for important documents. My father has a great deal of respect for Kory. He himself started as a small trader." She took Kory's hand.

Ciellon said, "And therefore he understands how difficult it is to be a successful solitary small businessman." He sat back, holding his teacup in both hands. "It is bad enough to fear failure when one has only oneself to suffer for it. But to bind one's failure to another—that is difficult. And to see it happen to one you feel love and responsibility toward—that is sheer torture."

Reed said, "Do you have a wife, Master Ciellon?"

"I—" Ciellon stopped, smiled faintly. "No. I just talk too much." He set down his cup. "Now, I think, I should send you on your way. Jagg?"

The bulky blue man was standing against the door, cup and saucer looking absurdly fragile in his hands. "Master?"

"Hire a pony-trap and take the Lady ais Ariom home. Then, Master Li, if you will guide Jagg to *The Vessel of Dreams*, I shall be indebted."

Kory said, "The master will not meet with Thomorin Wiln . . . ?"

Ciellon said, "Jagg knows what to ask for. I am certain that Thomorin Wiln will have no difficulty. Oh." He reached inside his quilted black gown, held out his hand again, and pressed a coin into Kory's palm. "For your recommendation." Kory knew the coin by touch, but checked it with a glance anyway; his fingers closed over a silver half-levar.

"A pleasure," Kory said, and then almost started giggling, "doing business with you, master."

"Not at all." Ciellon stood up slowly and went to

stand by the room's large window, which gave a truly excellent view of the Saltmarsh stretching out of sight to the southwest.

"If there is anything else . . . I happen to know that Thomorin Wiln can provide a much finer grade of Worrynot leaf than any . . . other establishment in the city."

"*Kory,*" Reed said.

Ciellon turned from the window. "I thank you, Master Trader, but that was just a small joke. Mistress Reed, did your mother never speak to you of Worrynot tea?"

"Sir? No, sir. I have never heard of it. The tea, I mean."

"But you are Hrothvekan."

"My natural mother was, Master Ciellon, but she died when I was five, soon after we came to the city. My stepmother is Liavekan."

"Ah. I am sorry. Truly sorry. Please forgive my lapse of tact, and taste."

"Of course, master," Reed said, puzzled.

Ciellon said, "I have one last request of both of you. I hope it does not seem . . . odd."

Kory tensed. Jagg was still barring the door; no way past *him*. Through the window it was four floors to the beach.

The wizard said quietly, "I would rather that my presence in Liavek not be made known for a little while. I don't expect anyone to ask you, and I don't ask you to lie; only not to speak. Will you agree to this?"

Kory said, "Of course, master."

Reed said, "Why, sir, if you are here for the End of Wine?" and Kory's heart skipped three beats.

Ciellon said, "That's a reasonable question, my lady. The most reasonable answer I can give is that I am an acquaintance of His Scarlet Eminence the Regent of Liavek, and I do not wish politics to complicate my visit to this most beautiful of cities, at least not yet. Do you understand?"

"Of course, sir," Reed said. "I will tell no one. If you will have your man take me to the apothecary's as

well, then Kory can take me home, and there will be
no need to explain your man's presence."

Ciellon laughed. "How can any businessman fail,
with such a reason to succeed? Good day to both of
you now, and please call upon me again if I may be of
help."

The Vessel of Dreams had its anchorage in the hazy
region between the raucous Old Docks, the even older
but newly fashionable Canal District, and the south end
of Wizard's Row, when Wizard's Row decided to be
there. The *Vessel* was a flatboat with a catamaran hull;
the hulls were snow-white, coated with something that
barnacles and worms couldn't bear the taste of, and the
superstructure was dark blue with a spangling of stars
on the deck and the roof. Its masts were removable,
and stayed in storage except for two months of the year,
when Thomorin Wiln took *The Vessel of Dreams* out
onto the Sea of Luck, to trade in faraway ports and fish
in strange waters.

The trap pulled to a stop before the *Vessel*'s gangway,
less than a bowshot from the posts of Canalgate. Kory
and Reed jumped down from the back of the cart as
Jagg hitched the horse to a post. Jagg wore gloves and
a raised hood, which kept his appearance from drawing
attention.

Kory looked toward the docks; he saw a familiar figure in green, but before he could be sure it was Ghosh,
the person had vanished. Which meant it probably was
Ghosh.

Jagg tapped Kory on the shoulder and pointed to a
sign near the gangway. It read, FREEHOLD BY LIAVEKAN
LAW. "I don't understand," he said in the strange, aton-
al accent. "Are not all ships so?"

Reed said, "The last Levar created Thomorin Wiln
a landed noble. He's really Vavasor of *The Vessel of
Dreams*. But whatever you do, don't call him that."

"Why?"

Reed smiled, said, "The Levar wanted Thomorin
Wiln to serve on his Council. But he couldn't be both-

ered, and never put his name in for election by the
Merchants' Society; so the Levar made him a noble,
and the chancellors appointed him.''

Jagg nodded. ''Rulers have a way of getting the things
they want.''

''Oh, but that's not the end of it,'' Reed said primly.
Kory bit his lip. He knew the story, too, but hearing
Reed tell it, with the calm manner of a counting-house
clerk, was priceless. ''The rule is that noble councilors
can send a representative. Thomorin Wiln sent a message saying that, since he couldn't serve, he was sending another chemist, of proven ability.''

''Yes?''

''He sent a civet cat,'' Reed said, voice still even.
''It got *very* upset. Do you know what a civet cat smells
like when it gets upset? The Council had to meet in the
Levar's Park for three weeks while the chambers aired
out.'' Then she laughed.

Jagg scratched his cheek. His expression might have
been a smile, or anything.

Reed looked up. ''I see someone I want to talk to,''
she said. ''I'll be right here when you come out.'' Jagg
bowed slightly and followed Kory aboard *The Vessel of
Dreams.*

Thomorin Wiln's boat was tightly packed, the shop
front no exception. There was a narrow counter with a
cased set of balances, and a strongbox built into the
countertop itself; there were wall racks for glassware
and pottery herb jars; there were lockers with brass
catches and extensible lamps and, in a corner, tin buckets with fresh material brought in that day; Kory set his
bucket near the others. And there were drawers, hun-
dreds, thousands of little drawers in ranks on the walls,
each with a tiny white label describing its contents.
Thomorin Wiln did not seem to need the labels; he just
went to a drawer and pulled it open. It always seemed
to be what he wanted. Kory imagined that if he leaned
over to read the labels, they would all read, THINGS
(ASSORTED).

Thomorin Wiln came in from the rear. He was tall and quite slender, with straight black hair streaked with gray; he wore it long, bound with engraved lead rings. He was wearing a rust-colored gown, somewhat ragged, covered by a heavy leather apron. "Kory," he said, and touched a hand to his forehead; he stopped, sniffed the hand, which was stained strange colors, and shrugged. "What were you out after? Spooks?"

"Clawfires. Got some smaller than your palm, too."

"I've got big palms. Wish it had been spooks, though. There's a— Oh, excuse me, master." He bowed slightly to Jagg, indicated Kory. "This gentleman is one of my suppliers."

Jagg pushed back his hood. Thomorin Wiln cocked his eyebrow slightly. Jagg said, "I am acquainted with Master Li. He recommended your services to my master." Jagg took a folded paper from his blue coat. "Can you make these preparations?"

"The sign says 'apothecary,' " Thomorin Wiln said. As he unfolded the paper, he added, "I won't make Universal Solvent, though. Not on a boat."

"I meant, master, have you the materials."

"Apology acc—" Thomorin Wiln stared at the paper. "Do you know what this says?"

"I do, Master Drugsmith."

"I mean, do you know what it *means*? These concentrations—excuse me. Kory, do you need your money now, or can it wait?"

"I'll be back tomorrow," Kory said, desperately curious but taking the hint. "Jagg, may I pick up my 'sailer tomorrow morning?"

"Certainly, Trader."

Thomorin Wiln's eyebrow went up again. Kory smiled and went out.

Reed was on the dock, and Ghosh was with her. Kory waved and ran down the gangplank.

Ghologhosh said she thought she was the same age as Kory and Reed, though she wasn't sure, and she looked older. She was very dark, with short, straight black hair and startlingly black eyes in an angular face that had been hit until it was no longer pretty. She was a little shorter than Reed, and even thinner, but incredibly strong for her build; Kory had seen her bend the iron bars of a window grille enough to slip through, then straighten them again when she had what she was after. She was wearing a leather collar (it would turn a knife and stop a garrote, and Kory knew she kept a set of lockpicks inside it), a coarse green tunic bloused above a wide belt, and matching loose trousers.

"If you're going to do business in the nice parts of town," Kory said, "you've got to put on shoes."

"The cheap kind are noisy and the quiet kind wear out too fast," Ghosh said. It was their greeting, like a handclasp or a hug; you didn't touch Ghosh. "So you all made it back again with your virtue intact. I swear I don't know what you two do all that running around for; it makes ais Ariom just as mad, and you sure aren't getting anything out of it."

Reed said, "We just like the sight of each other, Ghosh."

Ghosh nodded, spat over the edge of the dock. "Asie Blackfinger'll do your pictures for a copper each, and you can stare all day. Kory, you mind if I sleep on your floor tonight? One of the regulars 'round my place cut a noble outside Cheeky's, and there's a couple of Guards waiting to see if he's stupid enough to go home."

"Sure, Ghosh, come by when you want." Ghosh's "place" was a block of abandoned Old Town buildings, sometimes called the No-Copper Bazaar, or Gizzard's Row. It looked like living hell, but in its way it was safe enough—there was nothing there to steal.

"I don't believe you're having this conversation in front of me," Reed said in mock horror.

"If you were going to fight me over the Merchant, you'd have done it a long time ago," Ghosh said. "And if anything was going to happen between him and me, it would have happened already. But you aren't and it ain't, and *that's* what I don't believe."

Ghosh turned sharply, apparently at nothing: Kory saw Jagg coming out of *The Vessel of Dreams*. He was not carrying any parcels. Kory said, "Thomorin Wiln *couldn't—*"

Jagg said, "It takes some time to prepare. I will expect you tomorrow, Master Li. Well faring to you. And you, mistress. And—"

"Ghologhosh," Ghosh said, looking narrow-eyed at Jagg.

"Mistress Ghologhosh." Jagg pulled up his hood, boarded the trap, and drove away.

"Friend of yours?" Ghosh said.

"Tell you about it later," Kory said. "I'd better take Reed home now."

Ghosh said, "You really do ask for it every chance you get, don't you? Look, I'll see Reed gets home all right. Anybody asks, she gave me a two-copper as her bodyguard."

Reed said, "I'm quite able to walk myself home, you know."

Ghosh bowed low. "Oh, Lady not want to go there, Lady meet terrible fate, worse than death, maybe even better." She straightened up. "Besides, I've got to go over that way anyway."

Kory scratched his head. If Ghologhosh had business in a quarter of wealthy merchants' houses, it was better not to ask what it was. "All right. Knock when you come in."

Ghosh nodded. "Well?"

Kory said, "Well what?"

Reed said, "Well *this*," and kissed him.

Ghosh said, "I didn't think you'd finish that before dark. Come on, Reed, let's go make some pretty boys cry."

They started up the canalside path. Ghosh, who never moved without looking in all directions, saw Kory just standing by the *Vessel*'s gangway, looking in no particular direction.

"So is there any hope for the two of you," she said

to Reed, "or are you just going to keep on mooning and strolling until Dyelam finds someone rich enough to bring into his business, with you as the splice?"

"Kory will be rich enough . . . or maybe he won't. I really don't care. And my father isn't the kind of man you seem to see him as."

"Wouldn't know. All I ever see is money. Is Dyelam just gold-plate, then?"

"What do you know about anybody?" Reed said, almost angry. "You don't love or care about anyone but yourself."

"You give me too much credit," Ghosh said quietly. "Hey, don't get mad. You cry and streak up your face, we'll have to explain it to your family."

Reed said, "And you couldn't do that, could you? You don't know how to cry."

Ghosh could tell she wasn't angry any longer, which was good. Reed was smart and funny, good to be with—like Kory. If Ghosh had been either of them, she probably would have spent as much time as possible with the other. Which was exactly why this courting game of theirs was so Gholdamn dumb. There was a Bree Amal proverb: *The line between wealth and poverty is as thin as a half-copper. The line between life and death is as thin as the edge of a knife. So why waste time drawing lines?*

They were passing the Levar's palace, which glittered in the late-day sun. The canal was alight. Caught between sparkle and shimmer, Ghosh felt suddenly grubby. "Hey, stop a moment," she said, and took a black cloth bundle from her pouch. She unwrapped a pair of black kidskin slippers, pulled them on. "You see? Some of your boyfriend's advice is worth taking." Reed laughed. Ghosh wiped her face with the cloth, shook it out, and wrapped it around her head, tucking in the ends.

"Here," Reed said. She plucked at her clothing, and held out a small silver pin with a green-enameled olive tree.

"You'll want that back," Ghosh said. "Don't give it to me."

"No. Father had a lot of them made when he bought the grove. So no one will think it's stolen, either."

"Can I call you if I ever need a judge?" Ghosh pinned her turban. "Forget it. An honest judge is something I'm never going to need."

"Ghosh, I . . ."

They were at the bridge across the canal. Across it, the Levar's Park spread out to the right, the expensive houses fronting the Levar's Way to the left. "Not now, hey? You don't want people to think you know me, not this close to home."

The ais Ariom house was of gray stone with black ironwork, with decorative castings of sugarcane on the exterior walls. It had belonged to a sugar merchant, before Dyelam ais Ariom moved to Liavek and needed a fashionable old address. As Reed knocked, Ghosh slipped into the shadow cast by the doorframe. A Tichenese in eggshell-colored silk, carrying a butler's rod of black wood, answered the door. "Pleasant evening, Mistress Cadie."

"Hello, Xochan. Am I awfully, fearfully, dreadfully late?"

Xochan smiled. "Not so late as that, mistress. The master your father has had business all this day, and a private guest for noon meal, and has had no time to notice your absence."

"Happy birthday, Reed," Ghosh muttered.

Xochan leaned forward. "Is that Mistress Ghologhosh?" She slapped her rod into her palm.

Ghosh moved out of the shadows. "Night breezes blow you sweetness, O Source of Order."

Xochan's grin showed polished white teeth. "And may the moon favor your labors with her darkness, O Mover of Property. I would shower you with riches for the safe return of my willow mistress, but sadly I am only a poor servant. . . . However, there is warm apple pie in the kitchen."

Reed said, "Why does *she* get apple pie?"

Xochan said, "Because it is not yet the mistress's dinnertime."

Ghosh slipped inside. "Tell her the truth, Xochan. If you rob the house of a person who's fed you, you spend ten thousand years of the afterlife as a plum tree."

Reed snorted in a most inelegant way and ran up the curving, carpeted staircase.

Ghosh said, "And with the pie, might there be cream?"

"There might be cream, for speakers of truth," Xochan said. "Was she truly with Master Korik?"

"I'm the only one you saw her with."

Xochan nodded. Her eyes narrowed. "A *plum tree*?"

"Liavekans," Ghosh said lightly, "will believe anything."

A twentieth-watch later, Ghologhosh sat in the outer sill of a shuttered window, licking pie crumbs from her fingers. She reached down and wiped her hand on night-damp grass, then dried it on her shirt. She took a pair of thin gloves from her pouch and tugged them on. She started to take off the kid slippers, then thought better of it; she could cross the rock garden wearing them, then slip them off and leave no track inside.

Her contractor wanted a small brass mask set with yellow opals. Junk by itself, he said, only valuable to a collector. That was what contractors usually said; sometimes it was true and sometimes it wasn't. Ghosh could almost always tell how much an object was really worth, but she was never tempted to scout for higher bids. Unlike Kory's businesses, her trade didn't have much room for private initiative.

She slipped to the ground. The earth was cool, the air quite crisp for late Wine. There was a little low fog, and almost no moon. Fine thieving weather.

Ghosh crossed the rock garden without any sound. The garden was poorly tended, overgrown, rocks turned

over. It had been the hobby of the house's last owner.
Dyelam ais Ariom didn't have time for such things, and
as the garden was not visible from the street, there was
no social reason to maintain it. Ghosh's foot stirred a
pool of mist. She suddenly remembered a rumor that
the prior owner, ruined in the sugar trade by some Ka
Zhir intrigue, had gone into his garden and cut his
wrists. *Interesting story*, she thought. *When I get
wealthy, I must remember not to keep a garden.*

She came to another shuttered window, listened at
it. Silence. She took a thin tool from her collar, slid it
between the shutters, lifted the latch. No click. Very
slowly, she opened the shutter. Only a whisper of
sound. Praising fine craftsmanship, Ghosh examined
the window beyond. There was no curtain. It was entirely dark within. Her contractor swore, whatever that
was worth, that this storeroom had not been opened in
years—perhaps not since Dyelam had moved in. It contained, he swore double, only some of the sugar trader's
old trivia, not worth displaying or selling.

Ghosh wondered why he had told her that. Reassur-
ance that the mask would not be missed? Or that she
would not *really* be robbing ais Ariom? If it was starting to get around that she and Reed—well. She'd have
to worry about that later. There was enough to do now.

She undid the window latch. The window swung in-
ward with a faint groan. *Stay dead, Sugarman*, she
thought, *you can't spend it now.* And then she was inside.

There was a faint rumble of conversation from the
far side of the room, probably through a door, though
it was too dark to see. That was just fine. If no light
leaked through to this side, none would shine out. She
took a tiny spirit lamp from her pouch, unfolded it,
scratched flint on steel. The light was small but steady
and sufficient.

She could see that the contractor was right: the room
was cluttered with small objects on shelves, all of them
dusty, untended. That meant the need to move care-

fully, not leave too much written in the dust. She kept her slippers on; they were less distinctive than footprints.

She saw the mask. It hung on the wall, on a strip of leather with several other items of oxidized brass. She reached gloved fingers around it. There was a simple hook. It came away easily, went into her pouch with no protest at all. She turned. One of the voices beyond the door was raised. She moved to go. Her business was over. Dyelam ais Ariom's voice said, "—kill the Regent." Ghosh stopped still. She moved to the door. Spying was, she reasoned, only another kind of stealing.

Dyelam was talking with another man. Ghosh did not know the voice.

Dyelam said, "—but I *don't* want him dead. Only removed. He's a bad influence on the child."

"You mean Her Magnificence, the Levar," the other voice said. There was an accent, familiar, not quite placed.

"I mean a flighty child, impressionable, who in not many years is going to have outrageous responsibilities. But keep this quite clear, wizard"—Ghosh bit her lip— "this is not an attack upon the Levar. It is a measure to save her from a man with only his own ends, his own interests, in mind."

He could be talking about Kory and Reed, Ghosh thought.

The other man, the wizard, said, "It can be done without killing. And far safer to do it so, of course. I know certain . . . potent facts about His Scarlet Eminence, which can—"

"I don't want to know," Dyelam said.

"Customers so rarely do." There was a clink of porcelain. "It is necessary that it be done on the End of Wine, in Hrothvek."

"A magical reason?"

"You don't want to know." Ghosh knew the accent now: it was faint, but it was Hrothvekan. "The Regent may be reluctant to attend your celebration, but you will find a way to persuade him. After all," the man said, with acid irony, "his position isn't so *very* secure."

"His man, the Count—"

"Dashif will be elsewhere occupied. There is no extra charge. May I have some more tea?" The cups clinked again. "Oh, and speaking of which, I need to pay a chemist. One hundred levars will be sufficient."

"Do you think in amounts smaller than a hundred levars?" Dyelam said, frustration audible in his voice. There were heavy footsteps, a drawer being pulled open, the sound of coins. Ghosh could tell ten-levar gold by its clink.

The wizard said smoothly, "Have you never heard the aphorism, 'One must pay an assassin three times: once to come, once to kill, once to go away'? After all, merchant, if this scheme fails, you will have no further use for money. While if it succeeds . . ."

"If it succeeds no one will ever know!" Dyelam almost shouted. "I grew up in a warehouse. I know the price of doing business. If it succeeds, no one will—*what's that*?"

"This little light? One of the things your money goes to buy," the wizard's voice said calmly. "Protection from spies."

Ghosh had once been told that all trap spells contained a loophole: something about balance of luck. You always had one chance to escape.

She looked up and saw glowing eyes, suicide's eyes, staring at her from the window. She froze for an instant. And her chance slipped past.

The two points of light rushed at her from the mist. Ghosh held up a hand, reaching for her knife with the other. A mothmote whirled around her wrist: it trailed a streak of blue-white light that tightened suddenly and hard. She felt it burn. The other light bound her knife hand to her side. The motes spun round her knees, pulling them together; she fell. The lights continued to whirl around her, wrapping, constricting, searing. She couldn't move. She couldn't breathe. She opened her mouth to gasp, and the traces gagged her tongue; she heard spit sizzle. She felt the wire wrap her throat, and then she felt nothing.

The midnight watch had gone by, and Kory was still awake, wondering about Ghosh. She often worked all night, but since she had asked for a place to stay, then presumably tonight . . . well. Ghosh was not the most predictable soul on earth.

Kory stood up, chewed on a piece of apple, walked from one end of his room to the other. It only took a few steps. It was a basement room in a ship chandler's, in Old Town near the docks. The only air came from a tiny window near the ceiling, but it was cheap and fairly private at night, and he had the off-hours' use of the shop to work on his landsailer, which was built of broken spars and odd brasses bought at cost. He wished he had the 'sailer now. He could work on the spring and hub. It would be better than pacing. He looked out the window, getting a rat's-eye view of the street: nothing.

Ghosh didn't want to be owed anything, she had a funny way about debts, but Kory felt he owed her something. Kory had been tempted toward thieving more than once; it seemed so easy, the overhead was so very low. But Ghosh was good at it, very good, and you couldn't call what she had a good living. It wasn't exactly a debt, but—

There was a tap at the door. "Ghosh?" Kory said. There was no answer. Kory went to the door. "Ghosh?" Still nothing. Kory loosened the broad-bladed knife that hung near the doorframe. He opened the door.

There was no one there. A folded paper lay on the steps. Kory looked around; there were a few lights, a few walkers, that was all. He picked up the letter, shut and latched the door.

The room was furnished with a bed and a table and a chair and a lamp. Kory turned up the lamp and unfolded the paper, which was unsealed. He recognized Reed's handwriting at once, and as he read his hand began to shake.

Beloved Kory,

Father has finally done it. He plans to marry me off to some horrid Hrothvekan, so he can make sure he doesn't lose control of the old part of the business.

I am to have no say in this matter, of course. The Hrothvekan is, I am told, "not a horrid man." I suppose this means he is abominable.

I will not be property. But I will be yours, if you will have me, without goods or dowry. The wedding is to be announced at my father's celebration in Hrothvek, on the End of Wine. There is so little time. Please, tell me what we shall do.

I love you
Reed

Kory read the letter, and read it again, and again. *The merchant has finally done it*, he thought, *finally challenged me to a duel.*

He did not sleep that night, and never noticed that Ghosh never came.

Ghologhosh hovered in darkness, immobile, feeling pressures against her bones. Her normal senses were all useless: she could not move, but did not know if she was bound, or held, or . . .

Then there was the clear touch of a hand to her face. "You're strong, dollikin," said a voice out of the nothing. It was the wizard's voice, the Hrothvekan—

The hand slapped her, hard. "Yes," the voice said. "I am that one. You don't know my name, though, do

you? No. Good for you that you do not. Good for both
of us. You can be of use to me, dollikin, but I have to
lock some things up inside you for a while. And I
couldn't take chances of something as potent as a name
slipping out.''

The hand stroked her face, then slid down her body,
cold flesh on cold flesh. ''What a misused little dollikin
you are. All scars. All the pleasure used up. I could
mend you, of course, and start *all* over—but there's no
time. We must take such enjoyment as we can.''

The hand brushed her hair back from her forehead.
The fingers spread out on her brow.

The pain was like the edges of seashells scraping
across her naked brain, the salt sea flooding in upon
the wound. She did not scream. She did not cry. At
least, she did not think so. The voice had said she would
live. How? she thought. She wondered, if she did live,
how she would ever again imagine hell.

*Ghol, oh Ghol, make me a plum tree for ten thousand
years—*

Ghosh felt herself bathed in coolness. Her head hurt,
and her wrists. She lay on something soft. Something
struck her, but gently, gently. She opened her eyes.

There was a ball of spiky silvery filaments crouched
a handsbreadth in front of her face, filling her whole
vision. It stretched a pair of fibers toward her: on their
ends were tiny, bright blue eyes. Ghosh smiled idioti-
cally.

Then a foot kicked the dawn spook away and a hand
touched her shoulder. She looked up at the sky and a
figure dark against it: a broad-faced man with a strange
fringe of white hair around his head. His blue head.

''What is it, Jagg?'' another man's voice called, and
the blue-gray man pulled Ghosh to a sitting position.
Another wave washed around them. Ghosh looked
around groggily: they were on the beach at Liavek's far
southwest, down by the Sea Eagle Inn, almost to the
Saltmarsh.

''Half-drowned lady,'' the blue man said in a weirdly

flat voice. "Friend to the pair we met yesterday. Saw her with them at the drugsmith's barge."

Ghosh remembered him then, the one who had spoken to Kory. She turned to look at the other man. He was of average height, just passing middle age, with light hair and eyes. He wore a high-collared black tunic and rolled-up gray trousers; his feet were big and blue-veined and pale. He leaned on a black stick.

"How ever do you come to be here, mistress?" the blond man said, in a voice that said something else was on his mind.

Ghosh thought. She couldn't remember. She saw the blue-gray man, she walked Reed home, there was apple pie—then nothing but a feeling like pain that had passed by, the memory of an infected tooth. And she wasn't about to tell these two about it. "I sleep on the beach some nights," she said, which was no lie.

"Below the tide line?" the blond man said. "Careful you don't sleep too late. . . . Jagg, help the woman up. My name is Ciellon. Do I understand that you know Kory Li and Reed ais Ariom?"

"Yeah . . . yes."

"We met them upon the Hrothvek road yesterday. They were gathering—what was it, Jagg? Oh, yes, crabs, for the apothecary Thomorin Wiln. But Kory's windcar had a slight accident. We drove them home." Ciellon smiled. "Does that establish our acquaintance? I could show you the landsailer, but Kory came for it very early this morning."

"I . . . uh, pleased to meet you, Master Ciellon. Master Jagg. I'm . . . Ghologhosh. Call me Ghosh."

"Good morning to you, then, Ghosh. We were just going for a walk to the Saltmarsh edge to have a little breakfast. Pleased to have you share it with us, if you've nowhere better to go."

She didn't know whether she did or not. But it wasn't far. And she did know she was hungry. "Happy to join you, Master Ciellon."

"Splendid! You meet the nicest people by accident here."

They sat on the rocks, eating smoked fingerlings and spiced toast with kaf, tossing the scraps to the sea eagles, who caught them on the fly. Ciellon talked on, explaining that he was a wizard, born in Hrothvek but long gone from there. Ghosh was wary of all his talking. People who started off with so much talking usually thought they were paying in advance for something.

In one of the pauses, Ghosh said, "Ciellon isn't a Hrothvekan name," and was surprised at herself for saying such a dangerous thing.

"No. It comes from a Farlander myth. Ciellon is the herald who leads the Brightmetal Gods when they go forth at the end of time, for their last battle with the Gods of Rust and Sand. Bit pompous, I suppose. Ciellon isn't even very smart, for a god. He's the first to die, of a Rusty arrow through the heart. . . . Look, there's Crookneck Zal." He pointed at a cormorant, taking off from the reeds. "Our innkeeper's name. Excuse me; names are a hobby of mine, but I don't know yours. Can you tell me the meaning of 'Ghologhosh'?"

Ghosh blinked. She had been calling herself that ever since she was small, and no one had ever asked why. "He's a god too," she said. "The God of Throwaway Curses, the ones people don't really mean. He's not much of a god now, but every time someone says 'Kosker and Pharn!' or 'by the Red Faith, from pole to pole!' he gets stronger."

Ciellon's smile was absolutely joyful. Ghosh wondered suddenly if she had given up part of her soul to the magician, by giving up her name. "But that's wonderful!" the wizard said, and began to laugh. After a moment he stopped, wiping tears from his eyes, and looked across the Saltmarsh.

"Come walk with me a little while longer, Ghologhosh," Ciellon said, his voice again preoccupied and faraway. "Jagg, go on back. We'll be all right."

Jagg left. Ciellon stood up and gestured with his

cane. Ghosh supposed they were headed for a nice sloppy tumble in the marsh. That was all right. She'd paid more for breakfast.

But all they did was walk, and talk. Ciellon seemed to know everything about the marsh: the names of fifty kinds of reeds, "all slender, all supple, like your friend Cadie"; where to turn over rocks to send outlandish creatures scuttling toward the safety of the sea, how to get seven skips from a flung flat stone.

Ghosh found herself forgetting the loss of last night. All she wanted to know was what she could not ask— what did Ciellon want?

She thought, just maybe, she knew. Maybe he just wanted to talk. Maydee Gai at the House of Blue Leaves had once told her that many of the customers wanted nothing more, and paid for nothing more. Ghosh had never met anyone like that. She had certainly never been touched by one.

Ciellon said, "Oh my. We must head back, or we'll miss the noon meal."

Ghosh looked up, startled to realize it was past mid-day.

"You will take lunch with me? After we've both cleaned up a bit."

No sense in missing a meal. "Certainly, Master Ciellon."

"Honored, mistress. Damned honored. There's one for both Ghologhoshes." He paused. "Ghosh . . . do you have a place to stay tonight?"

Well, she thought, finally. "No, master."

"Ciellon will do. Then, I would be pleased to guest you this evening. Our room's big enough for a regiment."

"I—"

"Don't answer me now," Ciellon said. "I warn you, I shall insist on taking afternoon tea with you. It's my inflexible custom. Decide then."

* * *

Wrapping a borrowed linen robe around herself, Ghologhosh came out of the bath into Ciellon's room, which was in fact enormous. Ciellon was standing by the picture window, looking out at the Saltmarsh, as a man who has lost something precious into the sea will stare at the waves, knowing they give nothing back.

"Your clothes are rather far gone," Ciellon said. "Somewhere in that trunk there must be a shirt and pants that will fit you, with a little judicious sashing. You don't wear shoes, I take it?"

"No. But I don't—borrow things."

Ciellon said, "Then it isn't a loan. Though your things are where you left them." He pointed with his cane.

Ghosh did not refuse gifts outright. She found a black blouse of heavy fabric—winter was coming—and green trousers similar to her old ones. Her belts and gear did not appear to have been touched, her knives all in place.

Jagg came in then with lunch, and Ciellon began to talk again, and then suddenly it was the end of the afternoon.

"Tea," Ciellon said. "Shall we take it downstairs, in the parlor? I need a small change of scene. And then you may leave, or not."

Ghosh saw Zal the innkeeper look up as they entered the parlor, running fingers over the bald side of her head. As they passed, Ghosh heard a few words of the Second Prayer to Bree Amal the Great Madam, which is: *May These Events Not Cost Thy Servant Money.*

Zal najhi Zal showed Ciellon, Ghosh, and Jagg to a table with a sea view. "Tea, master?" she said, with just a little too much deference.

"Tea, innkeeper," Ciellon said. "I think the Incense of Fair Memory."

"I would have you know, master," Zal said with pride, "that at great expense we have procured a small quantity of the rare Tea of Worrynot."

Ghosh stared.

Ciellon said, "That's very nice, innkeeper. But I've

made my own arrangements about that. I suggest you save it for the appropriate occasion.''

To Ghosh's surprise, Ciellon did *not* talk during tea-time. None of them did. Ciellon looked at Ghosh with an unreadable expression, Jagg looked at Ciellon in an even blanker way, and Ghosh tried to look out the window at the declining light.

Ciellon said, ''Well, Ghologhosh?''

More from curiosity than anything else, she said, ''I would be honored, mas—Ciellon.''

The wizard nodded, waved Zal najhi Zal to the table. ''Innkeeper. Please add the surcharge for an additional guest in my rooms.''

There was only one bed. Ciellon slept in it. Jagg took a heap of silks and furs from a trunk, and another for Ghosh, and they slept curled up in those, all quite far from one another in the enormous room, its picture window silvery with faint moonlight off the sea.

Ghosh slept as she had never done in her life. Until the dream came. The voice, and the hand—

Her eyes snapped open. She did not stir. The dream—she could not remember the dream.

There was a black shape against the silver window. It was Ciellon in his nightshift, leaning against the sill as if a weight were crushing his shoulders. Ghosh could hear his voice, very faintly, speaking in rhythm. A ritual spell? She wondered, and then she heard the song:

Call to thee, Harmony, Saltmarsh's daughter,
Drink to our faith in a cup of salt water.
Come to me, Harmony, promise unspoken,
Follow your faith where the marsh reeds lie broken.
Never be, Harmony, healed or forgiven,
Salt in the wound where the promise was riven.

Ciellon turned away from the window. Ghosh held entirely still: she could feign sleep for a long time. It had saved her life more than once. Her knife was naturally at her fingertips.

Ciellon leaned over her. He touched her hair, ran his fingers through it. He knelt. He spoke some words she did not understand. He kissed her on the temple. Then he stood up slowly and got back into his bed.

Ghosh lay very quiet in her sleeping bundle. She was entirely awake. She was more than awake. She was beginning to remember. First a trickle. Then a stream. Then a flood. Ais Ariom's house. The Hrothvekan wizard. The Regent. Kory. The pain.

She opened her mouth in a noiseless scream and stood up in the silks, slashing herself free, and before Jagg or Ciellon could move, she was racing down the hall, down the stairs, away from the Sea Eagle, and into the twisting alleys of Liavek.

Kory woke to a hammering on the door. He drew the sheath knife, stepped to the side, and opened the door: Ghologhosh half fell into the room. She was wearing new clothes and her knife was out.

"Plan," she said, "remember, stop." She twitched like a puppet on strings. "You, letter, they, plan, chemist, kill, *wizard*."

"What's happened to you?" Kory said. She was jumping, whirling her knife wildly.

"Spell," she shouted at him, "spell-spell, *spell*. Wizard. You, plan. *Kill-not-kill*."

"Calm down," Kory said. He put out his hands, saw the knife he held, dropped it. Ghosh dropped hers. "Sit down, Ghosh. Be calm. Sit-down-on-the-bed."

Ghosh sat, calmer but still shaking.

"Who did this to you?"

"Wizard," she said, and shook her head violently. "Nuh-nuh-name. No-name wizard."

Kory understood then. It was a gag spell: Ghosh was under compulsion not to speak the name of the wizard responsible. "You said 'kill.' Kill who?"

"No-name-kill. But not-kill. No-name-not-kill."

This was getting complicated. Kory had a sudden awful thought. "Who am I, Ghosh?"

"You. You-you-*youyouyou*! No-name-you. No-name-*anybody*."

Kory let out a breath. The compulsion extended to the names of everybody and everything. This was going to be very difficult. What else had Ghosh said? "You said 'letter.' Letter from—oh, sorry. What kind of letter?"

"Love letter," Ghosh said quite clearly, and looked surprised.

"Reed's letter?" Kory shouted. Ghosh spread her hands in a desperate gesture.

Kory thought. "Maps," he said suddenly. "I'll get my maps." He brought out the small stack of maps he used for courier work and unrolled them on the table. Ghosh staggered over, squinting in the lamplight. Kory pointed at the location of Reed's house. "Letter from here?"

Ghosh opened her mouth. She strained. There was only a squeaking sound. She held out her hands, but the fingers curled up.

This was getting serious. Apparently she couldn't even act to betray the—*Conspiracy?* Kory thought, and thought of the letter.

Ghosh had taken Reed home. Reed must have given Ghosh the letter. Then Ghosh had been grabbed right off the street—only the kidnappers missed the letter—

Some horrid Hrothvekan, the letter had said.

Some horrid Hrothvekan *wizard*.

Kory shuffled the maps until he found his chart of the southern roads. He spread it next to the city map. He pointed to Hrothvek with his left hand, with his right to the Sea Eagle Inn.

Ghosh gabbled and choked and kicked the table over. Kory barely saved the lamp as it fell.

"That's all you had to say," Kory said.

The shadow of *The Vessel of Dreams* still reached to the wharf when Kory pedaled his landsailer to the gangway. Leaving Ghosh still fidgeting in the passenger seat,

Kory ran to the boat and pulled the FOR MEDICAL EMER-
GENCIES ONLY bellcord.

Thomorin Wiln appeared in a cloth coat tossed over
his nightshirt. "I'm certain there's an explanation for
this," he said.

"The man I brought in the other day—the blue one.
Where are the things he ordered?"

"What business is that of yours?" Thomorin Wiln
snapped, and looked at the end of the counter, where
a small paper box sat. More mildly, the apothecary
said, "Did he hire you to fetch them?"

Kory tensed. Ghosh had managed to choke out "One
hundred levars." If the payment was due now, he was
out of luck. "Yes," he said. "Sorry about the hour.
He insisted."

Thomorin Wiln nodded. "I hardly blame him. Well,
there it is. It's in glass, so be careful."

"I will."

Kory reached for the box. Thomorin Wiln caught
Kory's wrist in his discolored hand. "I mean *be careful*, Kory-of-All-Trades. I used up all the prepared rapture flower in Liavek for that bottle, and it'll be ten
days to ready more, plus the distillation time." He released Kory. "The other wasn't so hard. I just don't
get much call for it."

"I'll treat it well," Kory said.

Thomorin Wiln said, "I'm sure you will. Sorry,
Kory. Too early."

"Sure."

"If you're going to start rising at this hour regularly,
I still need some dawn spooks."

"Tomorrow."

"Fine. Oh. Tell the man a happy End of Wine, will
you?"

The box wedged between his hip and Ghosh's, Kory
drove up the canal to the first bridge, crossed, and pedaled back to the seashore, to an empty dock. He got
out of the car, lifting the box; Ghosh sat quietly. Kory
looked out at the water, the sails of the fishing fleet off

Minnow Island. He opened the box. Inside were a slender flask full of pale golden liquid and a jar of blue-black leaves. The jar said INFUSION TAXALIN AZIFLORA (WORRYNOT TEA). The bottle was not labeled, but Thomorin Wiln had said enough. Rapture flower was the most potent narcotic Kory knew of. He remembered the wizard, the addict, slurping from his flask.

"Kill-not-kill," he said to Ghosh, who looked at him with unfocused eyes. Kory grasped the delicate flask, cocked his arm to throw it into the bay.

Ghosh moaned and struggled. She fell out of the car.

Kory lifted her back in. "We go to Wizard's Row next. I hope I can afford—" Suddenly he had a better idea than smashing the bottle. He went to the edge of the dock, pulled the ground-glass stopper, and poured the yellow liquid into the water, being careful to avert his face from the fumes. He hoped it did not poison the fish.

He refilled the bottle. Fortunately, it was not too large. Then he pedaled along the shoreline, almost to the Sea Eagle. "Wait here," he told Ghosh, who opened her mouth uselessly. "Back soon. With money."

Zal najhi Zal told Kory that Ciellon was on the beach walking. When Kory reached the shore, Jagg was standing soldierlike on the sand, watching the wizard, who stood some distance away, alone out in the Salt-marsh.

"Jagg," Kory said, and the blue man turned. "I've brought Ciellon's preparation. From Thomorin Wiln. I had some other deliveries, and I thought—"

"The master will thank you well," Jagg said. "But your friend, the small dark one? Ghologhosh. The master must see her."

"I'm sorry," Kory said, trying to choke down rage. "I don't have any idea where she is."

"The thing is important." Jagg turned. "Master! The master Korik Li is here!"

Ciellon looked up, waved his cane, started toward them.

"I have other deliveries," Kory said. "It's medicine, it won't wait," and he shoved the white box into Jagg's hands and ran, waiting for his heart to be stopped, lightning to strike him; but nothing happened. When he got back to the 'sailer, Ghosh had gotten out, and dragged herself along walls almost forty paces. Kory led her back to the car, half carrying her. She seemed about to explode, like a gun stopped at the mouth.

"I'm sorry," Kory said to Ghosh. "I've brought what money I have. It'll have to do."

They drove to Wizard's Row—or rather, they tried. Wizard's Row was not there.

"Damn street's never around when you need it," Kory said. He spun the landsailer hard. Somebody dropped a parcel and swore at him. Someone else was interrupted in the middle of a pickpocketing; Kory saw the victim draw a pistol on the thief and he pedaled on hard, not listening for the bang. A few blocks on, he turned—and clearly saw the signs and rooftops of Wizard's Row.

"Happy birthday, Ghosh," Kory said, executed an illegal U-turn (knocking over a rubbish bin, which rolled into a one-legged beggar, who unfolded his other leg from his cloak and sprinted away), and pedaled for all he was worth.

There was no corner to turn. No signs, no rooftops. The Row was gone again. Kory looked at Ghosh, who looked miserable and furious. Kory pedaled on for a block, and got out of the car. "Wait," he said, and sprinted back toward the place where the street had been.

And still was, signs, roofs, dustbins, everything.

Kory stamped back to Ghosh, sighed. "That's a damned comprehensive spell. Is he a magician or a lawyer?" He looked at the sun. It had become terribly near midday. "I have to meet Reed, right away," he said.

Ghosh struggled. Tendons and veins stood out on her
flesh. Her clothes were drenched in sweat. Kory reached
out, cautiously, to her forehead. It burned. "I'll kill him,"
Kory said. "I don't care if he is a wizard. I'll stuff
his luck right down his throat, and then I'll kill
him. . . . I've got to get you home first. You'll be safe
there. Ciellon doesn't know where I live."

Ghosh shivered and sweated.

By the time they reached Kory's room, Ghosh was
too weak to walk. Kory carried her down the steps,
kicked the door open, put her gently on the bed. He
fumbled at her clothes, then let go and drew the blanket
up to her chin.

She grabbed both his wrists, lifted her head. "You
wrote letter," she rasped. *"You wrote her letter?"*

Kory nodded. "They're leaving for Hrothvek just after the noon meal for Dyelam's party. Reed'll have everything all packed. But there's a slight change in plans:
she's going with me. To Saltigos. The marriage will be
Liavek-legal, and too late for Dyelam ais Ariom. And
Company."

"Not her!" Ghosh said and fell back on the bed.

Kory was suddenly sad. "Always her and no one else
but her," he said slowly. "I'm sorry you never understood, Ghosh." He backed away from her. "We wanted
you to come to Saltigos with us, be our first witness
. . . but . . ."

Ghosh's head rolled.

"We'll tell the City Guard where to find you. Ciellon—
they'll take care of him, or I will. I—goodbye,
Ghosh."

The door closed behind him.

Ghologhosh tried to rise, to run after him, but her
arm would not lift, not a finger. The spell was like a
wire snare: the harder she fought the more tightly it
bound her. She could not even think the names of things
now, could not even pray.

The snare would choke her before she could break

it. But maybe—if she could relax, stop fighting—she could slip it. Just enough to breathe.

The wheels of Kory's 'sailer chirped by the window and Ghosh tensed again, and felt the sensation leave her feet. *Be still*, she thought. *Still. Calm. Nothing.*

Her right arm rolled off the bed. She felt her knuckles strike the floor. *Yes. Fall. Do nothing. Let what falls, fall.* Her right heel hit the ground. *Fall.* Her head tipped over; she saw the floor, her limp hand. There was blood on the scraped knuckles. *Scrape. Pain.* Her other hand moved. *Pain for him. He wants pain. Give him pain.* She clawed her hand around the bed leg, feeling the corners of the wood dig into her flesh. *Not against his orders to hurt.*

She pulled herself off the bed, landing with a thump face down. She got her hands under herself and pushed. *Follow the pain where it leads.* Like a disjointed doll, she got to her knees, shuffled around, grasped the door handle, pulled herself upright by the pain in her joints.

On the other side of the door, she knew, were three impossible stairsteps up to the unimaginably long street. She could not do it. She could not live so long.

You must live, said a voice inside her head. *You're doing fine. You're doing right. Think of nothing. Think of sand, sea, sky, all empty.*

"The hurt . . ." she said.

Here is pain enough. Something flowed through her, something cold as mountain water. She knew that it was someone else's pain, feeding the invisible hunger that the caster had put inside his spell.

She knew whose pain it was.

Sand, sky, sea . . .

"Sand, sky, sea . . ." she said, wondering at the rushing cold pain, wondering how anyone could live adrift in such a cold sea of agony. . . . "Sea, sea-sea, *Ciellon!*"

The door flew into splinters. Jagg stepped through, held out his blue hands to Ghosh.

No, Jagg. Let her do it herself.

She took three firm, straight steps toward him, and then she fell, but he caught her easily. He thumbed open a vial and made her drink; she felt better at once.

"Ciellon," she said, "Jagg, Ghosh," drunk on the sound of names. "How, Jagg, Ciellon, Ghosh, find?"

Jagg reached into her hair, drew out a tiny, shiny object. Ghosh tried to focus on it. It was a golden louse, tiny hooks along its legs. "Ciellon put this on you," Jagg said. "He tracked it."

Ghosh nodded. "Nice Ciellon bug." She struggled to think. "Track. Kory track Reed. Track Kory!"

Yes. Jagg, take her to him, quickly.

The ais Ariom house was surrounded by plenty of bustle, more than enough for Kory to hide among. Baggage was being moved, wagons loaded. Dyelam ais Ariom himself stood in the middle of the confusion, trying to look in charge.

The rock garden, Reed's letter had said. *It's invisible from the street.* It was exactly the route he would have chosen. He knew for the ten-thousandth time that he loved her.

He sidled up the alley that led to the garden. The old iron gate was open. Good; less noise—though galloping horses might have been lost in the caravan out front.

Kory paused at the gate. The day had become cool and damp, Fog coming early, and there was mist filling the garden. "Reed?" Kory whispered.

"Here, Kory," Reed's voice said from the mist.

Kory took a step. He looked up. A pair of glowing points stared back at him.

A spinning dagger flew past his head, toward the floating lights. It sailed between them; there was a long spark, and the lights were gone.

Jagg, the wizard's servant, stood in the gateway. In one thick arm he held Ghosh, limp as a rag doll.

Kory yelled and ran, drawing his knife. Ghosh's head bobbed up. "Kory, stop," she said.

"Let her go," Kory said.

"Yes, Jagg," Ghosh said. Jagg released her. She stood unsteadily.

Kory moved next to her, holding his knife level on Jagg. "Now, you're going to—"

"No time to argue," Ghosh said, and Kory looked at her just in time to see her fist knock him cold.

Thomorin Wiln closed his bag. "That's no substitute for rest," he told Ghosh, "but it should keep you on your feet." He looked at Ciellon, who sat up in bed against pillows. "I've given you the strongest pain medicine I have, if you won't let me put you to sleep—"

"I will be fine, thank you," Ciellon said in a thin voice.

Thomorin Wiln started to speak, then shut his mouth. On his way out of the inn room, he turned to Kory and said, "The next time you decide to go into the apothecary's trade, see me about an apprenticeship."

Kory stared at the floor as the door closed. "I don't understand—the caravan was just leaving; I saw it."

"An illusion, waiting for you to trigger it," Ciellon said. "The real party left early in the morning."

"But I had Reed's letter."

"Show it to me."

Kory unfolded the paper and held it out.

"Ghosh, read it," Ciellon said.

" 'My father wishes me to marry against my will. Let us flee.' It isn't Reed's handwriting."

"What do you mean? It says right here—about the Hrothvekan—"

"It doesn't even mention Hrothvek," Ghosh said, and Kory looked shocked at the coldness in her voice.

Ciellon said, "Mirage ink. The writer draws the intent of the message, and the reader's mind creates the text and handwriting. Only wizards can use it, but many chemists can make it. For a high fee. Now, you must go to Hrothvek, and quickly. Reed's life may depend on it. The Regent's certainly does."

Kory was still staring at Ghosh. "I don't know why—I guess I thought that—"

Ghosh turned away from him. She said, "What are they going to do to His Eminence?"

Ciellon's face was rigid for a few moments. Then he sighed. "Look out the window."

Ghosh opened the curtains. A storm was forming offshore—unnaturally fast, clouds boiling black, stabbing lightning. It was racing toward the shore.

Ciellon said, "Resh—His Scarlet Eminence—has a fear of high places, and of storms. A very strong fear."

Kory said, "Now even I understand. He was a sailor, wasn't he?" He looked outside at the dark mass. "And if he should funk in front of all manner of powerful people—he'd never be able to hold power, once that got about. But what does Reed have to do with it?"

Ciellon was silent for a moment. He put a hand against his abdomen and pressed. Then he said, "What only Resh and a few Hrothvekans know—myself, and apparently this wizard of Dyelam's, among them—is that the storm at sea was the second storm. It was the first storm, when he and I were your ages, that drove him to the sea, and me to the Farlands, and the young woman—her to the Saltmarsh on the last night of Wine, and to wherever the marsh hides its dead."

Ghosh said, "Harmony."

"That was her everyday name, yes." He shut his eyes and breathed shallowly. Tendons bulged in his neck. "And jhi Hisor means to play the tragedy out once again, with Reed in Harmony's part . . . poor Resh."

Ghosh thought, *Now there's a word for His Eminence I'll never hear again.*

Ciellon said, "And now you *must* go. Jagg will drive you. Jagg, if you must kill the horses, then you must."

Kory said, "The landsailer's faster." He pointed at the storm. "Especially running before that."

Ghosh went to Ciellon's side. "The other wizard. You used a name. Do you know him?"

"Phris jhi Hisor. He was only an unkind little boy when I knew him. I would never have believed him determined enough to succeed in investing his luck, but I've learned since . . . Oh, I am sorry, Ghologhosh. I removed the spell he laid to bar your memory—you fled before I was quite aware of the second spell beneath it. I was never . . . a very clever wizard. Go now, quickly." His eyes closed and his back arched with his pain, for which there was no medicine in Liavek—Ghosh knew there had been none since Ciellon had given the last diluted drops of it to Jagg, to give to her.

She said, "Why are you here? For Harmony? Or the Regent? If you knew about the plan—"

"But I didn't know, Ghosh. Nor was I told. It just happened— things do sometimes. Go. Go, before the wind rises too high."

"Why did you come back, Ciellon?"

"You know that already, Ghosh. Kory, take her and go. I can't concentrate enough to stop the storm."

Kory put his hand on Ghosh's arm. She shoved him away. She looked at Jagg, pointed at the storm clouds, which seemed about to crowd through the window into the room. "You see he doesn't try to stop it, understand? See that he's quiet, if you have to sit on him! We'll be back."

On the Hrothvek road, night had come hours too early, and the sky howled, and the lightning tore down the black walls of air with ragged-nailed hands, showing the Saltmarsh blue-white and the sea blue-black. Wind threw gravel across the road like grapeshot, and the first cold rain was falling hard.

In the landsailer, which was built for pleasure cruises on fair days, Kory held the sail, Ghosh the tiller and wheelbrakes, pumping them, with showers of sparks from the pads every time the car began to slew in the wind.

Ghosh knew that Kory kept snatching glances at her,

his eyes wide, as if he were trying to decide what she was, what she had become.

No wonder he didn't know; she didn't know herself. Reed had been saying for a long time that Ghosh didn't understand love. She had a sickening feeling that Reed might have been right after all.

"Look!" Kory shouted. There was a line of wavering lights ahead. A lightning stroke showed them as pavilions set up on the Saltmarsh edge. Dyelam ais Ariom's party. *See the End of Wine out with ais Ariom*, Ghosh thought coldly. *See His Scarlet Eminence the Regent out on his ear. But you never thought to see your only daughter out in the storm, eh, Master Dyelam?*

If only she were weaker in the arms. If only she had drowned in the sea. She had taken the first false letter to Kory, and then, at total war in her mind with the unhardened magics, staggered to the docks and jumped in. But she was a strong swimmer. She could swim in her sleep. If she had drowned that night, not washed up alive on Ciellon's beach, this all might still have happened, but safe in hell she would never have seen it. . . . *Make me a plum tree for ten thousand years, and all my plums will be poison.*

"Hold on!" Kory shouted as a sheet of rain hit the 'sailer. Ghosh leaned on the tiller and the brakes, and the car flexed and skidded off the road. Ghosh rolled into soft wet coldness, tasting salt that might have been marshwater or blood.

"Kory?" she yelled.

"Here—here, Ghosh." He had gotten a lantern alight somehow. "I'm all right. You?"

"That letter of yours—did you tell Reed to meet you *in the city*, or just to meet you?"

"I—just to meet me. She set the place—I mean, the letter I got said—"

Ghosh pointed marshward of the pavilion, to seaward. "Then Dyelam's sure to have seen your note. If you don't find her, you'd better just keep going."

"Ghosh—" He stared at her. The rain swept his black

curls down his forehead. "Luck, Ghosh," he said, and turned his lantern and headed into the darkness.

"Damn luck," she said, and hoped her god was stronger for it. She started for the pavilion.

There were guards at the entrance to the huge tent, but they looked at Ghosh, stamping in from the storm, and made no move to bar her way. She looked around. The whole scene within was frozen into tableau, all the elaborately dressed guests staring at an open flap that looked out on the Saltmarsh. Staring, Ghosh knew, after Cadie ais Ariom. Ghosh wondered what the wizard had put in Reed's mind, to send her walking into the storm; Kory, probably.

Dyelam ais Ariom was dripping jewelry and sweat, biting his knuckles. *You should have stayed in your warehouse, merchant,* she thought. *You didn't know the price of doing assassin's business.*

She saw the red-robed figure of His Scarlet Eminence the Regent of Liavek, his hands loose at his sides, staring out into the night. He was taut as a bowstring, ready to snap.

We need a diversion, Ghosh thought. *Thieves and pickpockets know all about that. Basic street work.*

"Hey-*yo!*" she shouted. Heads turned. "Hey-yo, hey-yo, my masters and mistresses, why so mum? 'Tis time for merry mischief! Ring bells! Sing songs! For is this not the last night of Wine, and we'd better celebrate before the Wine runs out?"

She did a handspring past the Regent, coming up right under his moustache. "Your Eminence! Oh, excuse me." She knelt at his feet, looked up at him. "Now I see what they mean by eminence."

Someone giggled. The Regent looked down, his face rigid. Ghosh said, "Don't you get scared of heights, with all that eminence?" She nodded, winked. The Regent nodded slowly.

Thomorin Wiln's drugs singing in her blood, her heart screaming on the edge of despair, she danced around the pavilion, tugging beards, punching playfully at bulging bellies, sipping at guests' drinks. "Whooo! What is that, shrimp cocktail?"

She looked back at His Scarlet Eminence, who had a small smile. Ghosh wondered how much he knew about this. Well, he would know a lot more very soon.

Ghosh pirouetted over to a table loaded with pastry. "And now, the centerpiece of tonight's entertainment, a masterwork of mystery, a syllabus of surprises, an astonishment of artifice—but first, I need a volunteer from the audience. Would that prince of conjurors, that most eminent sorcerer, that offspring of a Ka Zhir camel, Phris jhi Hisor, please show his owl-dropping of a face?"

It wasn't hard to spot him. She just watched for the blush. Ghosh took a cream pie in each hand and flung them, and that was easy, too—she pretended they were knives.

Jhi Hisor gaped and grabbed instinctively for a silver button on his gown. The pies struck him in eruptions of berries and cream. Ghosh cartwheeled toward him, slamming both feet into his breastbone. He groaned and went down against a side table, which buried him under an avalanche of sliced fruit.

Ghosh tore the silver button from jhi Hisor's coat, pulled his jaw down, and rammed the button down his throat. He swallowed involuntarily, and his face went slack as his luck went free.

"That was one of Kory's best ideas," Ghosh said. "If you've any luck left, you'll choke to death."

There was a disturbance at the other side of the tent. Ghosh looked up. It was Kory. He was carrying Reed. They were both soaked, but they were both alive. Dyelam ais Ariom went running to his daughter and inevitable son-in-law.

And the rain had stopped.

Ghosh stood up slowly and went to the tent flap. The storm mass was splitting in two, peeling back from a cut as straight as a knife could make, exposing blue-black sky specked with a few hard stars.

"No," she said in a small voice. "Ciellon, no, you don't have to, we're all right—"

"The wizard," Dyelam ais Ariom said. "She freed the wizard's luck, and the storm broke." Dyelam beamed at Ghosh. "My dear young woman, I—" He stopped when he saw Ghosh's face, and he took a step backward, and another. Ghosh looked at him for a long moment, thinking any number of things, which all boiled down to one.

"No," she said, "you live, to pay."

She turned and went to His Scarlet Eminence, who looked so stately and reserved that no one could have imagined him any other way. Ghosh spoke a name, and His Eminence gave her his hand, and in a moment they were aboard his coach and away up the road toward Liavek, as fast as horses could run.

Zal najhi Zal was just about to hand over the desk to her night clerk when there was the screech of a wagon braking, and the front doors of the Sea Eagle were thrown open by two men of the Levar's Guard. She promptly spoke the First Prayer to Bree Amal. Then there entered His Scarlet Eminence himself, and with him the short dark woman that the wizard had entertained the night before; he looked terrifying and she looked like a drowned rat. Zal spoke the Second Prayer.

The Regent and the soggy girl were met on the stairs by the wizard's ghastly blue servant, who actually looked like he might send His Scarlet Eminence away, though he led the pair upstairs instead. Zal najhi Zal stood at the desk for the next three hours, staring at the immobile guards by her still-open doors, being fed kaf and dry toast by the night clerk, until the Regent and the blue man came downstairs again and the blue man really did seem to send the Red priest away. The guardsmen shut the doors, and the blue man went upstairs, and only then did Zal najhi Zal utter the Third Prayer to Bree Amal, which is *May These Events Leave No Trace of Themselves in Thy Servant's Memory.*

* * *

"Prop me a little higher, Jagg," Ciellon said. "So I can see the Saltmarsh. I'm not going to have my last sight on earth be a plaster ceiling."

Jagg adjusted the pillows and said, "I believe the master intended to tour the Dreamsend Hills before his death."

"Did I? If a road were paved with intentions, Jagg, where would it lead? Come closer, Ghologhosh. I want to see you, too."

"Damn you," she said.

"Stop praying and come closer."

"You're a *magician*. Magicians live for centuries."

"Some of them do."

"Why not you?"

Ciellon gasped, exhaled slowly. "Because . . ." he said faintly, then coughed and said in a stronger voice, "because of birthdays. Do you know what every magician must do on his birthday?"

"He has to reinvest his magic, in his luck-charm."

"And has no use of it 'til he does. That's why, yes, some of us last for a long time, but not forever. Because on your birthday, you revert to your actual age. Investiture is very trying, without the added burden of being three hundred years old when you try it. . . ."

"But aren't there charms—bound things—"

"Yes. But another must make them, and they cost the binder his or her entire luck, all magic for the rest of the maker's life. And I was offered it—I think we all are, at some time. A reflection of our power. A test of what that power has done to us. I found the cost much too high.

"It is the nature of my disease—which is itself partly magical—that a spell can repress it, but not destroy it. So I could live without pain—until my next birthday, when the pain would arrive so suddenly and in such great measure that I would never be able to reinvest. So there was the choice: one year free from pain, or several with it. The choice is straightforward, but not,

I assure you, simple. In the event, it has been about eight years. I went many places in those extra seven years, saw many things. I think I did some good. I think I chose . . .'' His face tightened and he twisted against the pillows.

Ghosh said, ''But last night you did the magic. You took away the pain. So you could stop a storm you didn't have to stop, so . . .'' She clenched and unclenched her hands. ''And now you're hurting again. That means today's your . . . birthday.''

''I was born on the first day of Fog, a little after dawn. My mother was in labor some four hours. I am told that is a very bad pain, to have suffered with for four hours.''

''Then you did come back just to die.''

''I had to die somewhere,'' Ciellon said patiently. ''Not in Hrothvek—you can't really go home, not that way—but in sight of the Saltmarsh.'' He looked at the closed window. ''Though I've been struggling all night with the question of purpose. Was I brought here? What a grand thought, to be needed, and a terrifying one, to be summoned. . . . Well. I was here to do the good thing, and now it's done.''

''*Done?* And nothing else matters, not me, not Jagg—''

''Please. My precious Ghosh. Don't break my heart.''

''Why not?'' She put her hands to her eyes, but she did not cry; she really did not know how.

''Jagg,'' Ciellon said, ''open the windows.''

''It is cold out, master.''

''Of course; that's the marshmist. I want to smell it. Open them, Jagg.''

Jagg did so. Streaks of dawnlight ran across the Saltmarsh, turning it the color of iron in the forge. The mist was rising, smelling of reeds and salt. There might have been no storm at all. Jagg stood by the window, in the cold marsh breeze, as still as a cedar tree.

Ciellon said, ''The girl's name was Seva sei Varun, but she was called Harmony. Resh didn't think I would remember. He told me, before we both went away, that I would forget. But I didn't forget. I never forget names. The girl's name was Seva sei Varun, and things went so terribly wrong, and she never came back. Resh and I thought we'd never come back either . . . but we did. And . . ." Ciellon turned his cloudy blue eyes on Ghosh. "You see, Harmony, I did remember. And I heard you call, and I came."

Ghosh said, "Will you have tea with me, Ciellon? Worrynot tea?"

Ciellon smiled. "So you learned what it—" His body went rigid. He made a strangling noise. Ghosh leaned over him, put her hands on his shoulders. "Fight, why won't you fight? What do you want dignity for, without any life to—no *life*—" She felt the breath leave him. She let him go, took a step backward and bumped into the door, sagged against it. Outside the window there was a flutter of white wings, and Ghosh turned her head and stared—but it was only a white heron, only a cadie flying; and then a golden cormorant was flying with the heron; and then both birds were gone.

Jagg closed the window. He went to Ciellon's side, reached into his collar, and drew out a small pendant on a cord. He put the luck-piece on Ciellon's chest and folded the wizard's hands over it. He looked at Ghologhosh.

She said, "He didn't babble at the end. He didn't think I was anyone else. There was never one moment when he wasn't sane and wise and— Isn't that right?"

Jagg nodded silently.

"He just wanted me to know he was happy. I wish to Ghol-whose-curse-doesn't-count he hadn't been so happy."

Jagg said, "I must wait now with him 'til midday. So no other spirit can enter his body. It is my land's custom."

"That's a good custom. Show me where to wait with you."

* * *

There were four of them in the Sea Eagle parlor, taking afternoon tea: Korik Li and Cadie ais Ariom called Reed, Jagg, and Ghologhosh.

"We're going to live in Hrothvek," Kory said. "Reed's dowry is the old part of the ais Ariom business—but we won't be part of Dyelam's company."

Reed said, "We like Hrothvek. It's quieter than Liavek, but near enough that we can visit when we want."

Ghosh thought but did not say that it was very generous of the Regent to let Dyelam's children visit him in his house on the Levar's Way, since Dyelam's house would certainly be a kind of prison for the rest of his life. Dyelam would not suffer a hundred thousandth of enough, but he would suffer. And his heirs were good. Ghosh was satisfied.

Kory said, "We've got a big house . . . there's plenty of room for you. For both of you."

"I thank you, no," Jagg said. "I like your country, but it is not home to me. Any place was home when the master was alive . . . but now no place, 'til I find it again."

Reed said, "And you, Ghosh?"

"I'm going to help Jagg find his place," she said. "He's going to help me find a new name, too."

"Harmony?" Kory said.

"No, not Harmony," Ghosh said, gently because Kory didn't know any better. But he was learning. They all were. "Don't try to find my new name." More firmly: "I mean that. Don't try to find me."

Ghosh waved to Zal najhi Zal. "Innkeeper, I believe you said the inn had procured some Worrynot tea. Would you bring it, please?"

As Jagg filled the cups, Reed said, "I wondered about Worrynot tea. Ciellon was always talking about it, and calling it a Hrothvekan joke. So I asked someone at the End of Wine party, and she explained it."

"And?" Ghosh said.

"The way she told it—well." Reed imitated a matron giving out the story over teacakes. "The leaf, you know, the child-preventer, it's usually chewed, but one can make a tea of it, if one knows how. And mothers, you see, in the *older* parts of Hrothvek, their children would be going out, and no use to say 'Be careful,' because at that *certain age* one's quite deaf to such words, of course. But Mother could say, 'A cup of tea with me, before you go,' and that they'd hear, and that they'd do. You see, my dear?'' Reed chuckled. ''And I did. Worrynot tea is a care you don't know you're taking—a favor you do someone else that's really a favor to yourself.''

''And,'' Ghosh said quietly, ''the last cup of childhood, the first cup of responsibility.'' She reached over to the teacups; Jagg had filled five. Ghosh took one and poured it in the earth-pot the followers of Herself used for libations. ''For Ciellon.'' She raised another cup. They all did. ''For all of us.''

''For all of us.''

They drank.

''Gods, it's bitter,'' Kory said.

Green Is the Color

ARIANAI HAD GONE two blocks down the narrow, empty lane before she realized she'd missed Wizard's Row. Or it had missed her; sometimes the street vanished on a moment's notice. It was never individual wizards' houses that came and went, always the whole Row. She wondered just who decided the issue.

It was a gray, gloomy spring afternoon, matching her mood. She half hoped for rain, though she wasn't dressed for it, in white cotton shirt and pants and a thin flannel cape. Rain would at least be something definite—she could point to it and say, "Look, it's raining, no wonder we're all unraveled."

No, she thought. She didn't need cheap excuses. She needed Wizard's Row, and that meant she needed someone to give her directions.

There wasn't anyone on the little street, and all the houses seemed to be shut tight. Some of the doors were boarded up. But a little way ahead there was a glow of light, a shopfront, two high narrow windows and a high narrow door.

There was a rattle like bones overhead. Arianai looked up. Hanging from a wooden bracket, apparently as the shop sign, was a puppet on a string. It danced in the slight breeze—didn't just swing, but actually danced, throwing out its elbows and knees. The only sound on the street was a whisper of air. There was

something eerie about the marionette, dancing to no
music.

Arianai went inside. It was surprisingly spacious
within. The narrow storefront was only a third of the
shop's actual width.

There were shelves filled with stuffed animals of cloth
and fur, dozens of dolls, some with porcelain heads and
arms, little ships with linen sails. More marionettes
hung on the walls, and kites of paper and silk. A table
displayed boards for shah and tafel and other games,
dice, decks of cards; on another, two armies of toy
soldiers faced each other in precise ranks, brightly
painted in the liveries of Liavek and Ka Zhir four centuries ago. There were smells of sandalwood and hide
glue, and a faint taste of raw wood in the air.

A long counter crossed the back of the shop. Behind
it sat a pale-skinned man with long, slender limbs and
very black hair. He was working at a piece of wood
with a small rasp. Other tools and bits of carving were
laid out on the counter within his reach. Behind him
were more shelves, more toys; on the topmost shelf was
a wooden train, a model of the one being built along
the coast from Hrothvek to Saltigos. It had shiny brass
fittings and red-spoked wheels.

"Good afternoon," the man said, without looking
up. "Browsing is free. The prices are outrageous." His
voice was pleasant without being friendly.

Arianai said, "Excuse me, master . . . I am looking
for Wizard's Row. I seem to have gotten lost."

"You, or it?" said the dark-haired man.

"I'm not certain," Arianai said, and laughed, more
from the release of tension than the joke.

"Well," the man said, "the Row is either ninety
paces to the right of my door, or else it is not. Happy
to have been of assistance, mistress." He held up the
piece of whittled wood, blew dust from a hole. He
picked up a length of braided white cord and ran it
experimentally through the hole.

"That's a shiribi puzzle, isn't it?" Arianai said.

"It is."

"I'd always wondered where those came from. You see the White priests with them, but . . ."

"But you cannot imagine White priests making anything with their hands?"

"I'm sorry, I didn't mean to insult your faith."

The man laughed. "If I had a faith, that wouldn't be it." He put down the wood and cord, picked up another stick and a file, went back to work. He had long-fingered, spidery hands, quick and very smooth.

Arianai turned toward the door. An arrangement of soft toys drew her eye; in the center was a fuzzy camel as high as her knee, with a rag-doll rider perched on the hump. The rider, dressed in the robes of the desert nomads, had one arm upraised, with a yarn whip coiled down it—an ordinary pose, but there was something about the way the person was bent forward, and the camel's neck was bent back, that let Arianai hear the rider muttering and grumbling, and the camel—most obstinate beast that ever the gods devised—well, snickering. The toy was a perfect little sketch of a stubborn camel and its hapless owner, in cloth and stitches and yarn.

Perhaps, Arianai thought, there was luck in her wrong turn after all. "Who makes these toys?" she said.

"I do," said the black-haired man, "when I am not interrupted." Arianai was not certain if it was meant as a joke.

She said, "I am looking for something for a child."

"That is very usual in a toyshop." The man stopped his filing, but still did not look up. "Even if the child is oneself, many years late."

"This is a child who cannot sleep," Arianai said.

"Perhaps a music box," the toymaker said, examining the bit of puzzle in his fingers. "I have one that plays 'Eel Island Shoals' with a sound of waves as background, very restful. Or the flannel cat on the third shelf, beside the carousel . . . inside it are a cam and a spring; when wound up, it makes a sound like a beat-ing heart. Some people find it quite soothing." The toymaker's voice had warmed. "Then again, all your child may need is something to hold. A woollen mon-key, or a satin dolphin. A friendly caution—if the child has lost a pet, or greatly desires some particular ani-mal, choose something different. Toys should not come with bad memories or unfulfilled promises attached."

"Why have I never heard of you before?" Arianai said.

The man looked up. His face was fine-boned, some-what sharp, with hazel eyes of a remarkable clarity. "Why should you have?" The warmth was gone again.

"I am Arianai Sheyzu."

"Yes?"

"The children's physician. My house is just around the corner."

"Oh. Forgive me for telling you your trade, Mistress Healer. Please browse at your pleasure." He went back to his work.

"The child—her name is Theleme—is afraid to sleep." The toymaker said nothing, but Arianai went on, the words just spilling out. "She fights sleep for as long as she can, sometimes for days, until she falls into an exhausted sleep. And then she screams. Chamomile and valerian are no use at all, and she has become too frail for stronger drugs."

"I understand now why you were seeking Wizard's Row, Mistress Healer. I do hope that you find it."

Arianai bit her lip. "I'm sorry, Master . . ."

"Quard."

"I didn't mean to burden you with my troubles."

"I never accept such burdens," Quard said. "To the right, ninety paces."

"Thank you." She turned to go.

"Take the flannel cat with you," Quard said in a quiet voice. "It's wound through the seam on its left flank."

Hesitantly, Arianai picked up the stuffed animal. As

she moved it, she felt the springs inside loosen and the wooden heart pulse. Something in the mechanism purred softly.

"No charge for the loan," Quard said.

She looked at him. He was looking back, his eyes bright in his pale face like the eyes of a porcelain doll. Arianai tucked the cat under her arm, gave the man a hard stare back, and went out of the shop. Above her head, the sign-puppet kicked up its heels on a fresh wind from the sea.

Sen Wuchien was strolling through the Levar's Park when he heard the sentry call midnight. He paused for a moment, shivered, and felt an irrational impulse to touch the vessel of his luck. Instead he simply leaned slightly on his walking stick and thought on his vessel, drawing power into his bones to stop the chill. Foolish to have gone walking on such a chilly night, he thought, but the air was clean and pleasant, if damp. He would make tea when he got home, Red Orchid blend, and share it with his cat Shin; then all would be well.

His magic warmed him. With his empty hand he stroked the air, as if Shin's head were there, and tightened his abdomen, pulling power up to his eyes. Around Sen, the landscape brightened, sharpened. The images of catsight reminded him of an ink-and-water drawing; it occurred to Sen that he had neglected his brushes of late. That was not good. New rituals kept the magic responsive, the power fluid.

He stretched his vision, watched an owl gobbling a mouse, a badger waddling off toward its hole, a pair of lovers in deep consideration. He thought, amused, that he would do a pillow-book painting, the sort young people did, indeed the sort he had done as a young man in Tichen. And the text . . .

> Backs shape heaven's arches
> Dark hair braids with fingers
> As the tea grows cold.

Sen realized that he was tracing the calligraphy in the air. It was idle, no light trailed from his fingertips; he had moved, but not invoked. He was old now but not yet so careless. He wiped the power from his eyes, let the magic flush of warmth drain away, and walked on.

He heard a musical whistle, turned his head. There was a figure sitting on a boulder, a long white pipe to its lips. Sen Wuchien wondered that he had not seen this one before—he was not indeed so careless. There was power involved here. Sen looked closer.

The person wore a sashed full robe in the classical Tichenese style, all pure white with the sheen of silk, and white slippers. The face was smooth and finely featured, a young woman's or a beautiful boy's, Sen could not tell, with black hair in a long braid across one shoulder. The piper played a few notes, bowed slightly. Sen Wuchien bowed in return.

Sen said, "I had supposed to meet you in Tichen."

The piper gestured meaninglessly with the white flute, which Sen could see was made of a long bone. The bone of what? he wondered. It was too long to be a man's, or even a horse's. Sen said, "Pardon me. I spoke falsely without intent. I meant to say . . ." But he could no longer recall what he had meant to say.

The person in white stretched out a slim hand, pointing the bone flute at Sen, and spoke in Tichenese. "Come, if you are coming."

Sen smiled at the thought of having some option in the matter, and put his hand on the flute. It was very cold. Sen controlled his trembling without the use of his power, and looked into the face of the white piper.

"Oh," Sen said, "it is *you*—"

He looked at his hand. It glowed with a cool green light. He tried to let go of the bone flute, but could not. He reached for his power, but his mind was cold and would not move that far. Through the green haze that now wrapped his whole body, Sen looked again at the

piper's face, understanding now why he had been offered a choice, and that in fact the offer had been real.

But as the cold caressed his heart, Sen Wuchien
thought that he had already made the choice, thirty years
ago.

The Levar's Park was large and not heavily patrolled;
it was about an hour and a half before the two Guards
came by on their rounds. They saw the glow long before they could see what it came from.

The next day was still gray, and drizzly as well. The
puppet over the toyshop door seemed to clutch at himself and shiver in the wind, and there was a sad drip-
drip from his nose and his toes.

Lamps were lit inside the shop; Quard sat near a
lamp with a large glass lens that threw light on the
doll's face he was painting. As he stroked cobalt blue
on the eyebrows, he said, "Did you find Wizard's
Row?"

"Yes," Arianai said, "and a strange thing happened
there."

"Most who seek Wizard's Row are disappointed if
one does not."

"The Magician at Seventeen and Doctor Twist both
recommended you."

"As what?"

"As one who knows something about dreams."

Quard put down his work, wiped his brush with solvent. "In addition to an entire street named The
Dreamers', the apothecary at Canalgate calls his boat
Dreams. Maydee Gai at the House of Blue Leaves re-
tails them fairly and to most tastes; Cimis Malirakhin
is most to mine. Liavek has many splendid theatres,
though I do not attend them. I'm a toymaker."

Suddenly a chipmunk appeared from beneath the
counter, nodding and chittering, a blue nut in its paws.
"Yes?" Quard said to the animal, then, "I quite agree.
She has made a mistake." *Squeak, squeak?* "Yes, Doc-

tor Twist will probably refund her money, but Trav? Never. It would offend his moral principles.''

Finally Arianai realized that the chipmunk was a puppet on Quard's hand. ''You do that very well,'' she said, ''but I'm not so easily insulted.''

''No insult intended,'' Quard said, now sounding tired. ''I only wished to get a point across. Sometimes puppets are better at that than people.'' He pulled off the glove-puppet and put it on the counter, where it looked rather unpleasantly like a dead real chipmunk.

Arianai said, ''You haven't even seen the child.''

''I assume that you have confidence in your own abilities as a healer. And you have already named the most noted sorcerer in Liavek, as well as the craziest. What is there for me to look at?''

''It was the wizards who named you.''

''So you said. Perhaps I've upset them somehow. They are subtle and quick to anger, you know.''

''Surely you must care what happens to a child.''

''Because I'm a toymaker? Bad proof, mistress.''

''I think you did prove it to me. When you first spoke, about choosing toys.''

''As a children's healer, you must know a certain amount about lice and worms. Do you love them?''

She stared at him. He had picked up the doll-mask, and turned the lamp lens to examine it.

''She slept last night, master. With your cat in her arms, she slept for almost the whole night.''

''Then you have no further need for me. You may keep the cat.''

After a moment Arianai said, ''The girl is dying.''

''So are we all, Healer—with all due respect to your profession.''

For several minutes there was no sound in the shop. Then Quard said, ''Did Trav tell you I'd be difficult?''

''Who?''

''The Magician.''

''He did not tell me you would be hateful.''

"Trav is like that. Bring Theleme tomorrow at five hours past noon."

It took her a moment to realize what he had said. "There's a long night between now and then."

"True. Five tomorrow."

She felt puzzled and relieved—too much of both to be really angry. "Tomorrow, Master Quard. Thank you."

The wizard Gorodain sat in his attic room, contemplating a tabletop. The wood was covered with a disk of glass, etched with a six-pointed star and inscriptions in the language that had centuries ago evolved into the S'Rian tongue. From each of the points of the star, a line led to the center of the disk; above the intersection was a small, darting green flame that burned without fuel or ash. One of the points was empty. Small objects rested on the others: a small bronze mask on a chain, a leather shoelace coiled in a complex knot, an arrowhead, a wooden doll, a silver dagger with a wickedly curved blade and an emerald in the hilt.

The previous night all the points had been filled, a little paper scroll on the sixth.

Gorodain examined the objects on the glass as a man might look over a crucial position in a game of shah—which, after a fashion, this was. The creation of the board, the collection of the pieces, had occupied most of thirty years. This was no time to rush the endgame.

He picked up the mask. It had horns, and finely crafted eyes that were chips of carnelian in onyx. He put it down again on its point, looked out the garret window at the moon rising through torn clouds. It was nearly eleven o'clock. Time to start.

Gorodain concentrated on the vessel of his luck, reached out with an imaginary hand, closed fingers of power on the bronze mask. He began to push it along the cut-glass line, toward the flame in the center.

He met resistance. He concentrated again, pushed

harder. The mask wobbled but did not move. Gorodain felt his strength draining away. He ceased to push.

He raised his right hand, brushed his smallest finger against the boss of the ring he wore. A small blade, no bigger than a fingernail trimming, flicked out. He drew back his left sleeve, spoke some words, and nicked the skin of his arm. A drop of blood fell into the green flame.

The flame guttered, flattened, pooled on the glass. A darkness appeared, and Gorodain looked into it. He saw a man with pale skin, lying on a narrow bed, one arm thrown out straight, the hand clutching the bedpost.

So, Gorodain thought, the key was not yet fully in the lock, the door was closed to him tonight. It was possible still for him to send another nightmare, perhaps force the issue. But that would cost more of his already depleted magic, and the ritual of feeding the flame was exorbitantly costly. There would be time. He had waited thirty years; he could wait another day. He made a gesture and the flame went out.

It had rained all day, and by five in the afternoon showed no sign of stopping. Arianai and Theleme met no one on the street except a pair of cloaked and disgruntled City Guards, who looked after them as if bewildered that anyone would take a child out on a day like this.

They sloshed and bustled down the side street—it didn't seem to have a name posted anywhere—to the sign of the dancing puppet, which now stood nearly still, just shivering in the wet.

There was no one in the front of the shop, though lamps were lit. "Master Quard?" Arianai said. There was no answer. A small light came from a door behind the long counter.

Arianai took the damp cape from Theleme's shoulders. The girl was five, or perhaps six, but her face was ancient, hollowed under cheekbones and dull, unfocused eyes. "Wait right here, Theleme," Arianai said. "I'll be back in just a moment. Don't go anywhere, now."

Theleme nodded. Arianai went behind the counter. "Master Quard?" she said into the dimness beyond the doorway.

"No farther," Quard's voice came back softly. "How did the night go?"

"The cat did help," Arianai said. "She slept for a few hours—but then she began to scream again."

"All right. Go back to her. I'll be out."

Arianai did so. She saw that Theleme was slowly looking around the walls of the shop, at the toys. Perhaps, Arianai thought, they had made an opening; perhaps the key was in the lock.

Quard came out. He wore a long robe of blue and yellow, with a matching skullcap. Without a word, he went to the windows and lowered the blinds. The lamps were already lit. Then he bowed low to Theleme, and settled down to sit cross-legged on the floor before her, his clothes billowing around him. The effect was at once clownish and impressive.

"You would be Mistress Theleme," Quard said in a respectful tone.

Theleme nodded.

"I am Quard Toymaker, Quard of Dancing Wood, and your friend the healer Arianai has brought you to me, through the storm and the cold and the wet, because I need your help in a thing."

"Yes, master?"

"Sit down, mistress." Quard spread his arms above his lap. Theleme looked at Arianai, who nodded. Theleme sat down, cradled on Quard's knee.

"Now, mistress," he said, "do you know of the Farlands? The Countries of Always-Cold?"

"Anni has told me stories."

Quard shot a curious glance at Arianai, then said, "There is a princess in the Farlands—just about your age."

"What does she look like?"

"I have never seen her," Quard said, "but they tell me she has yellow hair like yours, and violet eyes like Mistress Anni's, and the pale skin of all Farlanders."

"Like yours?"

"There you have it. Now, mistress, the princess is to have a birthday soon. Lean close to me." He whispered in Theleme's ear, and she nodded gravely.

Quard said, "Now you understand how important this matter is?" Theleme nodded again. Any Liavekan, even the youngest, understood the seriousness of revealing a true birthday.

"Now, mistress, comes my problem. The princess must have a gift for her birthday. But there are so many things in my shop, and I know them all so well, that I cannot choose one for her. Do you think you can help me?"

Theleme put a finger to her mouth. She turned again to Arianai, who smiled and nodded.

Quard helped Theleme stand up again, and she began to wander around the shop, looking wonderingly at the toys. She put out a hand hesitantly, drew it back.

"Please touch," Quard said. "You will not break them."

Theleme searched among the toys for a third of an hour. Arianai caught herself fidgeting; Quard just sat, smiling crookedly, his hands crossed in his lap.

Arianai noticed that the backs of Quard's hands were entirely smooth, without a single hair. His face was just as bare below his eyebrows, without the shadow of a beard. Was Quard a woman? she wondered. The flowing robe made it difficult to tell. Not her business, she supposed. If this succeeded, she did not care if Quard was a troll.

Theleme had picked up a toy and was bringing it to Quard. It was the soft camel-and-rider Arianai had seen on her first visit. Quard held out his hands and received the doll. "Why, this is it, Mistress Theleme; that is just the present for the princess. I never would have guessed it.'' Quard stood up in a fluid motion, holding the stuffed toy in both hands. ''Perfect, perfect. I must arrange at once to send this to the Farlands.''

Theleme looked up at him, still as a sculpture, watching with dead eyes as the toy camel left her.

Quard turned away, then spun full circle, his robe floating out. ''Wait,'' he said, and sat down again. ''Come closer, mistress.''

Theleme did so. Quard said, ''My eyes are not what they once were, you know. Will you look closely at this toy, *very* close, and tell me if anything is wrong with it? A princess's gift must be perfect, you know.''

Theleme took hold of the toy, began to minutely examine it. As she did, Quard reached slowly to the back of her neck, began to rub it. Theleme leaned over the soft camel. Quard stroked downward. Theleme's head tipped forward and was pillowed on the camel's hump.

Surprised and a little alarmed, Arianai said, ''What did you—?''

''Let nature take its course,'' Quard said softly, and then pressed a finger to his lips. He leaned close to Theleme and said, ''They will ask me why, you know. Not the princess—she will be delighted, I am sure—but all the lords and ladies at court, they will want to know, 'Why that toy? Why a camel?' Surely you know how lords and ladies are, when they see something that is special to you. They always want to know why.''

Eyes still shut, Theleme said, ''Yes, Master Quard.''

''Tell me what the princess should say to them.''

Theleme said, in a startlingly clear voice, ''The green man is there. He has to go away.''

''Is the green man bad? Is that why he has to go?''

''He wants to hurt the princess. He wants her to die.''

''Do you see the green man, Theleme? Is he here?''

''Yes. Yes!'' The child struggled. Arianai bent forward. Quard hugged Theleme and said, ''Look away from the man, Theleme. Look away. Do you see something coming there? Do you see a camel, and a rider? I think they're coming. Do you see them?''

"Yes . . . I see them."

"And does the rider have a whip? Can you see the whip in the rider's hand?"

"Yes."

"Look, Theleme! The rider's reaching down for you. Catch the rider's hand as the camel comes by. Quick, now! Catch it!" He gripped Theleme's hand in his own.

"I have it!"

"I'll pull you up now!" He tugged gently at Theleme's hand. "Hold tight, hold tight! We have to ride fast!" He slipped his hand around Theleme's waist.

"I'm holding, master!"

"Now, we must ride for the green man. You have to be brave now, Theleme, for we must drive him out. Do you see the whip in the rider's hand?"

"Yes, I see it. I'll try to be brave."

"Very well. Here we come. And here comes the whip." Quard gestured to Arianai. She raised her hands and clapped them as hard as she could. Theleme twitched, but held tight to the stuffed camel.

"Here it comes again!" *Crack!*

"Is he running, Theleme? Can you see the green man run?"

"Yes! He's running! He's running away . . ." Theleme's voice faded, and she relaxed in Quard's arms. He rocked her gently.

"I think she will be better now," he said finally. "Here—can you take her?"

Arianai did, and Quard stood up, the stuffed toy under his arm. He put it in Arianai's arms beside Theleme, who cuddled it without waking. Then he walked to the door. "I'll go up to the corner and get you a footcab. There must be an enterprising few of them out in the slop." He opened the door, letting cool air in from the dark outside. "Well. It's stopped raining."

"Quard, I—"

"I doubt she'll remember the story about the princess as any different from the rest of the dream. If she does, tell her that I made another camel, just for her."

"Quard."

"Let me get the cab. You don't want to carry her home, do you?"

"I wouldn't mind. If you carried the camel."

"I'll carry the child if you carry the camel." Quard's voice was suddenly flat. "That must be the punch line to a joke, but I don't remember it."

"Come and have tea. I'd like to talk to you."

"What, and wake Theleme with our pillow conversation?" he said, sounding more sad than funny.

"Do you have other appointments?"

"There's your cab," Quard said, in a tone that made Arianai hug the child tight. He went running out the door, and was gone for minutes, and minutes, the door wide open. Then a footcab did appear. Arianai went to meet it, found the driver had already been paid. But Quard was nowhere in sight. Arianai closed the shop door and rode home. She put Theleme to bed, the camel still in the child's grasp, and then sat in her office making notes on the case and rereading medical books that had been dull the first time. Finally, at almost midnight, she went to bed, and her sleep was very sweet.

Shiel ola Siska blew through the narrow bronze pipe, sending a narrow jet of flame from the spirit burner onto the tinned wires in her left hand, brazing them to a circular copper plate as broad as three fingers. She tongued the blowpipe, spraying fire around the copper, producing a pleasing rainbow finish on the hammered metal. She slid her fingers to the other end of a wire, bent it around, then fused it to the plate. Another wire was curved and twisted over and under the first before being brazed in place; then the next, and the next.

The end product was a copper brooch bearing a coil of wires, tangled, complex, yet pleasing in form. The purpose of the item, the ritual, was antimagic: when luck was driven through the brooch, spells cast at the wearer would be ensnared in the coil, their energy twisted and untuned and dissipated. Certain spells, at any rate. "The most crucial of magics," ola Siska's instructor had taught her, "is the illusion that wizards are infallible, but their customers can foul up any enchantment."

And as with any magical device, it was temporary; it would lose its luck on ola Siska's birthday, or with her death. No wizard could truly create. A true adept could bind luck into a thing and make it truly magical—but only once, for the bound magic was gone from the wizard forever. The brooch was just a brief diversion of luck, as a spinning top that could stand impossibly on its point until it slowed and toppled.

Ola Siska stroked her finger across the wires. They played a faint series of notes, not quite music. She snuffed the spirit burner, took the brooch to a table covered in white linen. A high window let the light of the three-quarter moon shine upon it. She took up a pair of forceps, and with them lifted a small silver casting of a spread-eagled, naked man. She started to lower it into the nest of wires.

There was a slight rumbling beneath the floor. The copper brooch bounced into the air, rolled across the linen, and fell to the floor, where it kept rolling. Shiel muttered darkly and turned to catch it as it wheeled away—had she been thinking of spinning tops? Was that why the thing was acting so—

The brooch bumped against metal with a little tinny clink and fell over. The thing it had struck shifted; it was a boot, of lapped bronze plates.

Ola Siska looked up, slowly. Above the boot was a bronze greave, a knee-cover, then, resting on the knee, a jointed bronze gauntlet. The hand pushed down, and the knee levered up, and the figure of a man in full metal armor stood up, a bronze man shaded green with verdigris. His breastplate was heavily engraved with intricate designs, and his helmet bore winglike flanges at the temples. Its crown nearly brushed Shiel ola Siska's ceiling beams.

His faceplate was a mirror-finished sheet of metal,

without features, without holes for sight or speech or air.

Her throat felt tight. So it had not been time and chill night air that had taken Sen Wuchien after all, she thought. She should have known.

She should have been *told*!

The bronze man walked toward her, holding out its hands. Ola Siska saw that its forearms were spiked down their length, like a crab's arms. She was quite certain that the jagged metal points had not been there a moment ago.

She flexed her hands. If she had not been at work, there would have been a ring on every finger, half a dozen bracelets on each of her wrists, each one the ritual of a spell. But she still wore amulets, around her neck and ankles, in her hair. And most important, she had the vessel of her luck safely on her person.

She caught her full skirts in her hands, swept them upward like a butterfly's wings, then released the cloth and touched a square pendant of interlaced steel and glass rods.

As the skirts fell, a circle of something like stained glass, though impossibly thin for glass, appeared before her. Grainy color radiated from the center of the disk, and thin black veins.

The bronze man collided with the colored disk. There were showers of sparks where his armor touched it. Ola Siska reached to the top of her head, pulled out two long golden pins. She raised her hands and breathed deep, feeling the power rise from her vessel to the pins.

A bronze gauntlet punched through the disk in a spray of colored fragments. Cracks shot through the glass, and in a moment it collapsed to the floor, and evaporated.

Ola Siska stiffened, but did not break the incantation. She threw the two pins. They flew true as arrows through the air, and pierced the bronze man's hands, nailing them to his breastplate. Ola Siska raised her right fist, slammed it into her left palm, and the pins

shone with unbearable blue light, hissing as they welded
themselves into place.

The bronze man struggled to pull his hands free, as
Shiel ola Siska groped through her boxes of jewelry for
the proper ritual device. There was a grating noise,
then a rhythmic clinking, like a music box but deeper
and flatter. Ola Siska seized a bracelet and turned.

The bronze man's arms had fallen off at the shoulders, and dangled from his chest by the nails through
their gauntlets. From the sides of his breastplate, another pair of arms, thin and rodlike, was folding out,
oiled cables gliding in grooves along their length.

Ola Siska dropped the bracelet—no use now to sever
the thing's legs—and turned, and ran, out the door and
into the night. She could hear the clanking of the bronze
man behind her, and could not help but waste a moment in looking back: there were now spikes and hooks
and blades down all its limbs, and steam hissed from
its joints.

She ran up the street, trying to keep a grip on her
thoughts and her skirts, unable to order her luck with
the brazen thing behind her. She seemed to feel a dull
red heat from it, but that was only in her mind, surely
in her mind—

She paused, leaned against a doorframe, turned to
face the thing. It was twenty paces behind her, taking
slow long strides. There was no steam, no furnace glow,
and even its steps were not overly loud; it had a sort of
quiet dignity as it came for her. She held up a hand in
a warding gesture, saw that her fingernails shone bril-
liantly green.

Into the pit with dignity, she thought, and hiked up
her skirts and ran. She heard the clank of metal behind
her, dared not waste the time to turn but knew it was
gaining. Could it tire? *Metal fatigue*, she thought,
with—irony? Ha, ha, ha.

Suddenly she thought of a place to run, a thing to
run for. She had cast the spell away uncast, and now—

She stretched luck down to her right foot, felt the

anklet there rattle and loosen. There was no time to stop, take the thing off, do this properly; it had to be timed just right—

Ola Siska kicked off the loop of silver. It sailed out before her, spinning, expanding from a bracelet to a belt to a loop broader than her shoulders; it struck the pavement; she leaped into it—

And landed on her hands and knees, gasping, half the city away, where Park Boulevard met the Street of the Dreamers. The shop called the Tiger's Eye was dark, its awnings folded. There was only the slight glitter of streetlamps on the items behind its windows.

Shiel tried to stand. She couldn't, not yet; the spell had drawn most of her strength. She was terribly cold. And her nails and knuckles were greenly luminous.

She pushed herself upright and went to the door of the shop, groped at her belt for a gold-and-silver key that hung there. She rubbed the pendant, pulling hard at the last of her luck.

Her hand spasmed and the key fell on its cord. Of course the shop would be sealed against magical entry. She pounded on the door, still short the breath to shout.

Behind her was a sound like a key in an unoiled lock. She looked into the dark shop, and in the glass saw the bronze man reflected, tall and shining and severe, his arms stretched out to her.

Ola Siska leaned against the door. With just a moment to recover herself, she could break the glass, reach through . . . no, that was too obvious, the inner bolt would require a key. There was no sign of a stirring within, no lights, just a twinkling like stars on crystal and silver and brass. Only an inch of wood and glass between her and that whole constellation of life.

Something blurred her view: it was her face, shining green in the glass. Was that truly the way it was, then? Was she really so tired of running?

She turned, leaning back against the door, hands on knees that glowed greenly through her skirts. She looked up at the bronze man, who stood above her with his metal hands outstretched. His face was green as well . . . no, it was just her reflection.

"Come," said the bronze man, his voice rasping and twanging like a saw cutting wires, "if you are coming."

"I could have run farther still," she said, breathless but with dignity. "I could." She held out her hand, but remained sitting, so that he would have to kneel to her, like a courtier and not a conqueror.

Which he obligingly did.

The sun came out the next morning, in more ways than one; Theleme woke wanting breakfast, and almost smiling. Arianai gave her some buttered toast and juice, knowing the child would be hungry but that her stomach would be in no shape for a heavy meal, and then they tossed on light cloaks and went for a walk along the canal.

As they crossed the lower bridge, they ran into a cluster of people on the street, around the Tiger's Eye, and a line of Guards keeping them away from something. Arianai recognized the officer in charge, a tall, hawk-faced woman with straight black hair, and walked up to her.

"Hello, Jem."

Jemuel, captain of the Levar's Guard, turned. "Hi, Anni." More softly she said, "Keep the little one away. It's not nice, what's over there."

"Can I help?"

"Not any longer, Anni. It's another green one."

"What? A Green priest?"

"Another glowing one—you haven't heard? The half-copper rags have been full of it."

"I've been busy, and you know I don't read the rags."

Jemuel said, "We've got two wizards dead in three nights. Not a scratch on either of them—but the bodies are glowing green as fireflies."

"Just a moment, Jem." Arianai led Theleme over to

a baker's cart, bought her a sweet biscuit for distraction, then went back to Jemuel. "Glowing? Magic?"

"What it seems. Funny, though, you should even have to ask—Thomorin Wiln said that phosphorus could make a body glow so, but he tested, and there wasn't any, nor any other poison he could find. Phosphorus, imagine that. More ways to die than you'd think, eh, Anni?"

"Who were they?"

"Um? Oh. Two nights back was that old Titch who lived up on the canal, Wuchien; found him in the park. And this morning when Snake opens up, she finds Shiel ola Siska glowing on her doorstep."

"Snake," Arianai said distantly, thinking of Snake's skill with the camel driver's whip she always carried, thinking too of a rag-stuffed toy.

"—so there it sits," Jemuel was saying, "one not far from his house, the other a long way the wrong side of the canal; a man, a woman; a Titch and a Liavekan— no pattern to it except that they both did magic, no motive, no sense. And an ola Siska dead, so the nobility are demanding that Somebody Do Something." She sighed. "Guess who."

"Captain?" It was a young Tichenese, Snake's assistant Thyan. "There's kaf."

"Enough for one more?" Jemuel said, indicating Arianai.

"Of course. Hello, Healer."

"Well . . . will Theleme be any trouble in there?"

"I'll take care of her, mistress," Thyan said. "Part of the job. Do come in."

Jemuel and Arianai sat in wicker chairs, by a tiny brass table with the porcelain kaf service; Snake, wearing an embroidered abjahin with the long whip coiled incongruously at her waist, leaned against a cabinet, stroking her cup, looking as if she wanted to pace. Arianai recalled that the shopkeeper had quietly put out word that she was to marry shortly. Death on the doorstep must have been quite an intrusion.

"You did know ola Siska?" Jemuel said.

"Of course I knew her. Everyone involved with jewelry did. But I never carried much of her work. Mostly she sold through Janning Lightsmith, sometimes the Crystal Gull."

"Too expensive for your trade?"

"Thanks, Jem."

"Well?" Jemuel said, not apologetic.

Snake gestured with her fingertips. "Not to my taste. Shiel had a particular fondness for . . . well, strange images. Skulls. Human figures twisted up. And sharp edges: she showed me a necklace once that . . ." Snake ran a hand around her throat.

Arianai said, "There's a market for that?"

Snake said, in a more relaxed voice, "There's a market for everything. I'm no prude; I'll sell you a poison ring, or a pendant with a hidden dagger. But Shiel ola Siska's work seemed to . . . celebrate death, and pain." She looked around the shop, at the multitude of trinkets and oddments that crowded the place. "Let me show you something," she said suddenly, went behind the counter, and brought out a velvet-covered tray. She raised a spherical pendant on a fine gold chain. "This is one of hers. I bought it for the craftsmanship, before I quite saw what the thing was."

The pendant was an openwork ball of gold and silver pieces; the gold bars were straight, the silver ones coiled.

"It's a shiribi puzzle, isn't it?" Arianai said. "What's that in the center?" She put her finger to the pendant.

"Careful!" Snake cried, and Arianai stopped her hand, just as she saw that the object within the shiribi puzzle was a silver figure of a man, curled into a fetal position with one arm outstretched.

Then Snake's hand shook, and the metal sphere bumped against Arianai's fingertip; and the ball collapsed on its silver springs, into a tight knot of white and yellow metal from which a pale hand emerged in a gesture of pure desperation.

"Kosker and Pharn!" Jemuel said.

"It'll certainly be salable now," Snake said, "dead artists and all that. But I've wondered ever since I first looked closely at the thing, would I want to do business with anyone who'd buy it?"

"You think it had anything to do with ola Siska being at your door last night?"

"I've told you already, Jem, I don't know why she was there."

"And you didn't hear her knock."

"If she knocked, I didn't hear it." She put the pendant down. "There *was* a privacy spell on the bedroom last night."

"Thank you for saving me the question," Jemuel said. "Anni? Something wrong?"

Arianai realized she was still staring at the shiribi puzzle. "No, nothing."

From several corners of the shop, clocks began to strike nine. Jemuel said, "Pharn's teeth, it's three hours past my bedtime. If anything occurs to you—either of you—as a clue, you'll let me know, right?"

"Of course."

"Sure, Jem."

"Thanks for the kaf. I'll sleep better for it." She waved and went out of the shop, jingling the porcelain bells above the door.

Arianai said, "Snake, you sell some toys, don't you?"

"Sure. Want something for the little girl you've been—"

"No, I . . . have you ever bought from Quard?"

"Quard? Yes, some marionettes. He makes the best string-puppets I've ever seen. He'd have a reputation and a half, if his shop weren't harder to find than Wizard's Row in a dust storm."

"Hard to find . . ."

Snake put her hand on Arianai's shoulder. "Are you sure there's nothing wrong, Anni?" They locked eyes for a long moment, and then Snake said gently, "*Oh.*

Yeah. Me, too . . . guess you've heard.'' She smiled, a little sadly. ''It does make it harder to look at death, doesn't it?''

Arianai nodded and went out. In front of the shop, Thyan was demonstrating cat's cradles for Theleme, who watched in amazement as the knots appeared and vanished. Arianai said, ''Time to go, Theleme. Thank you, Thyan,'' and handed the young woman a copper.

''I shouldn't take this,'' Thyan said. ''It's part of serving the customers . . .''

''I didn't buy anything.''

''Oh. I guess it's all right, then.'' Thyan grinned. From within the shop came the sound of a single clock striking nine, and Snake's voice calling, ''Thyan!''

''Oops,'' Thyan said, ''see you later,'' and ducked inside.

Theleme held up her fingers, tangled in brown string. ''See, Anni? You pull, and snap she closes!'' She tugged at the figure.

''Yes, dear, I see,'' Arianai said, and licked her dry lips. ''Let's go home, now, and you can nap.''

''Well,'' Quard said as Arianai entered the shop, ''you are by far the most regular customer I have ever had.'' He had some of the miniature soldiers arrayed on the counter, with books piled up to represent hills and a blue scarf for a river.

''Tell me about shiribi puzzles,'' she said, trying not to look at the little metal men.

Quard shrugged. ''They involve rods and strings. The object of the puzzle is to take it apart, and then to reassemble it.'' He went to one of the shelves behind the counter, took down one of the puzzles; it was the size of a small melon, of dark oiled wood and white cord, with a blue glass ball caged inside. ''Some, like this one, have a thing inside them, which is supposed to be 'freed,' but the problem is the same.''

''Where do they come from?''

Quard looked up. "Toymakers, when they're not being interrupted."

"I mean—"

"I know what you mean. I was being hateful again. I don't know who invented them, but they're old, several thousand years at least. And most of them come from the far West, beyond Ombaya." He turned the puzzle over in his fingers. "The White priests have decided they mean something important, and wear them as symbols of whatever-it-is."

"You make them for the Whites?"

"I haven't yet. But then they haven't asked me."

"Have you made them to order?" she asked carefully.

Quard blinked his clear light eyes. "I was once asked to make one as a cage for an animal—a chipmunk, say, or a large mouse. I'd seen them before; the puzzle has to be made of something the pet can't gnaw, of course, but it can easily be fed through the openings, and when it runs for exercise the cage rolls around on the floor, which also cleans it . . . however, this customer wanted a bit more. The puzzle was to be designed so that a mistake in opening it would crush the animal to death."

In her mind Arianai heard the snap of metal. "Did you build it?"

"Is it any of your business if I did?"

She said slowly, "Do you know Shiel ola Siska?"

"The jeweler-mage. I know she's dead."

"It only happened this morning."

"They print the half-copper rags so fast these days, isn't it a wonder?" He put the puzzle back on the shelf. "Time I was going back to work. Theleme is well?"

"Yes. Theleme is well."

"I don't suppose I'll be seeing you anytime soon, then. Do come back if you need a toy."

"I'm still interested in shiribi puzzles."

"Well." Quard took down the puzzle again, spun it between his palms. "There really isn't much more to be said about them. Do you know the match take-away

game, where a player can always force a win if he
knows the right moves? Well, there's a general solution
to these, a set of moves that will unravel any shiribi.
Once you know it, they're no fun any longer."

"Any of them?"

"Quite simple and obvious, once it's occurred to
you." He brought the puzzle down on the countertop
and smashed it to pieces.

"Quard—"

"You *did* ask me for an answer, Healer. There it is.
Good day."

Gorodain looked over his glass gameboard. The
bronze mask was gone now; the flame had been almost
greedy to receive it. The key was in the lock, and
turned.

There had been a great deal of news-rag speculation
on Shiel ola Siska's apparent attempt to break into the
Tiger's Eye in her last moments. Gorodain was not dis-
pleased. It would confuse and distract the temporal au-
thorities in looking for an answer, which they would
not find. He had acquired the small mask from Snake's
shop some years ago, through a series of intermedi-
aries, all of them now comfortably dead; even if Snake
should recall the item's sale, there was no way of tracing it to him. And the thing itself no longer existed.

It was just like ola Siska, Gorodain mused, to try to
dispose of the thing by selling it, casting it to the winds
of luck, so to speak; it was Shiel's habit of playing with
sharp things that had brought her into the circle to begin
with.

Just as it would be the pretty young healer's boldness
that would bring them together, that would open the
bottomless spring of death and let it flow. There were,
in round figures, three hundred thousand living human
beings in Liavek. Three hundred thousand deaths! The
thought alone was wine to the senses.

Gorodain reached his magic to the carved glass and
touched the knotted shoelace.

* * *

Teyer ais Elenaith lived in the entire top floor of a squarely dull old building in the Merchant's Quarter, fronting on the Levar's Way. The ground floor was occupied by a firm of admiralty lawyers, and the level between was packed with the lawyers' files and records, so that no one but the occasional tired clerk or nautically inclined mouse ever heard the thump of a foot from above.

The loft was one large room, closets and a tiny bath-chamber along one wall, heavy trusses and skylights overhead. Folding screens could fence off sleeping or dressing areas as needed. On the walls, dancing shoes and performance props, canes and bells and caps, hung from pegs. There were several full-length mirrors and a balance rail, and in a corner were a stack of music boxes and a large metronome.

A few sweet-scented candles were burning, but most of the light came from the moon through the skylights. All the folding screens had been set up on the studio floor in rectilinear boxes and corridors. Moonlight, direct and from the wall mirrors, added panels of silver light and black shadow to the maze.

Teyer ais Elenaith leaned against the wall, arms folded, one foot on the floor and one on the wainscot, examining the puzzle she had set up. She wore a loose shirt over trousers, all crimson silk of Tichen, with a broad leather belt, something she had once fancied on a sailor's hard body, riding low on her hips. Her dancing slippers were red kid, laced around her strong slender ankles. A nine-strand braid of gold wire wrapped twice around her long throat; a compromise, but one had to keep one's luck vessel within three steps—ordinary steps, not dancer's leaps—*and* make certain it didn't go flying during a particularly active movement. Probably the reason there weren't more dancer-magicians; of course, it also required a bit more working room than most rituals. She looked up at the ceiling beams; ais

Elenaith was not a tall woman, barely five feet, and
still the trusses were inconveniently low at times. Better, she supposed, than having columns interrupting the
open floor.

She went to the corner and set the metronome tick-
ing, its brass pendulum catching moonlight on each
beat. She took a few loose-jointed steps, rolled her
shoulders. One, she thought to the rhythm. Two. One,
two, *three.*

She leaped into the shadow-maze, landing on the ball
of a foot barely a span from one of the screens. She
arched her back, stroked her hands down the screen
without touching it, spun on her toe and sidestepped,
froze again, leaped again.

Ais Elenaith worked the maze with her whole body,
threading through it start-stop-turn-leap, moving ever
faster, coming ever closer to the screens without touching them, the smell of sweat mingling with the candles,
the only music the tick of the metronome, the steady
chord of her breathing, the bang of her feet on the floor,
all in harmony.

She came through the maze, stepped, stretched, then
repeated it, faster. She came through and repeated, and
now there was music in the loft, instruments called up
through the luck around her neck, cittern and hammered harp and horn. Once again and there were bells
and drums; once again and there was a chorus, and
sparks showered from her hands and feet as she moved.

Once again, and she saw him, standing by the metronome, in front of the mirror, which did not reflect
him.

He wore trousers tight enough to show every mus-
cle—*every* one—of black silk that glistened in the
moonlight, and around his broad bare chest was a
leather harness with small gold bells, as the temple
dancers of eastern Tichen wore. One gold earring, one
bracelet, one anklet. He was barefoot, and his hair was
tied back like a sailor's.

So, ais Elenaith thought, was this why so many went

willingly? But she was more than a heart and a will. He would have to dance for her life. She spun, clapped her hands, stepped again into the maze, hearing the temple bells chiming behind her.

Step, turn, pause. Her music was now a bright passage for horn, counterpoint to the golden bells. One, two, leap, four. She waited for him to falter, to touch the maze. He did not. Perhaps he would not; it was not necessary. Arch, step, pivot, *kick*—

Her foot snapped out, and a panel swung on its hinges, slamming closed against another with a crack and a streak of red fire. She danced on, two, three, *kick*, and another screen closed up.

She circled the maze of screens, kicking higher than her chin, shutting the panels like a puzzle box, luck in her throat like the lump of arousal. Sweat spattered from her as she moved, the droplets crackling with waste luck. The candle flames were drawn toward the center of the room.

The spell drew close. Ais Elenaith cartwheeled heels-over-head three times and drove both feet into a painted wood panel. The screens all collapsed, one on another with a crescendo of slams. All the candles blew out.

Teyer ais Elenaith wavered on her feet. There were no more sounds of footsteps or bells or music, nothing but the metronome's tick, tick—

It stopped beating.

Ais Elenaith turned. The man held his finger on the pendulum. Then he held out his hand, palm up; he did not have to speak. She knew an invitation to the dance.

She bowed. She pulled the metal braid from around her neck; it only chafed, and she was out of magic for this night. It was a strain on the strength, so much more than dancing. She pulled the lacings of her kid slippers, kicked them off. Teyer ais Elenaith took the offered hand, and saw pale green light shimmer and bounce from the mirrors in the loft.

She began to dance. There was no hesitancy in it; she had always called hesitancy the death of the dance.

And it was not hard at all, even without her luck. The
stiffness that she had tried to ignore these last years was
gone truly. She moved with her partner like two hands
at the same task, and she danced for joy—what other
way is there?

They spun to the door, and kicked it open, and moved
lightly down the stairway to the moonlit street. The
partner held out his hands, and she leaped into them,
was lifted into the clear night sky. Something fell away
from ais Elenaith, the last concealment of the veil dance
she had done so long; it crumpled beneath her feet but
did not hinder her step, the green light of its bones
through its flesh only a backlight to her firework movements, as she danced away from Liavek with the partner she had always known would come.

The House of Responsible Life was a boxy building
at Liavek's northeast corner, between the Street of
Thwarted Desire and Neglectful Street. Though not far
from a city gate, it was not in a heavily traveled part
of Liavek. So the occupants of the House, the religion
whose color was green, did see the crowd around them.

The Green order did not do anything at first. It was
not their way to do anything: they were a faith of sworn
suicides, concerned only with fulfilling all their earthly
obligations and responsibilities before making an artistic exit from life. This was not too clearly understood
by most Liavekans, and crowds had stared at the House
before. The order simply took no notice; there was work
to do in the House and its gardens.

They noticed the first stone through the window.

Suddenly there were more stones, and angry shouts.
Glass was breaking, and people were running, and
wood splintered. A hole was battered in the garden
fence, and bodies crowded through, trampling vines
and crushing fruit, doing more damage by accident than
design. Someone tossed in a little pig, which ran about
rooting and squealing.

At the front of the House, a novice came out of the

main double doors and hurried to close the window shutters; a shower of stones drove her to cover. Voices were loud and without meaning. Someone lit a torch. The crowd, some fifty people, moved forward.

The front doors opened again, and a man in green robes came out. He was not tall, with long hair and large brown eyes in a soft face. He walked down the three green steps, and went straight toward the mob, to the man holding the torch. Missiles shot past him; he ignored them.

The Green priest put both hands on the burning roll of papers and jerked it out of the holder's grip. He threw it down and stamped on it.

The crowd faltered, fell back a step. They muttered in a low rumble that was not quite speech. The Green priest stood still. The crowd started to surge forward again.

There was a gunshot, and then a voice: *"All right, that's enough!"* To one side, pressing in on the crowd, was a line of City Guards in gray. Most had swords out; a few carried flintlock shotguns, clumsy but able to splatter men like thrown tomatoes. The shot and the voice had come from a Guard captain with black hair and a fierce expression. Her double-barreled pistol was still leveled, and people were backing away from her as from a plague carrier.

The crowd was breaking up, people colliding with one another, drifting away from the House, falling down, getting up and running.

It was over almost as quickly as it had started, the street emptying out as the line of Guards pressed forward. The Green priest had not moved. The captain walked up to him.

"Hello, Verdialos," Jemuel said. "Nice morning."

"I can recall better," the priest said, "and worse." He turned to survey the damage to the House, then walked quickly to the bush where the novice was still huddling. "Are you hurt, my dear? No, that's good. Go inside now, and tell Cook I said to give you two

honeycakes and some strong tea.'' He turned back to
Jemuel. ''The gardens?''

''I've got some people back there.'' She took her
pistol off cock and put it away. ''Dialo, I realize you're
sworn to kill yourself, but weren't you trying rather
hard at it just then?''

''Oh,'' Verdialos said, and his eyes went very round
and white. ''I didn't . . . well, it was their stoning the
girl. It made me angry.''

''Angry. You? If I put that in the report, no one will
believe it.''

''Would you then also put down that my order takes
complete responsibility for the green deaths, so that
won't be believed either?''

''We're doing what we can, Dialo. Do you want
guards full time?''

''I'll put it to the Serenities, but I don't think so. It
might only encourage another mob. We were fortunate
today.''

Jemuel nodded. ''I wanted to tell you that I've been
put on special duty to deal with this green mess. No
offense.''

''None taken. If we learn anything, of course we'll
let you know.''

''Thanks, Dialo.''

''Thank you, Jem. Good death to you.''

''I'll just say good day, thanks.''

Jemuel took a footcab back to the Guard offices in
the Levar's Palace; the runner grudgingly took a city
credit slip for the fare, but insisted on a cash tip.

Jemuel made out the reports on the night's dirty work
and the incident at the House of Responsible Life. The
riot—she had to call it that—was really bad news; the
Regent would want to know if Liavek were being
pushed to the edge by the deaths, and the truth, that in
a city of three hundred thousand you could get fifty
people together to throw rocks on any excuse at all,
would not reassure him a bit.

Only three deaths, she thought. More people than

that died every night in the Old City, of starvation or other sharp edges. But these were all wizards, and even people who knew better—like other magicians—tended to think of wizards as immortal. And it was certainly a creepy way to go. Sen Wuchien's body was four days cold in the morgue, with nobody to claim it, and still glowing. Somebody wanted to keep him on the slab, to see how long he did glow. There was a typically morgue-ish joke about saving money on lamp wicks.

Her pen was starting to wobble. So this was special duty: she was supposed to end her shift with the end of the night watch, and here it was morning with a vengeance. She shoved her chair back from her littered desk, put her feet up, and closed her eyes. Immediately there was a knock at the door.

Lieutenant Jassil put his red-haired head in. "Captain? Someone here to see you. It's Thyan, from Snake's place."

"Sure, Rusty."

The Tichenese girl came in. Jemuel gave her forehead a pat in greeting. "What news, mistress?"

Thyan held out a small shiny thing. "Snake thought you'd want to see this."

Jemuel looked at the object. *"Fhogkhefe,"* she said.

Thyan giggled and blushed slightly. "That's a good one, Captain."

Jemuel said, "You speak Bhandaf?"

"I work in Snake's shop, Captain. I can swear in sixteen languages."

"Come visit this office on a holiday night, you'll learn sixteen more," Jemuel said. "Come on, let's go talk to Snake."

Quard was reading when Arianai came in. He put the book down, said, "I'm sorry about yesterday. I was upset."

"Would you like to tell me what you were upset about?"

"No."

She nodded. "I guess the apology will have to do, then. Would you mind talking about Theleme?"

"She's not ill again?"

"No. She's fine. I wanted to ask—you seemed to slip into her dream so readily."

"You wondered if I knew something about green men?" Quard said, an edge in his voice. "Green men who kill?"

"That's not it at all," Arianai said. It was at least halfway the truth. "I was wondering . . . if we could work out where the nightmare came from, so she could be protected from having it again."

Quard nodded. "All right. What's the girl's family like?"

"She doesn't have one. She was left as an infant at the House of Responsible Life—"

"The suicides' order?"

"Yes, of course," Arianai said, startled. "I don't know why. Perhaps the person who left her misunderstood the name of the order, thinking it meant 'those who take responsibility for the living,' or somesuch."

"That is what the name does mean," Quard said, "in Sylarine . . . Old S'Rian."

"There's such a thing as *Old* S'Rian?"

"Everything has a past," Quard said softly. "What did the Green priests do with the child?"

"They thought about taking her in as a novice of the order. But it was decided that if she were raised entirely within the House, she could never come to an unbiased decision about her own death . . . isn't that odd, that a religion of suicides should be so particular about who actually dies?"

"Every faith excludes someone from paradise."

She laughed in the hope it was a joke. "Do you know, I cannot remember ever having heard of a member of the House actually taking his own life?"

Quard said, "They may not, until they have severed every link of responsibility to the rest of the world. The order isn't about death, really, but breaking links."

"There's a difference?"

"Yes, there is. That is another reason they would be unwilling to adopt a child, you know. Someone would have to take responsibility for her, and be bound again to life. To willingly take on such a bond would be practically apostasy."

Arianai paused. It was so hard to read anything from Quard's tone of voice. "Are you a member of the House?" she said.

"I once considered it. But we were discussing the child."

"Yes. . . . They gave her to the Levar's Orphanage. She lived there for five years. Until she began to sleep badly. Could the Green order have been the source of the 'bad green man' in her dreams?"

"It seems so obvious. But it was five years between the time the Greens had her and this . . . disturbance? You're certain of that?"

"Yes, certain."

"And she was only in the House of Responsible Life for a short time."

"A few days, I was told."

"Then . . . no. Surely that can't be it. Not with the dream so strong."

"*Does* it mean something?"

"No," he said, too quickly.

"You don't think—"

"Do you intend to adopt Theleme?"

"What? Well, I'd thought about it . . . or find her a foster family—"

"I think the best thing you can do to protect her from nightmares is to do just that. The Levar's Orphanage is, I'm sure, a fine place, but it surely can't be better than loving parents."

"I think you're right."

"Thank you. Now, please, I need to get some work done."

"All right, Quard." She held his hand; he looked at hers as if he were not certain what it was for.

* * *

When Arianai got home, Jemuel was sitting on the doorstep, in her officer's uniform.

"You're up early," Arianai said.

"I'm up late. I sleep when there's a chance these days."

Arianai said, "I've found a cure for—" and shut her mouth.

"So I hear. What does your gentleman friend do nights, Anni? Beggin' your right to privacy."

"Jem, do you know how long it's been since I've had a . . . gentleman friend?" She tried to laugh, but it came out forced and high.

"Your little patient told Thyan. Thyan's not very good about secrets."

"Third-hand gossip, Jem? Are you really so short of clues for your two dead wizards?"

"Yes. And it's three. The Hrothvek dancer, Teyer ais Elenaith, was found last night, in the middle of the Levar's Way." Jemuel reached into the pouch at her belt, put a small cool object into Arianai's hand. "Seen one of these yet?"

The item was a glass skull, not much bigger than the end of Arianai's thumb, filled with green liquid. The crown of the skull seemed to be threaded in place. "What is it?"

"Poison. Fast and neat. I'm told it doesn't even taste too bad."

Arianai sat down on the step next to Jemuel, with rather a bump. "Where are they coming from?"

"At last a question I can answer. Remember Old Wheeze the glassblower? His son, Little Wheeze, came up with the first ones. He claims it was his girlfriend's idea. Now there are five glassblowers turning them out so fast that there's a shortage of green poison. They're dyeing white poison . . . Pharn's fangs, I didn't mean that pun."

"But what's the idea?"

"Random green death, according to Little Wheeze's girlfriend. If you never know when you're going to suddenly glow green and drop dead, well, why not carry your own?"

Arianai looked at the skull. "And are they actually using these?"

"Not yet. I'm not going to worry until they stop shocking the grownups. When that happens, the kids'll need a new shock. And then we might be in trouble."

"Are you going to do anything about it?"

Jemuel produced another of the skulls, tossed it in the air, and caught it. "Legal age to buy poison in Liavek is fourteen. So far, that's been strictly observed. There's no legal minimum to *carry* poison, because who would have passed such a dumb law? And if you use the thing, you can't be charged with much, except maybe littering, or blocking a public sidewalk, which come to think of it we're guilty of now. Move along, please, mistress."

They stood up. "We *did*," Jemuel added, "put the lid on a fellow who wanted to do them in rock candy and lime."

Arianai shook her head. "Would you like to come in for tea and a biscuit?"

"I'd rather come in for tea and a clue. . . . Anni, I do need help. Is there any chance that this friend of yours knows anything?"

"I don't think there is."

"Are you not thinking there is, or can you provide him with an alibi?"

"Jem, there's a line. Don't cross it."

"All right," Jemuel said, sounding nearly sorry. "I'll see you around, Anni. Say, what's your luck time?"

"Three hours. Why?"

"You might want to study magic. I think there's going to be a shortage." Jemuel went off down the street, juggling a pair of glass skulls and whistling "Positively Cheap Street."

Prestal Cade thought that her life had a rather marvelous symmetry to it: she had become a magician on her fifteenth birthday, successfully forcing her magic into a wooden doll in one long and nervous night. Then for forty more years she had practiced the mysterious and confusing art, leaving her birthplace in Ka Zhir for some time at sea, a few years in the Farlands, a few more in Tichen, before finally arriving in Liavek to stay as a quiet practitioner of the luck-craft.

She worked through dolls, composing her spells in carving and painting, dressing and detailing them; as a result, her magic was mostly involved directly with people—cosmetic spells, protection from hazards (while at sea, she had crafted a doll of cork, whose spell preserved absolutely from drowning), and the occasional bodily complaints, though always with the assistance of a healer.

And of course there had been the special doll, her part of the spell that they had all cast together, that was now coming back to them all and dressing them in green.

Well, she thought, that completed the symmetry. For after fifteen years without magic, and forty with, she had had fifteen again without. Fifteen years ago there had been a man who was jealous of her luck, her dolls, her craft. Durus had loved her, she still did believe that; she was convinced that it was because he loved her that he found the vessel of her luck and broke it, set her magic free so that all her spells failed at once.

Prestal Cade had been walking home from the greengrocer's when it happened. She felt her heart squeezed, she fell and was sick into the gutter as fruits and cabbages rolled away from her. *So this is it*, she thought, *the knock at the door and me without my magic to answer it*. But the Liavekans on the street, used to the vagaries of luck, knew better than she what was happening; someone, she never knew his name, gathered up her groceries and led her home.

There she found Durus on the floor, a knife in one hand and a small cedarwood doll without its head in the other. Had he only waited a few more months, the break in his heart would have healed, and the patch she had put on could have failed without harming him; but Durus was always impetuous.

He had not, of course, destroyed her vessel on her ill-luck day; on any given birthday since that night, Prestal Cade could have stuffed her luck into some new vessel, been a practicing magician again. But she had not. She was, she thought (when she thought about it at all), becoming old, and would inevitably start using magic to confuse that inalterable fact. She had seen all the places she had meant to see, except the Dreamsend Hills (and who ever got *there*?). She would only begin to repeat herself, another this, another that, another Durus.

Still, there was the one small thing, each night.

Prestal Cade stood in the largest room in her not-large house, as she did every night just before midnight. The only furnishings were a chair just big enough for her, and a table just large enough for a teacup and a cake plate. The rest of the room was filled with dolls, more than three hundred of them, tiny dolls made from a single piece of wood and some as high as her waist, with jointed limbs and eyes that moved; dolls clothed as kings and jesters, sailors and fops, heroes out of legend and beggars from the Two-Copper Bazaar. Some of them had been spell dolls, a luck-twisting purpose in their every feature, but most of them came after that. If not for those she had sold or given away, there would be twice as many of them in the room.

For most of those in Liavek who knew Prestal Cade, she was the Doll Lady, had never been the Doll Witch. It was, she thought (and this she thought rather often), a satisfactory name to depart with.

She looked among the dolls on their shelves, took one down. It was a little lady as tall as Prestal Cade's forearm, with a porcelain head and arms and a cloth-stuffed body, under a long, full gown of blue velvet. It had been the style of court ball dresses two centuries ago, preserved in children's stories. Prestal Cade adjusted the hem of the gown, saw that the tiny fur slippers were securely in place. She stood the doll on the floor, and waited for midnight to strike.

A wizard who could invest, but did not, had one trick left: on the minutes of each day corresponding to the moment of birth, the power flashed by. Only a little luck, the most immediate of all the instant magics, but sufficient, perhaps, to hold the line between power and the void.

The hour came by. Prestal Cade felt her luck rise. She reached out with it.

The blue velvet doll straightened up, began walking in stately fashion toward the door. When she reached it, she raised a porcelain hand, and the door swung open. The doll curtsied to the figure beyond the door; Prestal Cade bowed.

The doll did not rise. The moment was gone. Prestal Cade looked up, smiling. The room was already suffused with green light.

"Verdialos, you're crying."

"Oh. Am I?" His eyes went wide, which stopped his tears. He was sitting in the dining hall of the House of Responsible Life, over a cup of cold breakfast tea and a half-eaten slice of melon. "I'm sorry, Serenity." The title did not mean a great deal; the hierarchy of the Green order was loose at best. It just was necessary to have something to call the people with more authority than others.

"Don't be sorry. Do you mind telling me what the matter is?"

"I was just told that Prestal Cade had died. Did you know her?"

"I don't believe so."

"She was a dollmaker."

"A wizard?"

Verdialos smiled slightly. "She had been. But her vessel was destroyed."

"*Oh.*"

"Well, no, not like that, not *quite* like that, Serenity. Her luck was just freed, not lost. She could have reinvested, but she didn't."

"Do you know why?"

"Not so well that I would be comfortable saying so." He picked up his piece of melon. "I was there the night her luck was freed, you see. It was fifteen years ago, and I was just barely a novice of the Order, and I saw this woman fall down. . . ." He examined the melon rind. "She had a bag of groceries."

"Groceries."

"I picked them up for her. I remember thinking, as soon as I'd sorted out what had happened, that I should convert this woman to the faith, that I should at least preach the truth to her. . . ."

"But you didn't?"

"No, I didn't. There was so much going on at the time, you see."

"And now the woman is dead, and it's too late to preach to her. You shouldn't cry over what can't be mended, Dialo."

"I'm not," Verdialos said plainly. "I'm sad because I've lost something, and I can't decide whether it's a reason to live, or to die." He shook his head. "One would think after fifteen years as a priest I'd be beyond such ambiguities."

"I've been a priest rather longer than you," the Serenity said. "If it weren't for ambiguity, what need would we have for faith?"

Verdialos nodded. "Thank you, Gorodain."

"That's what I'm here for," the Serenity said, and started up the stairs to his attic room. "That's what we are all here for."

* * *

Arianai went looking for Wizard's Row, and was rather surprised to find it present.

Present, but scarcely all there: in place of the usual outlandishly styled houses, there were plain stones, shuttered windows, and silence, except for a raw wind blowing dust and trash up the street.

Number 17 was on this day a modest stone dwelling with lead-paned windows that admitted no view. A small enameled sign by the doorway arch carried the street number. The knocker on the heavy oak door was of black iron, and as Arianai reached for it, it rattled of itself and the door swung open.

Arianai entered a narrow corridor with a worn red carpet, hazy light filtering through small windows high up. The passage led to a room with one small lamp on a table: it was otherwise so dark that the objects on the walls, the walls themselves, were uncertain.

In a large leather chair next to the lamp sat The Magician. He wore a long red gown with brocade trim, black leather slippers. His face was difficult to see in the glare of the lamp, but his hands were as youthful as always. His small silver-blue cat was in his lap, the fat black one curled up at his feet.

"Arianai," he said, and that was all.

"Magician."

When he did not answer, she said, "Your hospitality is usually better than this."

"Times are usually better than this."

"What's the matter with the times? It doesn't seem to me to be a bad time at all. Unless of course you're a wizard."

"You are acquiring a bitter humor, Arianai. I wonder from where." His voice was that of a very young man, but it was shot through with ancient weariness, so terrible that she had to pause before answering him.

"You sent me to Quard."

"I referred Theleme's case to him. There is a difference."

"I'm tired of hearing about all these subtle differences! Is Quard involved with the dead wizards?"

The Magician was silent.

"You want a fee?" She threw a handful of silver on the floor. The sleeping cat jumped up and ran away into the darkness. She took a step forward. "I think you're scared. You're afraid you're going to die, too."

"Young lady," The Magician said firmly, "I *know* that I am going to die. It taunts me every year with its presence. I ceased to be *afraid* of it before your several-great-grandparents were conceived." He stroked his cat. "That is why these . . . colleagues of mine are dead: because they had no fear."

More quietly, Arianai said, "Is Quard a murderer?"

"No."

She licked her lips. "But is he the wizard-killer?"

"There is no way to answer that question in a way you will understand."

"Then tell me enough to understand! Please, Magician . . . Quard said your name was Trav."

"I've thought about changing it." He sighed. "What you are seeing now are the last in a long series of actions. Call them moves in a game. The object of the game is power . . . a power as much greater than our magic as the sun exceeds this lamp."

"Are you playing the game?"

"At present, only observing it."

"So who are the players?"

"Originally—thirty years ago—there were seven. Their leader's name was Imbre. He was an extremely powerful wizard, with a luck time of almost two full days. There was, in fact, a time when he might have become The Magician of Liavek in my place. But he had an obsessive streak in his nature that led him into . . . experiments. And not long after the start of the one that interests you, he died."

"Did you kill him?"

"Thank you for your confidence. His closest associate in the seven killed him, fairly or not, I've no idea.''

"And took over.''

"There was nothing for him to take over.''

"But you said the power—''

"It is not that kind of power. Not something that any of Imbre's group—or all of them together—could use or control to their own ends. All they could do was release it on the world.''

"And if they did?''

The Magician said nothing.

"And if they did?''

"Do you pray to a god, Healer?''

"I . . . pray. Healers do that quite a bit.''

"And what happens when you pray to whatever god it is? Does some actual being use its power to touch you back? Or does your own wish, your own prayer, give shape to some abstract power?''

"What difference does it make?''

The Magician made a gesture over the cat in his lap. It began to rise, levitating almost in front of The Magician's face. The cat seemed to enjoy it, curling and stretching in midair. "I reach into myself and do this,'' he said, "but I am not a god.''

"How do you know?''

The cat sank back into The Magician's lap, presented its belly for scratching, and was rewarded. The Magician said, "Because I look back and regret my wasted efforts. Only mortals look back.''

"Is Quard mortal?''

"If you cut him, he will bleed. But Quard is also a gateway to the power that Imbre's seven reached for.''

"He has the power?''

"No one *has* the power!'' The Magician's voice softened. "Because Quard has a mind and a will, he may not simply be walked over. Think of his will as being a lock on the gate. Imbre's successor has spent thirty years assembling the key to that lock.''

"And the glowing dead—they're the first light coming through the keyhole?"

"Spoken like a wizard."

"But if you know all this—if you've been 'observing the game'—why in all the gods' names haven't you *done something*?"

"Because I believe that the play will fail, and by interfering I would do no good and might cause many more deaths."

"All right! Tell me what *I* can do."

"You have already done it," The Magician said tiredly. "You put the key into the lock."

Arianai stared. "I . . . what did I . . . do you mean Theleme?"

"Imbre fathered Quard to gain access to power. Imbre's successor fathered Theleme to gain access to Quard."

Arianai's throat clamped shut. The Magician just sat in his darkness, stroking his cat.

Finally she said, "Theleme . . . ? The . . . green man is her father?"

"Planted in her dreams for Quard to find."

"But you sent me to Quard!"

"I sent you *back* to Quard. His sensitivity to dreams is real. Theleme would have died without him, and the unlocking process would still have begun. Now do you start to understand just how complex this game is?"

"Tell me the rest of it! *Please.*"

"The rest of it is Quard's story. He will have to tell you."

"You could tell me more, but you won't."

The Magician sighed again. "I could tell you to leave Liavek, to have nothing more to do with Quard, but you won't. That is one mistake that I have made, and am bitterly sorry for: I forgot what it meant to be lonely, and not be proud of the fact."

"At least tell me the name of the green man."

"If I tell you, you will go to him. If I do not tell you, you will discover it anyway."

"Then you might as well tell me."

"No. I will not. So that I may pretend that my hands are clean. Good day to you, Healer Sheyzu."

The lamp went out. After a moment of darkness, Arianai found herself standing on Healer's Street, at the intersection with Wizard's Row; but the intersection, and the Row, were gone.

"I've been to see Trav," was the first thing Arianai said to Quard.

He did not look up from the piece of wood he was whittling. "On first-name terms with him now? That's good. Did you get your money's worth?"

"He told me you were involved with . . . some sort of power."

"I thought Liavekans always called it luck."

"Don't be hateful to me, Quard."

"I'd be glad to do it in your absence."

Arianai breathed hard. "Forgive me for wearing sandals," she said. "If I'd known the self-pity ran so deep around here, I'd have brought my boots."

Quard put down the rasp. "That's not a bad line."

"The Magician said I was learning."

"How long is your luck time?"

"What?"

"I didn't ask your blessed birthday, just the span of luck. How long was your mother in labor?"

"A little more than three hours."

"Not long for a Liavekan," Quard said.

"My family are healers, not magicians," she said. "We don't believe in prolonging pain."

Quard said, "Then you know that it *is* done."

"Of course. A student magician has access to power only for the duration of his mother's labor. I've heard of it being stretched out for forty, fifty hours." She shook her head in disgust. Then she thought of what The Magician had said about Imbre—two days' luck— and shivered.

"Is labor pain really as terrible as all that?" Quard said, with a sort of distracted curiosity.

"It is."

"Then to extend it for . . . say, twelve days . . . that would be a very bad thing, wouldn't it."

She stared. *"Twelve days?"*

"It would have been twelve weeks, if they could have done it. Twelve months, if only they could have. Imagine that: an unending luck time. But it does leave the question of one's ill-luck time, at the opposite pole of the year. I think they might have been satisfied with six months and a day . . . just to see what happened on that day when luck and counter-luck overlapped. An irresistible force and an immovable . . ." He gave a nasty, barking laugh.

"But your mother—twelve days? That's impossible!"

"No. Not impossible. With drugs and magic and clever surgeries, not impossible for the pain to last that long. But impossible to survive, yes." His voice rose. "My father and his little clutch of wizards stretched my mother's pain until there was no more flesh to cover it. And then, as she was dying and I was being born, just when any *human being* would have thought the obscenity could not be increased, they cast a spell. It took all seven of them, because the luck of a birthing woman is overwhelming—how else do you think the thing happens? These seven people, with enough power between them to have done anything, *anything* their souls desired, they, they—" He gestured wildly. "—they *stopped* my birth instant, my mother's death instant, and we *hung* there, me struggling to be *born*, she struggling to *die*, for an *hour* from midnight—"

He fell forward on the counter, sobbing without tears. He reached up and clawed at his hair, pulling the wig away, displaying a skull utterly smooth but for a few strands of false hair stuck in spirit gum. He tugged at an eyebrow, and it came away as well.

"Quard—" She reached around his shoulders.

"Three of them—" He shuddered, pulled away from her arm. "Three of them were *women*."

"Quard. You have a will of your own."

He straightened up. "A small one. . . . I destroyed my vessel of luck, years ago. It was almost harder than the investment had been. I did it at the wrong time, though. The luck is only loose, not gone."

"As long as you use your will, your mind, no one can use you. The Magician told me that."

"You don't understand. I was created for a purpose."

"I don't doubt your power. But the power belongs to you. No one else can use it, if you don't let them."

"No. No. That was the experiment, but not the experiment's purpose. Do you remember when we talked about the Green faith? And I mentioned what its name meant, in the old language?"

"Yes."

"When that language was spoken, the Order was different from the one you know. Now they spend their time plotting their own deaths—and rarely succeed. But not so long ago, they contrived the deaths of others, and they did achieve them. Do you see?" He leaned toward her, and his clear light eyes shone feverishly. "Death as an art form. The death of the whole world as their masterwork." He stood up, turned away from her, braced his hands against the wall as if to keep it from collapsing upon him. He took a deep breath. "My father didn't want a powerful magician, you see. He wanted to create a god. To have Death as his own obedient son."

Arianai went around the counter, put her hands on his knotted shoulders. "But he failed," she said gently.

"No!" He twisted away from her, pulling the shelf from the wall. A shiribi puzzle and a stack of alphabet blocks crashed to the floor. "No, he *didn't*! The death is in my soul, just waiting to come out in the world. Don't you see? Don't you know who the rest of my father's gang were? Sen Wuchien. Shiel ola Siska. Teyer

ais Elenaith. Prestal Cade. All of them dead, and still they control me. I've killed them, in my midnight dreams, and I'm still the slave of their wish.'' Quard stared at the shelves of toys, and began to sweep them aside. Puppets were tangled and broken, music boxes spilled their tinkling clockwork, porcelain dolls shattered.

"Stop it, Quard,'' Arianai said firmly. "Do you think I haven't seen an unhappy child throw a tantrum before? I said, *stop it*.''

Quard's shoulders slumped. He looked up. There were tears and dust on his face, and he smiled, a joyless doll's smile. "Tantrum? It's midnight, Mistress Healer. Allow me to show you a tantrum such as gods throw.''

He stretched his hand toward a pile of ceramic bits that had been a doll's head. There was a flicker of green, and a small tornado swept the pieces into his palm. He closed his fingers around them, and squeezed; green light leaked from his fingers, and the bones showed through the skin. The hand relaxed. He flipped something to Arianai, and she caught it.

The object was a perfectly formed porcelain skull just smaller than an egg.

She threw it down. "Come home with me,'' she said quietly. "I'll change your dreams.''

"What, in *bed*?'' he said incredulously. "Wrestle and gasp and pledge the world, and then wake up counting the days till the world ends?''

She was too angry to turn away. "I'm not frightened, Quard.''

"Then you're stark mad.'' He circled around her. "I can't stay here any longer,'' he said. "If I can't get away from my destiny, at least I'll be the death of someplace less than Liavek.'' He went into the back of the shop, paused in the doorway. "The toys are innocent,'' he said in a hollow voice. "Give them to children who will love them.''

The door closed, the latch clicked. Arianai knocked

at it, called to Quard, for half an hour. Then she went
home.

Theleme was sleeping fitfully, tossing and turning.
Quard's stuffed toys were beside the bed, apparently
knocked aside by Theleme in her sleep. Arianai wound
the spring in the flannel cat, listened to the soft beat-
beat of its wooden heart, put it carefully against Theleme's chest. Theleme curled her arms and legs around
the cat. Her breathing quieted.

Arianai picked up the camel and rider, carried them
from the bedroom into her office. Some of the stitches
on the rider's hood had broken, and it was askew; Arianai straightened it, put the toy on her desk. She poured
a cup of nearly-cold tea, sat down behind the desk, and
looked for a long time at the stuffed beast and its har-
ried driver. As ever, the cloth tableau made her want
to laugh out loud.

But she didn't. She put her head down on her arms
and cried herself to sleep.

When Obas came to Liavek from Ombaya, he brought
with him six shafts of ebony from the tree behind his
house. The tree was old, and strong, and lucky; it had
been planted on the grave of Obas's thrice-great-
grandfather Udeweyo, a mighty wizard of earth and air,
and the black tree's roots and branches kept his luck
alive. Obas's mother had gone out into the yard where
the tree stood to give birth to him, done the labor that
gave Obas his birth luck on the ground that fed the tree,
in the shade of its leaves.

Obas shaped his luck in the making of arrows, and
when he left home his mother gave him the blackwood
shafts, sealed in a pouch of moleskin, saying, ''These
are for no ordinary magic, not for wealth and not for
power, not for the people of the lands you visit, for
their own trees in their own earth will be strong enough
for that. Someday, my son, you will need the luck of
the house you were born in; these will touch you to
Udeweyo's luck.''

That had been fifty years ago; and in that span Obas had been hungry and poor, and he had been afraid, and he had needed luck that had not come to him; but he had not touched the ebony shafts.

Tonight the moleskin pouch was open and empty, and Obas was crafting the last of the six black arrows.

Their points were silver, and their flights were from a red flamingo, taken without harming the bird. The smooth black wood was carved with words and symbols, the carvings then rubbed with a mixture of herbs and Obas's blood. Each arrow had a name, and the names were Seeker, Binder, Blaster, Blinder, Flyer, and Slayer. Each arrow had a purpose—and the purpose would come for Obas at midnight, but Obas would meet it armed with ancient luck.

Just before midnight he put the arrows in a quiver and strapped it to his back. Around his left wrist he tied a band of oxhide. He put on a short cloak of skin, and went out into the Levar's Park in the city's northwest, the place where Sen had died. He did not have to go to the park; he did not have to go to his opponent at all. He knew that he could be found. But he wished to meet the enemy in the open, under the sky, earth under him. Sky and earth might strengthen the gift of Udeweyo's luck; Obas did not know. But if he was to die, let it be in the room he was born in: the room of the world.

The park was quiet, and bright with the light of the nearly full moon. Obas smelled damp grass and cedarwood, heard a fly buzz past his ear; he turned, but the fly—if fly it had been—was gone. He was alone.

No, he thought, feeling luck stir in the soles of his feet, not alone.

Obas drew out the first arrow, the one named Seeker. The vessel of his luck, a broad silver arrowhead on a cord around his neck, was cool against his chest. His heart was slow and his breathing was even. He twirled the shaft in his fingers, filling it with his luck. Little lightnings flashed from the silver head down the shaft, making the carved chants glow, sparking from the red feathers.

With a snap of his wrist, Obas cast Seeker. It flew from his fingertips, trailing behind it a ribbon of silver light. The ribbon arched, bent, dove. Then Seeker began to whirl, spinning a ring, a braid, a column of light. The arrow struck the ground, its magic spent, and fell apart in black ashes.

Within Seeker's windings stood a tall warrior with a shield and a spear. He wore a striped skin, and his own dark skin was painted with figures of white and red and yellow.

In Ombayan the warrior's name was Barah. He was the First Hunter, the one who had learned to use wisdom to overcome prey stronger than himself. Obas felt suddenly old, and weary, and small. At the same time, he had hope: he did not fight an *inisha,* the wind or the earth, but the Hunter, who though a god had been a man. Barah could fail. A hunter might abandon the kill, if the prey proved too strong.

Obas raised the arrow Binder, spun it. It flashed and flew, striking the earth between Barah's feet. The shaft swelled, and sprouted branches, growing into a tree with its trunk at Barah's back. The branches reached for Barah's arms, the roots coiling to trap his legs. Barah struggled, but the tree drew luck from earth, and held him.

Obas drew the next arrow, Blinder, gave it magic, and cast it. It whistled like a diving shrike and flew toward Barah's eyes. The Hunter tried to raise his shield, but the branches pulled his arm aside. Blinder reached his face, and opened into a hood of blackness that tightened over Barah's head, covering his eyes, his ears, his nostrils, his mouth, so that Barah's face was a smooth ebony sculpture, all senseless.

Obas raised Blaster, whispering his luck into it. The silver arrowhead grew warm against his chest. The luck was there, the luck was strong. Hunter and prey had changed their skins. Obas cast the arrow, and it flew for Barah's chest.

Blaster erupted in fire that flowed down Barah's body, along his pinioned limbs, melting the skin from his bones. Dark flesh fell away, and the bones beneath showed green.

The fire spread to the binding tree, haloing it in the night. Bark began to slough from the branches, dripping thickly, like black mud.

Where the molten bark struck the Hunter's bare green bones, it clung, shining red over black over green, clothing the bones, muscling and fleshing them.

Barah stretched out his new limbs, still held in the tree's branches and roots, and tightened his new muscles. The tree groaned. Barah bent his back, and brought the tree up by its roots.

Earth fell away from the dead tree's roots, and tangled in them, Obas could see white bones: the skeleton, he knew, of Udeweyo, the breaking of his luck.

The First Hunter shook off the tree as a man throws off a cloak. Its trunk and Udeweyo's bones crunched together into black and white splinters. Barah struck his spear on his shield and took a step toward Obas.

Feeling his heart pound, his lungs strain, Obas raised Flyer. He cast the arrow, and as its flights brushed his fingers he grasped the feathers. Flyer lifted Obas, carried him into the sky.

He was afraid, he was fleeing. Could it be cowardice? The prey was too strong.

Far below, Obas saw Barah drop his shield to the ground, stand upon it. The wind rose, rippling the grass. Barah's shield rose on the wind, carrying him aloft. Barah raised his spear and flew after Obas. Together they soared above the housetops of Liavek, curving over the shining pan of the sea, riding the wind toward distant Ombaya.

Barah rose above Obas, stood on air, a dark shape against the moon. His spearpoint flashed in the moonlight. He threw the spear.

Obas raised his left wrist. The band of hide around it began to grow, until it was a shield. Obas raised it as the spear flew toward him.

Barah's spear struck Obas's shield, and pierced it.

And stopped, the spearhead barely two fingers' breadth from Obas's heart.

Obas let the shield and spear fall away. They caught fire, a green shooting star toward the roofs of the city. Obas grasped his last arrow, the one named Slayer. He pulled at his magic until his heart burned, and then he cast the spell. Slayer shot burning at Barah's heart, and the First Hunter's shield was between his feet and the wind.

Barah reached out and plucked Slayer from the air. As he held the arrow, it seemed that neither he nor Obas were flying, but simply standing, two men face to face in the darkness. Obas looked into Barah's eyes. The Hunter was mighty. The prey was not.

"Come," said the voice of Barah, louder than the wind, "if you are coming."

The moonlight took on a green cast; Obas looked at his open hand, empty of arrows, and saw that the green light came from him.

Barah cast Slayer back at its maker.

Obas's vessel of power melted, and the liquid silver trickled down his skin. If he cried out, it was lost on the wind. He lost his grip on the arrow Flyer, and he fell. Below him, the towers of Liavek thrust up like the bones of Udeweyo, and embraced him.

It was nearly noon when Arianai awoke. She dressed at once and went out to buy a *Cat Street Crier*; the front page had the news of Obas the Arrowsmith, found dead in the Levar's Park with the ground dented beneath him, though the earth there was not soft and there was no mark on Obas's body. Excepting of course the green glow of his bones.

Arianai crumpled the paper, shook her head. She

carried the sleeping Theleme next door, leaving her in the care of that healer's nurse, and went to the toyshop.

The sign-puppet showed no more motion than a hanged man. Arianai tried the door, found it unlocked. Quard was not in the front of the shop; quietly, Arianai went around the counter and into the back.

It was a mess even by young-bachelor standards, shelves and tables and most of the floor haphazardly covered with paint jars and glue pots and tools, partially finished toys and drawings for others, odd books and dirty dishes, with dust and wood shavings filling all the gaps.

Quard was asleep. The bed was small and hard, but so finely carpentered it must have been his own work. He was sprawled on his stomach, head turned to one side. His wig was off, and the smooth complete hairlessness of his head and neck and face made him look like an unfinished doll.

She put two fingers to his temple. His pulse hammered. His eyelids twitched as he dreamed.

"Who killed Imbre?" she said into his ear. "We can stop him if only we have his name."

"No," Quard muttered. "Can't go there."

"Imbre. Who was Imbre's friend? Who killed him?"

"Die, all die."

"We have to drive out the green man. Who is he?"

"Gorodain," Quard said. "Friend, priest, kill. Gorodain."

She kissed him and went out, went north, to the Street of Thwarted Desire, and the House of Responsible Life.

She asked to see Gorodain. The clerks sent her to a small office, barely big enough to pace comfortably. Its walls were painted a pale green. Arianai thought that she was becoming quite physically sick of green.

After a few minutes an unprepossessing man came in. "Are you Gorodain?"

"My name is Verdialos," he said, in a lame little voice. "I am . . . oh, say that I deal with requests."

"I'm not here to die."

"But you are looking for someone who is?"

"I want to talk to the priest called Gorodain. Tell him it's about five dead wizards."

"I will tell him that. But he won't see you on that matter."

"Then tell him it's about Imbre."

"All right," Verdialos said equably. "Dead wizards and Imbre. Please wait here. Sit if you like."

"Your chairs aren't very comfortable."

"Most of our visitors have other things on their minds." Verdialos went out.

He was not long in returning. "Serenity Gorodain regrets that the press of duties keeps him busy for the next several days. If you would care to make an appointment, or leave your name . . ." He sounded vaguely uneasy.

"Arianai Sheyzu, eighty-five Healer's Street." Then she recalled what The Magician had said, about her discovering the green man's name. The Magician was one of the murkiest of an opaque lot, but what was in the fog was always truth.

Verdialos had started writing the address. He looked up. "Are you well, Mistress Sheyzu?"

"Yes," she said. "I've got no intention of dying anytime soon."

"A good death to you nonetheless," Verdialos said.

Shortly after the Healer Sheyzu had gone, Gorodain came into Verdialos's office. "Did she leave her name and address?" the Serenity asked.

Verdialos gave him the paper. "Forgive me for asking, Serenity . . . but my schedule is rather light this week, and if I could assist you . . ."

"I forgive you for asking, Verdialos. And I forgive you your ambition. You do know that you will succeed me as Serenity, when I finally"—he smiled—"achieve the goal?"

"I had supposed I was one of those in line."

"Good. One should not face death with false modesty." He glanced at the paper, then crumpled it. "If the woman should return, another dose of your usual kind firmness, eh, Dialo?"

Verdialos nodded as the Serenity went out.

It was in fact a busy day for Verdialos; the mob had done quite a bit of superficial damage to the House, especially the gardens, and the repairs had to be supervised and accounted. They were, Verdialos thought, very often an order of bookkeepers and tallycounters, and he wondered if perhaps the work they did for the House bound them to it, created exactly the responsibilities they were supposed to be severing in their quest for the regretless death.

And then again, he thought with a stifled chuckle, neither the tomatoes nor the tomato worms would feel guilt at the gardeners' passing.

It was quite late when the last note had been written on the garden charts, the last cracked window mended against the night air. There was nothing artistic about any death that involved sneezing.

Verdialos ate a light dinner, a chop from the rioters' poor pig, and began a discussion with his wife concerning the healer and the Serenity. She ended it shortly by saying quietly, "Asking an extra opinion never killed anyone." Verdialos laughed and kissed her warmly. Then he put on a cap and cloak of neutral gray (because prudence in troubled times had never killed anyone, either) and went out to talk to a City Guard.

He was directed to the Guard office in the Palace itself, and finally to Jemuel, who was studying reports and drinking kaf thick as syrup—"It's not supposed to taste good," she said, "it's supposed to keep me standing."

Verdialos told her about the day's events. "I am troubled by all of it," he said, "both the healer's interest in us, and the Serenity's interest in her."

Jemuel said, "It bothers me, too. I want to have a talk with your Serenity."

They shared a footcab back to the House, and climbed the stairs to Gorodain's chambers. Verdialos knocked on the door.

"Come in," said a voice that was not Gorodain's. Verdialos opened the door. His eyes widened. Captain Jemuel said, *"You."*

The Magician sat in a wicker chair, looking at a table with an etched-glass top. There was no one else in the room.

"May I ask," Verdialos said, "how you come to be so far from your usual, um . . ."

"A fool's errand," The Magician said. "I came to talk a priest out of his faith. But I arrived too late; he has already gone."

Jemuel said to Verdialos, "I have the right to commandeer the fastest horse in the neighborhood. I hope you have it."

"I have a faster horse," The Magician said, "and we all may ride. Open the window, please."

"Trav—the Serenity—"

"Is a branch of the Old Green Faith," The Magician said. "Those Who Assume Responsibility."

"Yes. I had been rather afraid of that. In our defense, he was never allowed to—well. Nothing to say now, is there." Verdialos opened the window.

Arianai had been dozing, nearly dreaming, when the knock came at her front door. It was a faint tap, hesitant. Shaking herself awake, she rushed to answer it, swung the door open. "Qua—" she said, before seeing anything in the dark, and only gurgled the rest.

Gorodain's hands were crossed in the grip called the Butterfly; they closed easily around Arianai's neck, fingertips thrusting into the hollows at the base of her skull, tightening, lifting. She lost the power of speech and movement at once. Her toes scraped the doorstep. Gorodain held her for several heartbeats, wishing that there were time for something more elaborate. So often he felt like a master chef who knew a thousand exotic recipes and was forced to prepare a single bland pudding for a toothless stomach patient.

Then, he thought, minimal art was still art, and this was the brushstroke that would complete his masterpiece, to confound a metaphor. And there simply was not time. Gorodain flexed his wrists, and there was a single sharp *crack* from Arianai's neck.

He lowered her, turning her on her back so that she lay across the threshold of her front door, her head draped—quite elegantly, Gorodain thought—over the edge of the step. It might well be taken for an accident. Not that it mattered what it was taken for. Then, on impulse, he knelt beside her, stretched out a hand, tapped into his luck. The green glow would be simple enough to induce. Closure, that was what a work of art needed, a bright green line to link all the deaths.

There was a cold pressure at the back of Gorodain's neck. For a moment he thought it might be Quard—but the time was not right, it was still most of an hour until midnight. Then the touch resolved itself into pistol barrels. Gorodain looked up, saw Verdialos approaching, and with him The Magician—himself, out of his house!

The gun pressed hard against him, and a woman's voice said, "Just move, you dirtwad; just do us all a favor and make one little move."

"Don't, Jemuel," The Magician said, in that irritating pretty-boy voice of his. "The favor would only be to Gorodain."

Gorodain grinned involuntarily. The Magician was right. There was nothing they could do now, any of them. Death would come for his dead lover, and to save her be forced to admit that he was truly Death, take the power that could not be controlled. In less than an hour, Imbre's son would be loosed upon Liavek; before dawn, Liavek would be Necropolis. He wondered if the glow of all the dead would shine out upon the sea, like a green dawn.

* * *

Quard was sitting on the floor of the toyshop, arms and legs at odd angles, like a marionette cast aside.

He had intended to go away. He had started to pack a bag with everything that was meaningful to him, and then realized that such a bag would be empty. He had been sitting on the floor for most of the day now, waiting for night, for midnight, the hour of his birth and his power. There was nothing for him in Liavek but Death, but there wasn't anything more for him anywhere else.

So he would stay, and when next someone came into his shop they would find him on the floor, green.

The door swung open and Theleme came in. "Master, master! You have to come, master!" She rushed to him, and without thinking he opened his arms and hugged her.

"What is it, Theleme? What's wrong? Where's Anni?"

"Anni's sick, master, sick. The green man. You have to come. You have to ride the camel for Anni."

Quard's throat tightened. He tried twice to speak and failed. On the third try he said, "Where is she, Theleme?"

"Home," Theleme said. "Come, master. Captain Jem will take us."

"Who . . . ?" Quard stood up, walked with Theleme to the door.

Just outside was a woman in Guard officer's uniform. Her face was pretty, but hard as a cliff. She had a pistol out, casually ready. "Good evening, Toymaker," she said, in a cold voice. "I've been wanting to meet you. But we've got some other business first."

Quard walked mechanically down the stairs. The Guard captain pointed at the toyshop door. "Aren't you going to lock up?"

"Why?" he said. "There's nothing in there that isn't mine."

It was not far to Arianai's house. There was a sphere

of luck-light illuminating the scene, in the grainy, un-real fashion of magic.

Arianai was lying on the doorstep, half-in, half-out. The healer Marithana Govan was there, kneeling next to Arianai. Quard looked around at the rest of them: The Magician, Verdialos the Green priest . . . Gorodain.

"Welcome, son of Imbre," Gorodain said, and pressed his palms to his forehead. No one paid any attention.

Jemuel took Theleme inside. Quard said quietly, "Give her something to make her sleep," and Marithana went inside as well. The others stood out in the cold, around the body.

When the two women came out again, Jemuel said, "Well?"

"Her neck's cleanly broken," Marithana said. "She didn't suffer."

"I am an adept of my order," Gorodain said.

In a tightly controlled voice, Jemuel said, "If you speak out of turn one more time I will surely shoot your balls off."

"Can you mend the break?" Quard said abruptly.

Marithana said, "Young man, she's—"

The Magician said, "I can mend the bones, with guidance from Mistress Govan. Marithana, if they're splinted by magic, will they knit?"

"Trav, she's *dead.*"

"If that changed?" The Magician said, and all of them stared at him, except for Gorodain and Quard, who looked at one another with unreadable expressions.

"In time," Marithana said. "Perhaps more than a year. Your birth time . . ."

"If it takes that long, Gogo can renew the spell."

"You're serious."

Quard said, "More than you know. Do it."

The Magician said, "Marithana, concentrate on the bones as they should be. We'll do it together."

Marithana Govan put her hands on Arianai's throat, straightening it, massaging it. There was a faint sound of grinding, crunching. Verdialos looked worried, Jemuel impassive, Gorodain positively merry.

The healer and the wizard moved back. Quard stepped forward. He said to The Magician, "If something goes wrong—if I come back before she does, it'll mean that—"

"I'll do what I can," Trav said.

Quard knelt by the dead woman. Gorodain was speaking again; Quard shut him out, looked up. Full moon at the top of the sky. Close enough to the crease of midnight. Quard stared at the moon, feeling the weight of luck tug at his heart, the tides of fortune raising his salt blood.

He stepped from his flesh and into his birthright.

Around him was still Liavek, still streets, houses, windows, rooftops, still just as lovely and hideous as any other Liavek; if anything, perhaps a little more precisely defined, cleaner of line and truer of angle, small where it should be small and grand where grandness was deserved. For it is not true that the dead know all things—indeed the dead know nothing that the living do not. But the dead have perspective.

Quard was surrounded by wraiths, human figures in translucently pale shades of green: not the dead but the living, dwelling here in their minds as they wished for death, in the degree of those hopes. Marithana Govan and Jemuel were barely even visible, delicate as soap bubbles. Verdialos was nearly solid, but without luminance; certain but not eager.

Quard looked at The Magician, who stood there with one hand already in the quiet world; Quard examined the rest of The Magician, studied his wish, and almost laughed. He did not: laughter and tears were things of the full world.

Quard looked with interest at Gorodain, who flickered, wavering to and from oblivion. Quard reached out and touched Gorodain's shade. Its eyes opened wide, and the figure knelt out of Quard's way, growing fainter as it did so. As ever with the voyeur, Quard thought, recoiling at the actual touch. He walked by.

There was no source of light in the city: it was uniformly dim, dull perhaps, though the effect was not drab but soothing. And there was no glass in the windows, nor glasses on the walls, nor puddles on the ground—nothing at all that might cast a reflection.

He moved easily on the dustlessly clean streets, passing among the shades of the still living, looking up at windows luminous with their death wishes. "I felt Death breathe on me," their living selves would be saying, in the full world; "someone is walking on my grave." Quard could see easily through the windows, or the walls for that matter, and no door was closed to him: even Wizard's Row would be present, should he desire to travel it. Nor did he have to walk; others rode, he supposed, or flew, but walking was the one way he knew.

Quard paused at a house on Cordwainers' Street: in an upstairs room, a crowd of shades stood around a man on a bed. The supine figure was deep green, and his shade was very thick.

Quard held out his hand. "Come if you are coming," he said, and there was a sound somewhere between a sigh and the pop of a cork, and the shade on the bed was suddenly a body dressed in clothes of subdued color. The man rose up and followed Quard, as the shades they left behind—some fading, some thickening—threw themselves upon the empty bed.

There were others after that, the sick, the old, the murdered and suicided, a Vavasor who had eaten a spoiled fish, and nine sailors drowned off Eel Island. Some of their bodies were young and robust, some old and elegant in appearance, but they all walked steadily, and there was among them no mark of decay, no wound, no lesion, bloat, nor worm.

They all followed Quard, winding through the streets of that other Liavek like a streak of smoke, pointing and touching and talking among themselves in a low murmur, passing through the green shades of the wishful living without notice—as indeed they could not see them. That was for Quard alone.

Finally, after he had fulfilled his duties among the lastingly dead, he returned to find Arianai, in her house, searching through the rooms cluttered with what she loved. "Theleme," she said, "Theleme, where are you?" She ran her hands over Theleme's bed, touching, seeing nothing.

Quard saw Theleme, asleep on the bed even as Arianai's hands passed through her shade. Theleme clutched the cloth camel and rider to herself, and her wish shone in the cool-colored room. Quard shook his head and took Arianai by the wrist.

She looked at Quard, and in an instant she understood. Quard did not know what the dead saw in him, and there were no mirrors to show him. He led her from the house, to the street where the column of dead waited. Arianai saw them, standing patiently and calm, but looked right through the shades of the living clustered around her, each of them waiting for some kind of miracle.

Quard knew there were no miracles.

Arianai said, "You came to bring me back."

Quard said, "This is not the story you think it is. I did not charm you free from here. There was an exchange."

"Who? *Not Theleme!*"

Quard was silent.

"Is it Theleme? Or is it you? I won't accept such a trade."

"You are dead," Quard said, "and have no choice in the matter."

"If someone will die in my place, surely I have the right to know."

Quard said, "No knowledge is ever taken from this world." He pointed at the street, where he could see the shade of Marithana Govan kneeling. "Go, if you are going. We have a final destination, and you may not see it.''

Arianai looked at the column trailing behind Quard. She seemed to be trying to recognize individual faces, but Quard gestured again, and she lay down on the ground. The air shuddered, and in place of the solid Arianai there was now a shade, even less substantial than Marithana's.

He had not lied to her. Gods never lie, even if they then change the world to suit their words. He had struck the bargain with himself.

Quard turned and left the square, the dead in quiet files behind him.

"Is he dead?" Jemuel said.

Marithana held a bit of polished metal to Quard's nostrils. "To the best of my ability to tell." She looked down. "Dear Lady around us," she said. "Anni's breathing."

Jemuel said, "He *could* do it, then."

Gorodain said, "Ah, but that is only the beginning."

"Shut up," Jemuel snapped at him, then looked at Quard, crouched motionless over Arianai, who was now only sleeping peacefully. "Gods, how are we going to tell her?"

"I'll tell her what needs to be said," Quard said, unfolding and stretching his limbs.

Marithana said, "You were—"

"I slept. I sleep very deeply."

Gorodain said, astonished, "You *return*—"

"You are a complete fool, Gorodain," Quard said, in a voice that made Gorodain step back from him. "You wished for Death to take the whole world down with you. But Death serves no man's wish, nor does it wear one face. Death is particular to all it touches."

The Magician nodded. Then Quard turned to face him. "And you sigh with relief, Magician, because your guess was right, because the city did not die for your miscalculation? What of my mother, who was tortured for nothing? Of my father, who died for nothing? Of the other five?''

The Magician looked Quard in the eyes, and nodded again. "But Anni and Theleme live," he said, without any force. "And I suppose I shall, too."

"Kind of a shame," Jemuel said, poking at Gorodain with her pistol, "all those other wizards dead, and not this green toad."

Quard said, "I am . . . what I am. Justice is another thing entirely."

Jemuel said, "Fair enough. We'll see to justice," and pointed at Gorodain. "I know a nice little cell just your size."

Gorodain shifted his hands. The Magician said quietly, "Don't trust to luck." Something appeared between his fingers, and was as quickly palmed.

Gorodain smiled grimly, shrugged, lowered his hands. "Do you think," he said to Verdialos as if the others were not there, "that you could provide me with one of those little green skulls the youth are so fascinated with? Think of it as your first task as a Serenity."

"Pharn take that," Jemuel said. "You'll die on Crab Isle."

"True enough," Gorodain said, "for I am old, and once you destroy my magic—as you must—I will be older still. Better that Death come quickly for me."

Quard began to laugh. Gorodain looked at him, and went very pale. Quard threw his head back and laughed from the bottom of his lungs. Gorodain put his hands to his mouth, and his eyes were wide and black. Jemuel looked bewildered, Verdialos turned away, and The Magician was simply gone. Quard just kept laughing as he picked up Arianai in his wiry arms and carried her into the house.

Arianai woke damp with sweat, her neck stiff and sore as if she had slept with it twisted. Her scalp prickled, and she struggled to recall what her dream had been, but it had melted and run away.

She rolled over, pulling free of the sweaty sheets. Quard was on the floor across the room, cradling Theleme in his arms. Theleme shifted a bit, giggled in her sleep. Quard didn't move.

Quard didn't stir at all. He just sat, eyes shut, pale limbs wrapped around the child.

Arianai felt a chill touch her eyes, her spine. Draping a sheet over herself, she went to Quard's side, crouched, touched his shoulder. His skin was quite cold. She bit her lip and tightened her grip.

Quard's eyes snapped open. Arianai nearly screamed.

"Hello," Quard said softly. He shivered. Theleme stirred, but Quard rocked her to sleep again, then put her gently down, her head pillowed on the toy camel.

"You scared me," Arianai said.

Quard's face was mostly in shadow, but two little reflections stared her straight in the eyes. "Well. The world is full of possibilities this morning."

He got to his feet, and they went out of the room, with a last look at Theleme asleep and dreaming sweetly.

Arianai turned up the lamp in the office. Quard blinked in the light, then said, "Is that really what you want to be doing?" and looked down at the soft, thick carpet.

She chuckled. "Then you've no other appointments."

"Not this midnight," he said, in a different voice, and looked her in the eyes again: in the better light she could see that his eyes, which had been hazel and clear as water, were now the color of green olives.

She turned out the light before she could see anything more. She felt Quard embrace her, felt him stir.

"You're like fire," he said, and pressed his cold lips to hers.

Only mortals look back, she thought, and knew that she was mortal.

He pushed her away to arm's length, said distantly, "How can you love me?"

"Day by day," she said, "until the end of the world," and pulled him close again. She felt Quard's tears, freezing down her cheeks, and prayed she would not wake up counting the days.

The Illusionist

THORROW CREPT INTO the smithy, feet silent on the straw-littered floor, the short white knife in his hand catching the light from the forge. The smith was sleeping in the corner, a fat heap covered with a horseblanket. Thorrow spun the knife in his fingers, raised it.

A thick strong hand thrust out of the darkness and locked like a vise on Thorrow's wrist, bending it down. The blacksmith rose up like a demon from the forge's shadow. He shoved the knifeblade into the fire, held it there.

Thorrow screamed as the heat ran up the metal, let the knife go. The smith released him. Clutching his burnt hand, Thorrow staggered, half fell against the anvil. The smith's right hand came up, holding a steel-headed sledge; he whirled it, as lightly as Thorrow had twirled the dagger.

"It is reckoning time," the blacksmith said. "Know you not that a man who rides on stolen horseshoes risks his neck?"

"Blacksmith, stop! You do not know the truth—the truth is that your sister lives—"

"She does not," the smith said.

"She does! We only played at her death—to fool you—"

"Then I was fooled twice, and the second time most gravely," said the smith, "for the second time it was I who killed her."

"—and your wife was never unfaithful—"

"But she was, though not with you."

"—it was only a game, a game, *a game*!"

"I am good at games," said the blacksmith, with the calm tones of the irretrievably mad. "And I always win."

The smith raised his hammer. There was a sudden hissing wind, and the lamps in the smithy were snuffed at once, leaving it completely dark except for the glow of the forge. The hammer whistled, and Thorrow screamed.

The hammer clanged on the anvil, then struck again, and again, like a heartbeat, the puff of the bellows like straining lungs. Clang, clang, louder than any man could possibly scream, even in dying.

The sound stopped.

The audience applauded.

The lights came up. The cast stood lined up along the stage, hands linked, taking their bows. Flowers were thrown at the players' feet, among them a few blue blossoms with notes attached.

A tall, broad-shouldered man joined the players on stage, and the applause rose in volume. The audience stood. Virshon ola Vivar, Liavek's most successful playwright, took a bow with his company. Thus ended the two hundredth, and final, performance of *Hammer and Anvil, A Game.*

Aritoli ola Silba, Liavek's most successful art critic, paused outside the door of the Red Mask Theatre to hail a footcab. There was a show of bowing and scraping at his silk-clad elbow, and he turned: standing there, bent in either obsequy or severe rheumatism, was a little man with printer's ink grained into his fingers.

Aritoli stretched out his "Yes?" for most of a breath.

"Representing the *Salt Grove Clarion*, Master Observer . . . we should like to know your opinion of the play just seen."

"Don't you have one?" Aritoli said. "Or didn't you see it?"

"Alas, Master Critic, the pressures of assembling our journal are so great . . ."

"You mean, you couldn't afford a ticket."

"At a half-copper a copy, Master Perceiver, we must sell a great number of papers even to purchase ink, never mind entertainments." The newsragger held out his stained hands. "On the other hand"—he rolled his palms over—"the opinion of such as yourself qualifies as news by its very existence. And surely the Master Arts-Analytic is in favor of the dissemination of news . . . ?"

Ola Silba smiled, stroked his moustache. "You have a nice line in flattery, at least. Which rag—your pardon—news-sheet did you say you represented?"

"The *Salt Grove Clarion*, master. We are distributed primarily in the Levar's Park area."

"Very well then." Ola Silba cleared his throat. " 'A review, by Aritoli ola Silba. Once again, Virshon ola Vivar has left his particular mark on the Liavekan stage. Again he has used a cast of players unknown before now; again he has presented exactly two hundred performances and closed the play, though he could surely have filled the theatre two hundred times more. And again he has given us a tragedy—not the good old-fashioned melodrama of murderous kings and scheming courtiers, but a vision of people betrayed by a small trait of evil into a bottomless pit of madness and death. Ola Vivar's horror is extravagant enough to make it entertaining. He knows that we are afraid of small, sordid, meaningless deaths, while being destroyed by the gods—or the gods' favorite instrument, the indestructible madman—has to it a kind of exaltation.' You do have that, don't you, Virshon?"

"Of course, master, I . . ." The newsman coughed, straightened up (gaining a full head in height), pulled back his cap. "So you saw through me."

"Of course it's you, Virshon. What are you using for the inkstains, lampblack?"

Ola Vivar rubbed a thumb against his blackened palm. "And blue oil. Was it really so poor a costume?"

"It's perfect, Virshon . . . but as I should have expected you to know, none of the real ragmen would ever ask me for an unrecompensed interview. A few of them still have burning ears." He twiddled his fingers on the handle of his cane. "Now, if you'd appeared as a bright young trainee . . ."

"I'll make a note of it."

"Well, Ari?"

"Well what? Did I mean the review? You know I did. Five years and seven straight successes: what is a critic to say? I *will* say, five years ago I'd never have believed anyone could make a career out of tragedies. Not in Liavek. Liavek has never liked tragedy."

"You did say that, five years ago."

"Hmm. Did I say it for publication?"

"No."

"Thank Shianpar for that. So, may I announce that you are at work on your next triumphant tragedy?"

"You may announce that I am at work. But the play won't be a tragedy. It will be a comedy."

Ola Silba inclined his head. "Andri Terriot will be very nervous to hear of that."

"Why? Terriot's perfectly secure at the Levar's Company. He can't think I'm offering him any competition."

"You have it the wrong way round," ola Silba said, twirling his cane for emphasis. "Not that Terriot sees it that way. But never mind him. Why a comedy? Change of heart? Change of pace, change of mind?"

"A little of all of those," ola Vivar said. He no longer seemed to be paying full attention to ola Silba. Few things irritated Aritoli more, but he was a patient man in the presence of artists. Good artists, anyway.

Ola Vivar said absently, "Do you hear someone laughing?"

"*Laughing?* After that production? Release of tension, perhaps."

"Yes, perhaps that. . . ."

"Or anticipation? Come on, tell me, Virshon: why a comedy?"

"You said you wouldn't have thought a writer could succeed at making Liavekans cry. But I've done that. Now I want to make them laugh. Is that news, Ari?"

Ola Silba tapped his cane. "It might be. But I'll make you a trade, Virshon. Don't repeat any of my old predictions and I won't repeat any of yours."

"Fair enough," ola Vivar said, and extended his hand to shake ola Silba's. Then he paused, waved his blackened, oily palm, and said, "Just good night and my word on it, eh, Ari?"

"Ola Vivar's a good old name," Aritoli said. "Good night, Virshon."

The following morning a poster went up in the theatre district:

The Red Mask Theatre of Liavek
is pleased to announce

OPEN AUDITIONS

for its next production

All actors not currently members
of existing companies are invited

Beginning Moonday, 12 Wind 3320

Appointments at the Theatre

Virshon ola Vivar, Director

By five that Moonday afternoon the line was two blocks long, a string of players that began at the theatre door and trailed away to vanish in the spring fog.

Two days later on Rainday (and it did), eight of those called back from the line were in the theatre lobby, standing against the curtained walls, sitting on the red-cushioned chairs, pacing the patterned carpet, waiting for their turn within, trying to look disinterested. A short brown Tichenese in a long red housecoat came and went by the stagehands' door, paying no attention at all to the waiting actors.

"Porter," one of them said finally, "would it be possible to get a cup of kaf while we're waiting?"

"I am the dramaturge," the Tichenese said.

"Look, fellow, I don't keep up on what the Titch call servants these days. I'd just like some kaf, if it can be managed."

"Perfectly manageable," the small man said. "In truth, I would like some tea myself." He crossed his arms, tucking his hands into his sleeves; when they came out again, he was holding two steaming porcelain cups. "Kaf for the gentleman, tea for your servant."

"You—"

"Are not the porter? No. My name is Oten Chitaru. I was recently hired as dramaturge by my lord within; that is his name for the theatre company wizard. Your kaf is burning my fingers."

The actor took the cup. "Uh . . . that is, I didn't . . ."

"Of course, Master Player. Good day." Chitaru went out again.

The actor holding the kaf looked around; the others were carefully examining the carpet. "Well," he said, and raised his hand. It was empty.

The doors to the auditorium swung open and a man came out, the applicant who had gone in perhaps a quarter-hour earlier. He had been rather jaunty then. He wasn't now: his cap was crooked and there was a rip down one of his trouser legs. He had a look of mingled horror and relief and rage, as a fish must look after being thrown back as too small.

"Hey, Pollo," one of the other applicants said, "how'd it go?"

"I am going to retire from the stage," Pollo said in a drum-tight voice, "I am going to learn an honest and valuable trade, such as marrying rich widows and then strangling them." He tugged at his cap, deranging it even further, and walked straight out of the theatre.

Another waiting actor, a young man with brown hair swept low over his eyes, looked after Pollo intensely. His graceful hands were knotted together.

"Wirrel Skye," said a voice from within, and the young man's head came up, his hands jerked apart. "Yes," he said, "yes, I'm here," and went inside. Someone said after him, "Break something, kid," and more softly, "I mean it, break something."

The doors closed behind Wirrel Skye, shutting off every sound from outside. Ahead, past the rows of cloth-draped benches, was the bare stage of the Red Mask. It was the second largest in Liavek, thirty feet wide, extending perhaps five feet out to the footlights before the twenty-foot-high framing arch, and thirty to the rear. He had been here twice, with Dijade, to see *The Moon's New Coat* and *Middle Distance*, but he had never seen it without scenery or backdrop or proper lighting, naked. There were iron fittings against the brick back wall, thick vertical beams, a series of pulleys, and ropes tied to wooden pins, like something on a ship. Wirrel had never seen so many ropes in a theatre before; he wondered what they were all for.

A space just before the apron had been cleared of seats. There was a small desk, and behind it a man in a black jacket and white shirt, hunched slightly over a paper. "Wirrel Skye?" he said, not too definitely.

"Master ola Vivar," Wirrel said, and walked forward.

Ola Vivar turned. His face was pale and blank. His dark gray hair was pulled back and tied with a black ribbon. "You're rather young," he said. "You are an actor?"

"I've had training, master. As I told you before."

Ola Vivar looked at the paper again. "But you are not with any company."

"No, master."

"That is an absolute rule of this theatre. No one who is employed elsewhere is permitted."

"I understand that."

"Many actors do not. Or they pretend . . . they act, if you like, that they do not. I have known players who were appearing lead-billed in productions right up the street come in, wearing a bit of grease and a silly hat, and tell me, 'No, master, I have never played a role more exalted than Bo'sun's Brother in *The Pirates of Port Chai.*' "

Wirrel smiled. That was an old actors' joke: the Bo'sun in *Pirates* talks incessantly about his brother, but the brother never appears on stage.

Ola Vivar looked hard at Wirrel. "You take my meaning, young man?"

"I've told you the truth, master."

"It has happened," ola Vivar said, settling back into his chair, "that actors attempt to lever their way into roles through other actors . . . understudies in reverse, you might say: the puppet takes the text home to the puppet-master, until sometime deep into rehearsals the puppet disappears, and there stands the master with lines learned and makeup drawn, and what is the company to do but say, 'Aye? The show must go on.' You've probably heard that."

"Yes, master."

"Then you do know some actors."

"Of course, master."

"Anyone I've ever heard of?"

Wirrel took a breath. *Breath is to an actor what luck is to a wizard,* Dijade had taught him, *control it and you can work miracles,* "Surely the master ola Vivar must know a great many actors. Doubtless you—"

"Doubtless. I think I have seen you here before, Wirrel Skye. And accompanied. Was it Skaya Altaire? Or the Dayzell?"

"I do not know them, master."

"No, of course not. Skaya is careful to be seen only with women, and you're too healthy to be on the Dayzell's list." Ola Vivar stood up. "Show me your hands."

"My hands?"

"You've had some training, you must know where they're located."

Wirrel held out his hands, long fingers spread. Ola Vivar came over, grabbed Wirrel's left wrist and held it tightly. Wirrel looked up—ola Vivar seemed suddenly very tall—but did not pull away. He could feel ola Vivar's fingertips close on the pulse point in his wrist, feel the throb of blood.

"I'm certain I've seen you with someone," ola Vivar said. "Ais Ophiri? Dijade? Il Umiel? There's the Acrivannish fellow, who once said he'd kill to be in one of my tragedies; him being Acrivannish, I should take him at his word." Wirrel breathed smoothly—he was not certain how—and his pulse stayed hard but regular. Even as the playwright named Dijade.

"I am an actor, unknown but I believe not unskilled," Wirrel said firmly. "I am here to audition for your play. I understand your rules and conditions, and I am willing to live by them."

"*You're lying,*" ola Vivar said, very close to Wirrel's ear, and then suddenly dropped Wirrel's wrist and stepped back. "But you're lying as an actor does, that's good. And you do *not* understand the rules and conditions here. You don't have any idea of what they are. But I'll tell you one: if you do join this company, from that moment on you will lie about what you learn here. And not just for the run of the play: you will lie for the rest of your life, to your lovers and your family and the people who want to help them become famous actors. Do you understand that?"

"Yes," Wirrel said.

"You don't understand, so that's a lie. But it's a lie, so you've accepted the rule. Very good, Wirrel Skye.

Go home now. It's a cold, wet evening, and you can't keep yourself from sweating for much longer. Come back on Moonday next, and don't have a cold.''

"Master.'' Wirrel bowed, smoothly as he could, turned, and went out of the theatre, not even seeing the others in the lobby as he went past them, into the street, one block up and into an alley, where he threw up.

A little over three hours later, the rain over and the moon high, Wirrel Skye slipped into his house, shutting the door behind himself as softly as he could. The house was dark. Possibly Dijade was not—

"Ah, there you are, Wirrel,'' she said, standing in the parlor doorway. "Did the audition go well?''

"I think so,'' he said, more bravely than he felt.

"I'm glad. Did you mention my name to Virshon?''

"No.''

"Ah. So proud, still, Wirrel.''

He could see that she was wearing the green crepe gown; the moonlight shone through it as through clouds. Her hair was brushed into a red-gold nimbus, and in this light there were no lines in her flesh. He said, "Should I not be proud, then?''

"Oh, you should. Tonight, yes, you should. Hungry?''

"I—yes, I am,'' surprised at how hungry he suddenly was.

"You didn't eat this morning, and of course you didn't at midday; by afternoon you wouldn't have recognized food. But it's all right. You know what's on the kitchen table, don't you?''

He knew. There would be the sweet farm sausage, just as he had grown up with, that he loved and Dijade detested. She hated even the smell of it, but she would endure it, on his breath. There would be sausage on the long table, and crisp greens, and a silk pillow.

It was a good life, Wirrel thought, it was all the life most farmboys dreamed of and then some. Dijade was beautiful enough to sting the eyes—as Wirrel's stung now—and if she was twice his age, what was that? A role, a mask, that was all that age was. She had taught him that, as part of teaching him to be an actor. One way and another.

Dijade drew him toward the kitchen, brazen jewelry chiming as she moved, and he followed willingly.

Late on Luckday, a name was called in the lobby of the Red Mask, and a woman, who had been standing away from the crowd of applicants, walked to the door. She was of less than average height, quite thin, with long black hair and large, dark, gold-flecked eyes. She wore a hunter's jacket of tan deerhide, light wool trousers of the same color, low boots. Someone saluted as she went in.

The auditorium was dark. The bare stage was brightly lit, by a row of small lamps along its front edge and larger lights with reflectors hung above. A large man in a formal black velvet gown and hat, such as a doctor or city wizard might wear, was sitting on top of a small desk at the front of the stage, arms crossed. Behind him was a clutter of ladders, paintpots, bits of wood, coils of rope, as if some builders had downed tools and gone to dinner.

"You're Nin il Craith," the man said flatly.

"That's right."

"You're sure that's all of you? Or does more arrive by the second post?"

"I'm here to try out for your play."

Virshon ola Vivar jumped off the desk, landing with surprising lightness. "Oh, just like that," he said. "You're here to try out for my play. You're here to *try out*. For *my* play. Well, you're here. That's objective. Let's start with that, shall we?"

Nin said, "What would you like me to do?"

"Anything other than stand there at attention. Why don't you jump, so I can see a little of you below the eyebrows?"

"My lord?"

"That's easy for *you* to say. I'm up here. I think you

must be that chorus invisible I keep hearing about."
Ola Vivar walked up to a footlight, and his silhouette
was thrown against a side arch, twice life-size. "Perhaps we could give you an arrangement like this, Mistress Nin, and they could see you from the second row."

"Good day, Master ola Vivar," Nin said, and began
walking away.

"Wait," ola Vivar said. "*Wait. Please.*"

Nin il Craith stopped.

"I saw you in the little theatre at Mystery Hill," ola
Vivar said quietly. "I was not unimpressed. Do you
have something to read for me?"

"I did."

Ola Vivar walked down the narrow steps at the corner of the stage. He bowed to her, gestured upward.
"Then step up and read it. Please."

Nin went up the steps, stood by the desk. Ola Vivar
was hard to see, behind the glare in his black clothes.
Nin said, "Shall I stand here?"

"As you like. What are you going to read?"

"The soliloquy from *Softer Times Than These.*"

"I wrote that."

"Yes, I—"

"Just wanted to be certain you knew. Go ahead,
Nin."

She took the page from a pocket of her coat, unfolded it. The lights made it difficult to see. Mostly
from memory, she began to read.

Softer Times was the only one of ola Vivar's plays
she had seen. Her brother Kel had given her the ticket
two birthdays ago. The soliloquy took place a few
scenes before the end: the heroine Imire has charmed
her way free of enemy privateers with her statement of
love for the young Marine Caldon, and the crew leaves
her on a tiny paradise island from which she is certain
to be rescued. She sits on the beach, looking at a strange
light across the water, and speaks to it as if it were the
spirit of Caldon, "my own fire upon the sea." She does
not know that the light is a sea-battle, in which Caldon,

believing Imire murdered by the privateers, is sailing a
fireship into the midst of the enemy fleet, to their and
his own destruction.

Imire tells Caldon that when the war is over they will
return to the island, "here to live in light, drink from
one spring, and know no other company: and if the
guns sound any more, we'll hide within these groves,
and they shall not know us as we not them. . . . Now,
if these lands were not so small and rare, upon the
loveless sea, I think we'd all know private paradise; and
when the gods of war grew hungry once again, and
blew the call to fill their bloody ranks, the horn would
glance from living palisades. . . .

"Though yet we'd pass, as mortals, it would be
  As one sweet sleep, departing company,
  And not abandoned, left like weeds to die
  On stones someone once wanted, Gods know why."

Nin stopped.

Ola Vivar was laughing, pounding a fist into his
palm, laughing out loud.

Nin threw down the prompt-sheet, took a hard step
forward. "What in the name of Tracati's shot and powder do you want?" she shouted. "What am I supposed
to be here for?"

Ola Vivar was not laughing now. He vaulted up on
the edge of the stage, looked straight up at Nin. She
took a step back. Ola Vivar walked forward, seized Nin
by the shoulders, forced her back several steps farther,
to the center of the stage; then he danced away, around
the desk. He held up a hand, stabbed a finger toward
her. "What do I want, Nin? What do *you* want? What
is it you'd like to do, just now?"

She held entirely still. They were in a cube of light
surrounded by darkness, a dark that seemed to be deep-
ening, hardening like ice.

Ola Vivar said, "Do you want to kill me, Nin? Do
you think you could do it, if you had the means to

hand?'' He pulled open the desk drawer, took out a flintlock pistol and held it out to her butt first.

She took the gun.

"Means," ola Vivar said. "Opportunity you have. Now motive. You're going to shoot me. Through the heart, you've only got one bullet, and if you don't kill me dead on the spot with it I'm going to close the distance between us and—''

Ola Vivar kept talking. Nin shut her ears, examined the gun. It was a Fiesole copy, not fancy but well made, an ordinarily efficient killing machine. The pan was primed, and she could tell by the balance that it was loaded and tamped.

"Through the heart, Nin. Or I shall introduce you to things you never imagined in the little theatre. I shall show you the extinguishing of the lights.''

She cocked and leveled the Fiesole in one easy movement. Ola Vivar looked huge, a blot of darkness invading the light. Nin aimed at where a man would have his heart.

"So little. And now nothing.''

In her mind, flint snapped, sparks flew, there was an explosion.

Then her finger twitched the trigger and it all happened.

Ola Vivar stiffened and fell. A wave of sound and dust puffed out; a thin twist of smoke, shining in stage-light, whirled away into the darkness overhead.

Nin raised the pistol, said to ola Vivar, "When a gun doesn't recoil, it hasn't fired a bullet.''

Ola Vivar pushed himself up on one elbow. "Never let the audience know that. It'll spoil every play with a shooting in it.'' He rolled over and was suddenly on his feet, brushing dust from his velvets.

Nin said, "This gun has no vent from the pan to the chamber.''

"It's a stage weapon, can be loaded on stage and touched off without the possibility of terrible accidents.''

"Accidents." She threw the pistol at him; he turned and it crashed somewhere to the side of the stage.

"Don't you believe in accidents?" ola Vivar said mildly as she passed by him and stamped down the stairs from the stage. "Nin il Craith."

She stopped, turned. "You've had your entertainment, master. I'm quite aware that I have no reputation as an actor. I'm *very* aware of my size. Did you call me here just to make me angry enough to—to—"

"Yes. That's precisely why you're here."

"What?"

Very calmly, ola Vivar said, "I wanted one moment of authentic anger, Nin il Craith. If you have that moment available to you, I can teach you everything else you need to condition it into a performance. Sometimes, people who have . . . borne much . . . have lost their anger, trained it out of themselves. Those people may be better, wiser than you or I, but they will never be great actors. You are here so that I could find this out." He went back to his desk, examined a paper. "I would like for you to return next Moonday evening."

Nin said uncertainly, "I'll have to think about it," and turned to go.

Ola Vivar said, "If you don't come back, we'll both always wonder what would have happened if you had. We will both be unhappy for it."

Nin hesitated for just half a step, and kept walking.

When Nin reached home, the shop was dark and bolted. Nothing showed behind the barred windows but empty green display cloths and small white cards with descriptions and prices. The guns were in the back, she knew, locked in the heavy cabinet, safe from the cobblestone discount; but the emptiness of the window seemed symbolic, like a premonition. She went around to the back, up the short ramp to the apartment.

Kel was asleep in his chair, the lensatic bench lamp turned low. He stirred as she went past. "Nin?"

"Yes."

Kel rubbed his eyes. "I meant to stay up for you."

He pushed the chair back from the table; its wheels made no noise. He turned it with pressure from his right leg. He had no left.

"No reason you should have," Nin said.

"Yes, there is. I sold the Beyaret three-barrel today. I'm sorry."

"What on earth are you sorry for?"

"I know how fond you were of it."

"How much did it bring?"

"Three hundred levars."

"But that's wonderful!"

"It'll get us out of serious debt," Kel said. "But we can't replace it, and the Beyaret was the last really unusual piece we had."

"What about the lock design?"

Kel pushed some bits of brass and spring steel aside with his left hand, which lacked middle and little fingers. He picked up the board with the gunlock model, pushed at the trigger with the first finger of his whole right hand. As the trigger went back, the flint-holder began recoiling. Then it snapped forward, striking the flint against a bit of rough steel.

There were a couple of sorry little sparks, that was all.

Nin frowned, then hid it as Kel looked up at her. He said, "You see, that'll never light. It's something to do with the spring tension, I think."

"Have you thought of a hesitation lock at the top of the travel?"

"Thought of it. It'd be slow, though. Defeat the purpose of the double action." He put the model down, squeezed his hands together. "Thanks for the thought, though, sister."

"That's all right, Kel. Have you had dinner?"

"Oh. There wasn't—I mean, there's some of the potato-leek soup left. You have it, I'm not hungry."

Kel was never not hungry, Nin knew very well, but there was also never any point in arguing with him.

"All right," she said, "I'll have the soup, and then I'll go to the market tomorrow. We'll stock up."

"Hmm," Kel said, staring at the gunlock.

She put her arms around his shoulders, kissed him on the scarred cheek.

"I'm being stupid," Kel said. "How did your tryout go?"

She had been hoping he would forget to ask. "I don't—" Kel looked unbearably sad. "I mean—I might—"

"What's the matter, sister?"

"He's asked me to come back. I don't know any more than that."

"But you know that means it's good news. Good news never shows itself all at once."

She said, "Yes, you're right," because Kel needed so badly for the news to be good today. And suddenly, so did she.

Baren Baragon ducked his head to pass the theatre door and turned a little sidewise to get between the draped benches. They made him think of a formal garden, a hedge maze. He thought of another room, where the benches were ranked high above a small bright stage, but the garden kept him away from that place.

Virshon ola Vivar was on the stage, wearing cavalry trousers, boots, a loose white shirt. He had a jacket over one shoulder, a thin dueling sword in his right hand; he was waving and thrusting. The stage was hung with sheets of white canvas, and lamps threw ola Vivar's shadow on them, so that it seemed he was fencing with a ghostly opponent.

"Won't be a moment, Baragon," he shouted, and slashed furiously at the air. Then, with a shout of "Take *that*," he shoved the sword into one of the canvases, released it, and turned away, leaving it stuck in the cloth. He ran down the stairs, put his hands to his forehead in greeting, shook hands with Baren. Ola Vivar was only slightly shorter than Baragon, though rather less broadly built. The playwright's gray hair was pulled straight back and tied with a wide black ribbon; prominent blue veins showed at his temples, and there were stress cracks around his eyes and mouth. Baren could see the tenseness in his neck muscles, feel it in his hand. This was a man who did not sleep well.

Ola Vivar went to a small desk before the stage, examined a paper. "When you were here a few days ago, you were a bit vague about your acting background. You say you have some experience."

"I have never performed in Liavek, master."

"No, I know that." He looked up, smiling pleasantly. "Fish, for their reasons, swim against the current to spawn, but I don't use actors who are known in Liavek. . . . You said you're a gardener?"

"I lay out gardens, yes, master."

"Don't be ashamed, man. That's an astonishingly respectable trade for an unemployed actor. But we're still—you'll forgive me this—dancing round the bush. Is there somewhere you *are* known, Baragon?"

"No, master."

Ola Vivar tapped his hand on the desk. "I know it's a prying question, and most people with pasts of any interest whatsoever want that fact kept quiet. Now, I do teach—that's a reason for the curious conditions of employment here—but I haven't time to teach the raw elements to stagestruck gardeners."

There was a creaking sound from above the stage, and something like a whisper. Baren looked up; ola Vivar did not, and said, "We're entirely alone here. This is a condition, I'm afraid."

Baragon said, "I was a street entertainer. In Saltigos. As a child."

"O-o-oh," ola Vivar said. "Were you good at it?"

"I earned enough to go to school. . . . Not acting school. I—"

Ola Vivar slashed his hand down. "That's all I wanted to know. Street entertainer, yes, that's very good . . . tell me, Baren, did you juggle?"

"No, master. I did acrobatics, mostly, and sang, and told some fortunes."

"You aren't a wizard."

"No, master."

"Doesn't matter, we have one, I just wanted to know." He gestured toward the stage. "Please go up. Do you have something to read?"

"Some poetry."

Baragon took the stage. A crowd of shadows accompanied him. Ola Vivar blew out a footlight, extinguishing two members of the chorus, then sat down at his desk, just visible in the dark spot.

"Now, Master Baren," ola Vivar said, "I would like for you to put away your poetry and tell me a story."

"What sort of a story, master?"

"One I'm not likely to know. *And*—I want you to tell it to me without speaking. Make sounds, if you like—but not a word. Understand?"

Baragon nodded. Ola Vivar saluted with his hands again and sat back.

Baragon stood still for a moment. Then he looked upward, shading his eyes from an imaginary sun. He reached into a pocket and brought out his fingers pinched on something tiny. He knelt, scraped at the ground, put the seed into the hole, and covered it over. Then he mimed the weather, wiping summer sweat, bending against wind and rain, huddling from a storm— all the time "raising" the plant with hand gestures.

Soon the plant was taller than Baragon. He took a few steps away, began honing an invisible axe. He hefted it, went back to where the plant stood. He paused, lowered the axe. He touched the stalk, traced out the shape of a leaf. He knelt with his hands about it.

Then he exploded into motion, seizing the axe, slamming it into the plant, one, two awful blows, three— and the stalk gave way; Baren, stricken, let the axe drop and caught the stalk as it fell, holding it in both arms, lowering it to the ground as if it were a human body.

He raised a cupped hand, reached into it with the other. He drew out a handful of seeds, let them trickle back.

Then he bent and began planting them, one by one.

Ola Vivar said, "Be here on Moonday evening."

Baren Baragon walked the long way home to the Street of Rains, up the three floors to his loft. It was furnished with canvas cushions for sitting and sleeping, louvered screens for the privacy he had no need for, inked plans and penciled renderings of gardens done for hire tacked all over the walls, and something like a hundred plants. There were ferns and florals, ivies crawling up the screens and creepers dangling from their pots, a pan of vetch like some strange casserole, and a few exotics: barrelsticker from the Great Waste, Silverspine nightweb in a lightproof box, a tabletop forest of the little Tichenese trees.

There was no one else home. There never had been, except for a white cat that had insisted on following Baren home; it was friendly, and had gotten fat very quickly, but no amount of food would keep it from nibbling the plants at random; rather than come home to find it choked or poisoned, he had given it away.

It was the only living thing that had ever left him unwillingly.

Baren had just hung up his jacket and lit a fire beneath the teapot when he stopped quite still; he suddenly recalled that the playwright had saluted him with both palms to his forehead. The Liavekan style was one. The Saltigan style was two.

Baren brewed some Nine Joys tea, sat on a cushion, and wondered if he had made a terrible mistake. Saltigos was near: when the new Railway was finished, they said, it would take less time to reach Saltigos than to walk the length of Liavek. Someone was certain to see the play who had known Baragon when he lived in Saltigos, when his name was not Baren Baragon.

That man had saved enough copper from turning cartwheels in the streets to study medicine in Tichen.

He had rights of surgery at the Saltigan Lying-in Hospital. He had a comfortable home, with a fine garden that there was plenty of time to tend. He had a beautiful wife.

And the wife had a handsome lover, and the lover had tumors in his chest and his gut and his brain.

The cancer was beyond surgery, magic, hope. But once it had reached that point, become an indivisible web of love and death and sex and disease, it was inevitable that it should climax with all the players in the Saltigan surgery, the theatre where the seats looked down on the stage.

It didn't end there. It ended when the lover died, a month later, screaming through toxic doses of rapture extract, and the surgeon went home to find that the wife had gone. The last thing she had done before leaving was to spade up the garden. It is rare for one cancer to kill so many people at once.

So, Baren Baragon thought as he poured himself more tea, he was going to put himself under the lights, beneath the faces, again?

Yes. He was. There are only so many times a man can turn the same earth before he learns that lost gardens cannot be restored.

Lisel Solenti's name was called late on Sunday night. She glanced around at the few other people in the lobby: they all had desperate looks, rather frightening. The Tichenese wizard had been kind, had given her tea. One of the applicants had said that was all very fine, but the wizard had already been hired, had nothing to fear. That was when Lisel realized the others were frightened too: of her as much as anyone.

She went inside. The place was dark, and huge. She had never been in the Red Mask. Her mother had been an actor before Lisel was born, and when Lisel was small she had been taken to puppet shows and children's plays—she vividly remembered *Three Drops in the River*, at the Canalside—and introduced to people she learned later were famous. But that was a long time ago, and her parents had died in a coaching accident before the Red Mask was opened.

Lisel had not been to a play since then. Pirth didn't like the theatre. He took her to the Canalside once, but it had been for some sort of political meeting. She sat between Pirth and a terribly fat man who seemed to have no hair at all, and while the speakers talked she remembered lines from the play years ago.

She moved between the covered benches, gray shapes in the dark. Darkness didn't frighten her, but she didn't want to fall, appear clumsy. Ahead she could see the stage: one lamp hung over it, casting a cone of dusty light straight down. In the light a man was sitting, his chair tilted back, his feet up on a little desk.

"Come closer," he called to her. "Up on the stage."

Virshon ola Vivar was wearing high soft boots, tight trousers, a loose white shirt with the lacings half undone. The light around him was grainy, twinkling with dust.

"Hello, Lisel," ola Vivar said. "That's a very lovely dress."

"Thank you, sir." It was of pale blue silk, that went well with her fair coloring. Pirth usually didn't like her wearing it, pointing out that it was easily damaged and difficult to clean. Sometimes he complained that it was just the color of Worrynot, the blue flowers one chewed to prevent childbirth. But tonight he'd insisted that it was the only thing, along with the gold cord shawl that just matched her hair.

She waited for ola Vivar to say something more, but he just sat, the vertical light shadowing his face. Finally she said, "What would you . . . that is, I—"

"You've never had a formal audition, have you, Lisel?" ola Vivar said, very gently. He raised a hand. "No, I know you haven't. But you're very well spoken of. By Skaya Altaire especially."

"But I hardly know her, master."

"She knows you. Don't misunderstand me, Lisel.

You aren't here because anyone recommended you."
He swung his feet off the desk, opened a drawer, and
took out some papers. "Do you know what a cold reading is?"

"Yes."

"Fine. That's what we're going to do." He handed
her the papers. "This is a monologue from *Sunphase*.
That's one of my old plays. Have you seen it?"

"No, sir."

"That's fine. I want to hear you read these lines, not
an imitation of some other actor." He sat back in his
chair. "Read them over until you think you've got the
idea, then just go ahead. There's no hurry."

Lisel read over the text. She felt the skin of her palms
tighten, the sweat start. Hesitating wouldn't help, she
knew. She opened her mouth to begin.

"One more thing," ola Vivar said suddenly. "There's
some background I should have given you. The person
you're speaking to is the one you love, always have and
will love; but your country's been overrun by an enemy
king who wants you for his own—and you've agreed to
that, to save your lover's life. The king has given you
one last meeting before sending the boy into exile, but
he's watching you from hiding . . . and if your friend
expresses any affection for you, even uses the word
'love,' he'll die. Horribly. Got that? All right, go
ahead."

Lisel paused, but ola Vivar gestured for her to begin.
She started speaking:

"Here's this moment. I can't see through it, I can't
understand it; life's full of moments that all pass by, so
why does this one stick in my throat so, refuse to digest
like the others?

"Stop before you say the word I know you're going
to say. Swallow it; it's only one syllable, it'll go down
easy, smoother for certain than my feelings. You think
it's a pearl now, but swallow it, I'm sure you can, and
the next time you see it, it won't be so pearly or pure.
Am I being unfair? Confusing the coating with the un-

changed pearl within? Maybe I am, but how many washings will it take before you can swallow it so easy again?"

She looked up at ola Vivar. He was standing now, just on the fringe of the light, so that it sliced down his face, his open shirt. Lisel read on:

"No, you shan't make me say it, either. It's a mouse to an elephant, it runs into the ear and chews the brain; when an elephant dies it can crush something, and maybe there's hope to be squeezed from that, but I'm too small to do likewise; too small to be drawn hard to the whole earth, why then this pull from another weightless body. . . .

"It is no use. The moment has me now, I am not to be suffered the movement of time until I take it. This is the choice time and matter gives us: to be consumed, or to be tortured until we beg to be consumed. Either way, a kind of destruction. . . ."

Ola Vivar stood only a step away from her.

"But better destruction than oblivion . . . better ruins . . . than nothing."

She looked up at him. His knees were a little bent, his eyes nearly level with hers; she felt heat from him, or perhaps it was the hard down light.

"You do want to act, don't you," ola Vivar said, and licked his lips. "Not to 'be an actor.' Anyone who can crawl up on a stage and remember one line can be an actor. You want what only an audience can give you, if you will only give them what they need in return."

"Yes," Lisel said.

"Even if it's only an audience of one? Even if you have to play a hundred nights to stones and beasts and cattle for every one to human beings with souls?"

"I've never wanted anything else."

"That's good. That's right. You can't want anything else. Or you'll never have it at all."

He was impossibly close to her.

Then he turned and walked back to his little desk.

"The callback is for tomorrow, Moonday evening. You can make it, of course?"

"Yes. Of course."

"I cannot use you if you don't appear," he said, and raised his head, and smiled.

"I'll be here."

"Yes," ola Vivar said. "I know you will."

Lisel walked home by lamplight. It might have been cold, or not; raining, or not; she never noticed.

"Did he accept you?" Pirth said as Lisel entered the house.

"I was called back," Lisel said. "Others were as well. I don't know how many, so I don't know if we were . . ."

"But you had a great smile as you left the theatre," Pirth said, taking Lisel's shawl, locking it in the closet.

"You were there?" she said.

"I had to be certain you'd gone." Pirth put his fingertips on Lisel's cheeks, thumbed the hair away from her forehead. "Your career's at too fragile a stage to risk on a passing butterfly in the belly. . . . Speaking of which, you've had your blue flower?"

"Yes."

"There's my girl." Pirth hugged her. "Now I know you'll be hungry, so I brought home some splendid lamb and kidneys; they're all out on the table, with the flour and the potatoes. You haven't made pie in weeks now, so it'll be special."

"I'm tired, Pirth. Couldn't we go out . . ."

"We will, Lisel, we will. When you're an actress, we'll go out every night, so everyone will see you; and how they'll envy me then."

"What if I just fry the lamb and kidney, Pirth? With oil and peppers. You always like them that way."

"More than you know, my dear, I was thinking of it all the way from the butcher's, but then I thought, 'Oil and peppers, on my girl's stomach, after the day she's had?' No, I couldn't bear that. The pie is what you need."

Lisel took a breath. "I'm not hungry, Pirth."

"Nerves. Soon as you've relaxed a bit—"

"No, Pirth. I'm just not hungry, and I'm much too tired to cook."

There was a small, cold pause.

"Oh," Pirth said. "I believe I understand now. You do want this job very badly. And I'm sure that Master Virshon ola Vivar has very persuasive ways."

"What are you saying? What do you think I've done?"

"Only what you needed to do, my dear, that's all. There's no blame, not a copperworth. Now, you're very tired, and can't eat a thing, so you must go on to bed. I'll clean things up in here."

"I'll have some kaf with you."

"No, no, no, I won't hear of it. Come along, off to bed." He led her to the smaller bedroom, gave her a slight push through the door. The lamp was out, and when the door closed behind her the room was entirely dark. The scratching click of the lock was immensely loud.

She waited for fifty heartbeats, for her eyes to adjust, for Pirth to move away from the door. She felt her way past the bed to the nightstand, hoping the lamp and the striker were still there. They were, and she got light by touch and showers of sparks.

There wasn't much in the room: the little bed and table, a small closet with her cotton nightdress, a dozen books. Pirth never touched her books: he was almost superstitious about it.

Lisel took off the blue silk dress, hanging it carefully in the closet, putting on the nightdress. She sat up in bed, with a book of poetry that had been her father's. She had practically memorized it, but tonight it looked different: the love poetry seemed to be written in an entirely new language. She read and read until her eyes were gritty and sore, then turned out the lamp and sank into a sleep like deep water.

* * *

Virshon ola Vivar sat at his desk before the Red Mask stage. It was an hour before Sunday midnight; he had just dismissed the last of the applicants. He had a few notes to make on the playtext, now that he knew the cast; then he needed a bit of sleep, since the four of them would be back tomorrow evening.

Wirrel Skye, he wrote, *Nin il Craith, Baren Baragon, Lisel Solenti*. Then he went back and drew a hard stroke under Nin il Craith's name.

A voice from the left wing said, "Are they all gone, Vrrshei?"

"Yes," ola Vivar said. "There's no one else here now."

There was the squeak of a pulley, a rope whispering down, a small thud. A man walked onto the stage.

"Haunting theatres is hardly good style," ola Vivar said. "Not in Liavek. They do most of their sets by magic; these scenery supports had to be built to my own specification, and they're still not suited to our home style of pulley-dancing . . . even less is this the set for *Black King's Conscience*."

The man paused. He was strongly built, dressed in a dark red jacket and gray trousers; his hair was black and quite short. His face was pale, almost gray, but then the light was bad. "Conscience?" he said. "Now there's a word that falls light from your lips, Vrrshei."

"Stage center, please," ola Vivar said. "It's quite late, but I'll hear your audition."

"You do not know who I am."

"You're the man who laughed at my best tragedy," ola Vivar said, sounding impatient. "You call me by a name I haven't used in ten years. That tells me *what* you are, and where you've come from, and why; but naturally I don't know your name. I'm certain you'll tell me, though."

"I am Mnoreon, whom you murdered."

"You're a ghost, then? You made quite a thud. Who are you really? Or rather, who were you, before the court hung Mnoreon around your neck?"

"I was called . . . Krtsotses."

"Don't recall the name. You weren't an actor—not a professional actor, I mean?"

"I was . . . Krtsotses was an apothecary."

"Nice profession if you can't be an actor. And your crime?"

"Providing poisons for the purpose of murder."

"I like that. Not too banal. Were you guilty?"

"Of the preparation. The woman who bought them—that is, her husband was—"

"A brute and a beast, yes, yes, and her voice was so softly pleading when she asked you for the aconite. It was aconite, correct? *Three Women in One*, act two, scene two. Always a favorite in summer repertory, but we can't allow that to sway us, eh, Krtsotses? No, I'm afraid I have my cast now. Thank you for coming, please find your own way out." Ola Vivar began gathering papers from the desk.

"*Vrrshei!*" the man shouted, thundering it through the theatre like a great sneeze. "I have come for your justice!"

Ola Vivar stopped still. After a moment he said, "Ah. That is indeed Mnoreon's style, you've grasped it well. Or should I say, Mnoreon has grasped you."

"You have run, Vrrshei, but you have not run away. You have sought out the darkness, but the dark would not have you. You have lived as though you'd killed Justice in the same stroke as Mnoreon . . . but see, here I stand."

"*Secret of the Missing Hand* is a potboiler that Mnoreon wouldn't have played in to keep from starving. You're going to have to do better than that, Krtsotses."

"There's only one more thing I have to do," the man on the stage said, and took a step forward. The footlights, burnt low and yellow, lit him from below, making his face a demon mask.

Ola Vivar said, "Yes, you're from Drstona, right enough. I can smell your paint from here. Do be wise, Krtsotses; if you're going to follow the home habit, at least use cake-base in public, it's far less obvious than grease.''

"Kothesa Vrrshei, you have been tried and convicted of the murder of the cast of *The Broken Seal*, a play of your authorship and direction. Under the laws of Drstona, the Fury before you has been sent, his mission to visit justice upon you in the name and role of your victims—''

"Do you have a gun?" ola Vivar said calmly. "The Inspector in *Missing Hand* uses a gun. The Lady in *Three Women* has a poisoned hairpin. What are you equipped with?''

The man produced a dagger with a long, thin blade. "Perhaps you remember this?''

"Is that actually the one that killed Hlane?''

"You do recall it. That is good.''

"I recall the one that Csasel was supposed to stab Hlane with. But it had a sprung blade that snapped back into the handle.''

"Before you exchanged it for this.''

"Before someone exchanged it. How do you know it was me, Krtsotses?''

The man jumped from the edge of the stage. "You were tried. Convicted.''

"Careful, hopping about with that long-iron. I was tried in my absence, Krtsotses. In the absence of any witnesses—since, as you say, the entire cast of *The Broken Seal* died during the premiere performance.'' Ola Vivar pulled his shirt open. "Here's a throat, Krtsotses. Here's a heart, here's blood enough to wash out your little sin's punishment. You've been chained to the soul of Mnoreon for ten years now. A long time to live with a ham actor. Well, come finish it. Ten years of hunting for one stroke in the empty dark; stick your little steel home and serve Justice.''

"Are you saying that you did not kill them?''

"Were you even at my trial, Krtsotses? Or did they just draw you at random from a cell, have the wizards brand you with Mnoreon, cast you out of Drstona with

my name on your lips and that knife in your hand?
You're in Mnoreon's role, man: a halt, a tongue-tied
Mnoreon, true, for ham that he was he was also an
actor—don't you know how you died?''

"The Chancellor . . . had prepared poison for his
mistress . . . but on learning that she had committed
murder and died under torture to save his name and
career . . . he drank it himself, under the eyes of the
Council assembled to honor him." Krtsotses turned his
head, sending his face into deep shadow. "I drank the
stage poison. And there was . . . oh, there was lye in
the cup. . . .''

"And then, Mnoreon?" ola Vivar said, quietly, intensely. "What happened then?"

"I couldn't speak. I had a brilliant dying speech—
you had allowed me to write it for myself—"

"I'm strange that way. Go on."

"It burned. And I couldn't breathe. Fire and no air,
I remember thinking, and no way to speak the words.
Then I fell, and someone caught me . . . who?"

Ola Vivar rose from his chair. "I caught you, Mnoreon. There was no one else alive behind the stage.
Even the dramaturge was dead. I caught you, when you
fell."

Krtsotses wavered. He looked at the dagger. "Csasel
stabbed Hlane with this. And then they tortured Csasel
to death . . . only the springs and the blades of the
machine were real . . . the bullet for Tyith, too? And
Mrazen, surely not Mrazen, that was only the dramaturge's illusion, wasn't it?"

"The wizard knew it was no illusion the moment the
lightning struck. Some matter of an alteration to her
working material. She killed herself."

"Killed herself."

"Wizards are unstable that way."

Krtsotses's knees buckled. Ola Vivar caught him below the armpits, knelt beneath him, his smooth cheek
against the other man's painted one. "Like this, I did

it," ola Vivar said. "Do you remember my hands, Mnoreon?"

"You killed me—killed us all—and then appeared for your bow. You stole even my death speech and my applause."

"Did I, Mnoreon? I'm certain the court said so, but you were dead by then. You never heard it. You know nothing that the court didn't tell Krtsotses when they impressed your soul on his. You never even saw the evidence, only the verdict."

"You ran away."

"I knew they would find me guilty, present or absent. The courts of Drstona exist to assign guilt, Krtsotses, if not to the accused then to someone: to hold a trial and find no one guilty would violate the dramatic unities. And I had no one to pass the accusation on to. You were all dead. On my stage, in my play, in my arms."

"And I?" Krtsotses said—Krtsotses's voice now, not Mnoreon's—and pulled away, sprawling on the floor. "For what do I exist, except to execute a sentence? The role is upon me, Director; it does not end until you end." His hand tightened on the long knife. "Your death makes me innocent, Vrrshei. Whether or not you are guilty."

Ola Vivar, on his knees, bent his head back, pulled his shirt wide, showing the bare skin of his throat and chest. "Then be innocent."

Krtsotses stared. His head wobbled. He stood up, took a step back from ola Vivar. "I will be watching you, Vrrshei. I will be back." He turned, collided with the desk, then ran from the theatre.

Ola Vivar leaned forward on his hands. He exhaled heavily, then got to his feet. He peeled off his shirt, shook sweat from it, tossed it on the chair. He closed his eyes, stroked his fingertips lightly through the moisture on his back, his flat-muscled stomach.

Ola Vivar looked up at the empty stage, the dark

scene-space above it. "Thank you all for coming," he
said to the theatre. "That concludes the auditions."

"Captain?" Eban the desk clerk said through the
door.

Jemuel, captain of the City Guard, was seated at her
desk, balancing a pen on her finger, and an inkwell on
the pen, when there was a knock at her door. The desk
serjeant's voice said, "May I come in, Captain?"

"Just a moment," Jemuel said, and Eban instantly
swung the door open. Jemuel managed to catch the inkwell. She looked at Eban, who was looking at the ceiling, and said, "Yes?"

"Captain, you knew the old ola Vivar, didn't you?
The playwright's father?"

"I knew him. Why?"

"There's a man outside who wants to know about his
death."

"His death?"

"Captain," Eban said, not too plaintively, "I've had
to deal with four lost cats, a dockside brawl, a report
of giant locusts in the Levar's Park, and two invisible
wizards hiding under nice old ladies' beds, and it's only
ten in the morning. This fellow seems nice enough."

"All right, Eban. What's his name?"

"Trice. He's a sea trader, in from Gold Harbor."

"He would be. Send him in."

Trice breezed into the office. He was a tall man in a
huge black hat and a sweeping black cloak lined with
brilliant yellow. His clothes were expensive, in that extraordinary bad taste that marked the better class of
Gold Harbor merchants. Jemuel saw his right hand and
reached for the gun clipped under her desk.

Then she looked closer, and let the pistol go. Trice's
left hand was a brass double claw, and pinched in it
was a smoldering twist of incense rope. She had taken
it at first as a matchlock pistol.

"Master Trice," she said. "You're new in Liavek?"

"Yes, my first occasion to visit." His accent was

foreign but nondescript, which meant nothing at all, given his stated origin; if men from the Moon came to Liavek, everyone would assume they were from Gold Harbor and ignore them.

Trice said, "I am looking to find someone who can tell me what has happened to my friend Risil ola Vivar. Naturally I think the police will know things."

"I didn't know Risil as a policeman," Jemuel said. "We were friends. How did you know him?"

"I at one time managed a warehouse in Port Chai. We were mostly acquainted on business . . . but, I am sure you know."

"I can't say I do. Tell me."

"Oh, I do not mean illegal. We were just in the same trade, his goods in my warehouse. Two people in that arrangement, well, they either respect one another, or they very much do not, you see?"

"Yes, I see that."

"Many times Risil tells me, 'See me in Liavek.' Now you know this is always said, but still, here I am in Liavek and I propose to see my friend. But at once I am told that he is dead, and a . . . son has taken him over, sold the business in fact. I don't know this son; I don't know that Risil had a son. I am wishing someone could tell me about . . . Virse?"

"Virshon."

"Yes."

"It's as you've heard, Master Trice. Risil's wife had died while he was abroad, and he never had shareholders, so when he died, the business passed entirely to his son. Virshon had no interest in running a shipping business; he gave the ships—there were only a few—to their captains, and built a theatre, the Red Mask. He writes and produces plays."

"Successfully?"

"Very successfully."

"You know Virshon, then."

"Not well. But if you'd like to see him, his theatre

is the Red Mask. It's only a few blocks from here, near the canal.''

"I think not. I think I would not have much to say to him. My friend is gone.''

"He was my friend as well,'' Jemuel said.

Trice said, "Did he talk to you about his son?''

"He taught me to juggle.''

"Juggle?''

"That's right. You?''

"No,'' Trice said, and took a step toward the door. "I thank you for your time and assistance. If ever you are in Gold Harbor, I hope that I can offer you the same.''

"If I ever need help in Gold Harbor, I hope you can offer me a reasonably sized army. Good day, Master Trice.''

"Good day, Captain.'' Trice raised his brass hand and went out.

Eban came in. "So what did he want?''

"He was here about information,'' Jemuel said slowly. "But I don't know if he wanted me to give it to him or if he wanted to give some to me.''

"Eh?''

"He was practically drawing a picture that something's wrong with Risil's death and Virshon's inheritance. He seemed to think I'd be very interested in that.''

"I'd think you would be.''

"Not enough to make guesses and tell Trice about them.'' She picked up the pen, balanced it on her fingertip. "I knew Risil when I was just a kid. Used to see him on the docks, before he had any ships of his own. Then he went overseas, and I didn't see him again until he came home to die five years ago, and brought Virshon with him.''

"Brought—then he *isn't*—''

"Virshon ola Vivar is Risil's adopted son, which is a matter of legal record that you have no business knowing and will not repeat to anyone, especially Master Trice. Virshon *might* be from the wrong side of the blanket, but that isn't *anybody's* business." The pen toppled; Jemuel snatched it from the air.

"Now what's wrong, Captain?"

"I'm thinking, that's what's wrong. I watched Virshon at Risil's funeral, and if it wasn't real grief he was showing, then he's the best actor in the world . . . but that *is* what Virshon does, isn't it? . . . Tell me, Eban, did you notice anything odd about Master Trice of Gold Harbor?"

"There was his hand . . . I tried not to stare at it."

"Of course. But you did anyway. You didn't look at anything else." Jemuel put a hand to her face. "Master Trice was wearing a thick layer of makeup, in the middle of the morning."

Moonday evening was cool and moist and not at all unpleasant. One by one, people arrived at the Red Mask lobby, until there were four of them; hesitantly they traded names and introductions, always glancing back at the door for more arrivals. Chitaru, the wizard, came out to introduce himself; he led them into the theatre, where five chairs and a tea service were set up on the brightly lighted stage.

"Please help yourselves to tea," Chitaru said, "and be seated. The Director will be here very soon."

Baren Baragon said, "What about you?"

"I have already had discussions with the Director. By his instruction, yourselves and I shall have the pleasure of working together sometime later in the production. Good evening to you." He bowed and walked silently into the darkened right wing, past lights and ropes and scenery panels, and disappeared.

The four players sat with teacups, regarding one another and the fifth, empty chair.

Nin il Craith said, "So who do you suppose the last seat's for?"

Lisel Solenti said, "Surely no one's late. No one *could* be late."

Nin frowned but said nothing.

"No one is late," said a voice from the dark where Chitaru had gone. Virshon ola Vivar stepped briskly onstage, in boots and a red cotton tunic, wiping something from his hands with a cloth. He tossed the rag away, pulled the empty chair toward himself, and straddled it, his arms folded on the seatback. "Good evening, cast. I'm pleased to see you all here. I trust you've made each other's acquaintance?" There were nods and murmurs of assent. "That's very good. Before we're done you'll know one another like slaves chained to the same oar: no sense in delaying the process."

Nin said, "But we're all the callbacks—you chose us days ago, and didn't say so."

"True. Would it have made a difference?"

Nin said, "The suspense was not very pleasant."

Ola Vivar stood up, went to the tea set, poured himself a cup. "On opening night, Mistress Nin, at the moment just before the curtain rises, I shall remind you that you said that. I expect you'll think it very funny."

Wirrel Skye said, "But still . . . you called only the four of us. You must need at least four players."

"The production needs exactly four players. Apart from the dramaturge, who is already engaged, and the musicians, who will be hired later." Ola Vivar walked around the group, back to his chair. "Tell me then why you were the only ones called."

Baren said, "To show us that you are certain of players coming when called. That we can be replaced."

"Correct." Ola Vivar sat down again, took a sip from his tea, propped an elbow on his chair back, and rested his chin in his hand. He said, very gently, "But I don't want to replace any of you, and I don't think I shall have to. You're here because you want to act. I've just spent a long and very hard few days weeding out people who wanted something less than that—to be looked at, to play fancy-dress, to display their egos or politics or sexual desires under a public spotlight. . . . I've also sent away perfectly competent, talented actors who wanted to use my stage as a device for the development of their own existing careers. That's no crime, but they'll have to hire their own halls to do it."

Wirrel said carefully, "You are very specific about your goals."

"That, Master Skye, is why I succeed." He pointed at the tea tray. "In the drawer of that table you will find your scripts. Will you distribute them, please, Wirrel?"

He did so. The scripts were stacks of perhaps a hundred pages, copied out in the even round hand of a commercial scriptorium, drilled down the side and bound with red ribbon. The top page read:

MAY THESE EVENTS

An Accidental Comedy

by Virshon ola Vivar

" 'Accidental'?" Baren said.

Ola Vivar said, "Not, I assure you, in its creation. At least, I hope not." He smiled, and the others relaxed a bit. "No, it's a comedy of accidents, of people mistaking one another, meeting at the wrong times, that sort of thing. The intent should be quite clear once you've read the text. Now, wait, wait; don't be distracted yet."

They paused, looked up at him.

"I want you to take these home and read them. Don't try to memorize yet, just read and think. There'll be changes made in rehearsal. And while I've indicated the parts I want each of you to take, that may change as well."

"There are twelve names in the cast," Lisel said.

"That's correct. You'll each be tripling the major roles, plus one or two of the walking-scenery parts. And, yes, this was intentional. We've already discussed the availability of players." He stood up again, clapped his hands sharply. "That just about concludes our business tonight. Our next meeting will be in three days, Luckday noon. We'll discuss the script over lunch here and begin rehearsals afterward.''

Ola Vivar reached into a pocket of his tunic. ''Also, as of today you are formally members of the Red Mask Company. The salary is two levars each tenday.'' He held out a handful of small gold coins.

There was a pause. It was somewhat better than a skilled laborer's wage, and several times what an ordinary actor could expect.

Ola Vivar jingled the coins. ''If you think this is charity, you're terribly mistaken. By the time we're halfway through rehearsals, you won't even call it generous. You're workers and this is your wage. You can bank it or drink it, stiffen your mattress or warm your bed with it, but don't think for an instant you won't earn it.''

They took the money. Ola Vivar said, almost gaily, ''Now good night, my fellow artists, until we gather again in three nights' span.''

The players bowed and started down the steps from the stage. As they filed past the draped benches, ola Vivar stepped to the edge of the stage and said in a voice abruptly very sharp, ''One final thing.''

The players all stopped at once.

''You may tell anyone you please about joining this company; I'm sure you all have someone who'll be pleased by the news. But I do recommend that you do not spread it too broadly, nor too thick. And I *require* that you not share those scripts with anyone, anyone at all.''

There was agreement, bows. One by one the actors went out. The last to go was Nin il Craith, who stood for a long moment looking at ola Vivar, then wrapped her arms around the playscript and departed.

Ola Vivar stood still, looking out over the auditorium, until a shoe scuffed behind him. Without turning, he said, ''You've never seen anything like them, have you, Krtsotses?''

"I have seen any number of novices," the voice came back.

"I was talking to Krtsotses, not you, Mnoreon. But you don't understand either, no more than that poor young man you call home. You've seen novices, by which you mean incompetents, the talentless, the ineducable. Not these. These are the raw stuff, Krtsotses, people waiting to fill parts not yet written, speeches no one has thought of yet."

"Drstona is crowded with—"

Ola Vivar spun, chopped the air with both hands. "There is *nothing* like this in Drstona! The time a Drstonan has spent in memorizing dead verse and learning the appropriate makeups for all social occasions, these people have used in being really alive. They want to act so that they can expand, not fossilize."

The other man looked at his shoes for a moment, then walked heavily to the tea service, poured a cup, sat down. "And you, Vrrshei? What is it that you want to do?"

Ola Vivar paused, then refilled his own teacup and sat facing Mnoreon. "What I am doing. Writing plays, staging them . . ." He nestled the cup in both hands. ". . . and creating, from the confusion of human life, instruments that can crystallize and shatter that confusion."

Mnoreon's hand trembled. He clutched it in the other. His head swayed, stiffened. "Instruments," he said. "And . . . how does the craftsman . . . treat his instru-ments?" His eyes were cloudy, staring at ola Vivar. Then he raised his cup and smashed it on the stage. "Does he *shatter* them as well?"

"That's my porcelain, not a stage property."

"This isn't a matter of stage blood."

"Krtsotses had a grip on you just now, didn't he? Let's ask him what he thinks of this. Are you there, Krtsotses?"

The voice came as from the bottom of a well. "I shall kill you, Vrrshei. I must do so."

"And who knows, perhaps you will. But not yet."

"No, not yet." He stood up. "Some time when you are not expecting it, as those you killed were not."

"Some time when I am not expecting to die. . . . I must be immortal, then."

"There is another thing, Vrrshei." It was still Krtsotses's voice, perhaps a little stronger now, with an actor's projection.

"I am listening."

"Money."

"That's the usual other thing. You need some living expenses? Yes, of course you do. I can't imagine what you've lived on, chasing me for all these years . . . and if it's all the same to you, I'd rather not know." He set aside his cup, took a leather purse from inside his tunic. "Here's a hundred levars. You should be able to live comfortably on that until the play opens, and buy some new clothes as well. You do need new clothes, Krtsotses. Old City will give you the best prices, but you'll have to bargain for them."

"Bargain." Krtsotses stared at the purse, but made no move at all.

"Mnoreon knows how to haggle. He played Plpel Profit in *Something on the Side* for over three hundred performances. Just ask him."

Krtsotses snatched the purse away. "A thousand gold coins cannot buy your life, Vrrshei."

"First *Missing Hand*, now *The Murdering Ministers*. I've underestimated you, Krtsotses; you have what amounts to a doctoral degree in tatty melodrama."

Krtsotses stumbled from the stage. Ola Vivar began to clap, slow and steady and loud, until the rear door opened and slammed.

Baren Baragon brewed a large pot of tea, crushing a bit of mint into it for alertness, turned up a lamp and sat down among green fronds to read.

He smiled at the title: *May These Events*. It was taken from the prayers to Bree Amal, who in Liavek (as Sal-

tigos, and other towns, amen) was deity to the keepers
of disorderly houses, places of assignation, and inns of
the jollier sort. There were many variations on the
prayer (as the goddess, amen, amen) but all took the
general form *May these events not make thy servant's
life any more complicated than it already is.* Baren had
known the phrase quite well, on the streets of Saltigos,
in his first life; in the second, there had been a ward
nurse at the Hospital who used it to good effect.

The plot involved a young man named Hiron and his
companion Locarius, who while supposedly diligent
students are actually notorious carousers. The father,
Hirander, intends that his son marry a sweet, innocent,
and very lovely young lady named Honoria; but early
on, the son mistakes an overbearing society matron for
his intended, and spends the rest of the play avoiding
her. At the same time, Honoria has confused a wealthy
but very silly fop for Hiron, and behaves likewise. Cir-
cling around them are a set of stock comic characters:
an elegant foreign ambassador, a blustering general, a
big-booted eye-patched pirate, and so on.

That was the first act, a rather conventional setup
except for the sharpness of the dialogue, and a hint of
hidden things—a touch of madness in all the characters.

In the second act, the hint explodes. Not only the
hero has a double life: the merchant father is actually
a former pirate turned dealer in smuggled booty, the
Ambassador is a spy, the General is a cowardly civilian
who wears the uniform to impress women—the entire
supporting cast in fact have double lives.

Baren put down his tea. His hands were ever so
slightly damp. He told himself that there was nothing
unusual in the plot; the hidden past was a very usual
part of plays. Ola Vivar's use of the device was perhaps
more extreme than most—but this was a comedy, correct? A study in exaggerations. Baren continued to read.

Except for the hero, companion, and heroine (who
spend surprisingly little time onstage), all these cheats
and frauds are engaged in a complicated plot to sell

military secrets to the Ambassador. The secrets are the General's, and therefore false—but that doesn't matter, because no one else intends to deal fairly for them anyway. Everyone has a plan, several of which involve using one of the young not-lovers-yet—and then either framing the dupe for treason or killing him or her outright.

Somehow, the thread of murder was woven into the action so gradually that it did not jar at all with the laughter; when at the peak of the act a professional assassin delivers a catalogue of methods of accomplishing death—''The gun beneath the cloak, the gun propped on the windowsill—must mind the sun for that one—the needle, the dagger, the sword, the axe, the very large sword that is effective as such things go but not recommended for use in confined quarters, the drop from a great height, the item dropped *from* a great height, poison in food, poison in wine, poison on doorknobs and pomanders and nosegays, poisoned lovenotes, poisoned love-*tokens*, poisoned cloaks as in the S'Rian story, poison in the sugar bowl when one pleads a diet at dinner, *never* poisoned daggers (as too much security's the mark of an amateur), slow poison, fast poison, accumulative poison, retchy poison, windy poison, itchy poison, sneezy poison, and the fastidious but effective serpent in the bath—''

Why, there was no horror in it at all, no more than a clown discussing which flavor of pie best suited throwing. Baren found himself reading the killer's speech aloud and laughing, entirely despite that the assassin's false identity was an addle-headed doctor.

The third act brings another explosion, of violence this time, as the conspirators annihilate one another by means both prosaic and ridiculously extravagant, always, of course, leaving the hero and heroine not only untouched but perfectly unaware of the destruction going on around them. With practically no one else left to get in their way, Hiron (now heir to his father's business) at last meets Honoria—whom he instantly recognizes as the proprietor of his favorite house of ale and delights. They depart together, leaving Locarius alone on stage to deliver a wry epilogue on romance and business mergers. He concludes:

So fare the fair. May gold with gold entwine!
As meet the ill-met with their ill-bought ends;
But gods forbid that either path be mine!
I'm bound for where the candle has two ends;
For new horizons, ventures, music, wine,
Bright hours in company with proof-coined friends.
Now that you've shared my view of these events—
I wish you all good night—and now I'm hence!

Baren flipped back to the list of players. Ola Vivar had indicated Baren should play the father, Hirander; General Maximenes; and the fop Pancrad. The last seemed a little strange . . . though on reflection, he supposed having a character who fancied himself slender and elegant played by a big man could be very funny. He thought a bit about it, how to hold himself like a man who *thought* he was agile and delicate, and he began to laugh again.

He was not to play the Doctor; Wirrel Skye was. That was fine. And if Wirrel needed coaching on how to play a doctor—well, of course Baren would leave that to the Director ola Vivar.

Wirrel Skye closed the playscript, took another few breaths to stop laughing, then opened it again.

He was alone in the house, upstairs in his own room with the door shut. Dijade had left a note in the kitchen that she had been called out suddenly, would be back as soon as she could. Wirrel was, a little ashamedly, glad of it.

He riffled the pages. It was an incredibly complicated play, with moving sets, collapsing props, guns going off, a wild death by sorcery: the wizard, the Dramaturge Chitaru, would certainly have his hands full. And magic aside, there were entrances and exits by door and trap and rope—he began to count the moves, trying to keep track of them in his head, and lost track before the first act was out. It was going to be hectic as a marketday morning backstage, with each of them having to dress and hit cues for three characters. Wirrel alone had more than a dozen changes of costume, playing the hero, Hiron; the doctor, Viscusi . . . and the society matron, Bibidiel, whom the hero mistakes for his assigned bride.

Now, how was he supposed to see himself? He flipped to the page, Act One, Scene Three. Aha: Hiron was concealed behind a tapestry in his father's hall. Presumably Wirrel ducked behind the drape and shucked into Bibidiel's clothes for her entrance a few lines later.

The stage directions for that were: *Enter BIBIDIEL, a woman so confident of her own wealth and refinement that she has quite failed to notice the loss of everything else. She is dressed at the height of the last decade's fashion.*

Not terribly polite, Wirrel thought, but then whatever Virshon ola Vivar's chief virtue was, that wasn't it. And then another thought followed, as he looked at the description; Wirrel tried to push the image away, but it wasn't the least use. He could see Bibidiel clear as winter lightning in his mind, he knew just exactly how to play her, her dress, her movements.

Oh gods, he couldn't.

Ola Vivar couldn't have done this to him, not deliberately.

Of course he had.

There was a light knock on the door. "Wirrel?" Dijade's voice said.

"Yes," he said, so completely lost that he just sat there, the script open in his lap, as she came in.

She was wearing an embroidered dress of red silk, a red-and-black shawl; her hair was up, a broad red hat under one arm. "You have a script," she said, "so you must have a role."

"Three, actually."

"Three?" She sighed. "You should have insisted upon a lead, Wirrel. You're no more unknown than anyone else in the company—haven't I told you, sometimes you have to make your own way in these things?"

"Lead? Oh—well, we're all leads, actually. We're all tripling parts, and they all seem about equal."

"Someone must be the lead, Wirrel. There can't be a tragedy without a tragic figure."

"It's not a tragedy. It's a comedy, and—" He closed the playscript, put it aside, he hoped with indifference. "It looks all right, for an early draft."

"A comedy? That's certainly unexpected. There's been no word of such a thing."

"I suppose he's trying to—"

"But I think I know who did know—crisp his little moustache." She turned, said softly, "A comedy. Well." Her voice picked up. "You understand that it's no different; my own teacher used to say to me that tragedy and comedy are the same music, played at different pitches."

"We've just barely started . . . but ola Vivar has some very strong ideas."

"Of course he does. Are you very tired, Wirrel? Would you like to go out? Celebrate? Just a little quiet noise, the two of us."

"That sounds wonderful. Shall I dress up?"

"I want you to dress to the limit." She smiled, bright enough to light the back rows of the biggest theatre in Liavek, and went out of the room with a grand-ball turn.

Something was terribly wrong, he knew, but she was a wonderful actress.

No. But she had made him a good enough actor to pretend so.

When Nin il Craith got home, her brother Kel was asleep with a light on, his wheelchair pushed away from the bed, a sheet partly across him. His three-fingered hand gripped the edge of the sheet, the stump of his missing leg stuck out at an unnatural angle: he looked like an unfinished sculpture, a casualty of war. He had been beautiful. But guns, as all gunsellers were fond of saying, are the great levelers: bullets and powder are no respecters of persons, permanganate of potash is nobody's fool.

A few years ago, their father Taz il Craith had died of a lung disease, slowly and wearily, coughing into handfuls of gunwadding instead of a handkerchief so he could dispose of the blood unseen. It might have been caused by something he breathed at work, or it might not. Their mother was a desert woman much like Nin in color and shapeliness and height, who had met Taz when he was trading muskets to the nomads. She gave all rights to the shop to her grown children, and returned to the Great Waste: not to die, she told them firmly and clearly—because she never lied and never wept—but to let the wind blow her a new life, as it had before.

Less than two months after that, Kel had read in the half-copper newsrags about the Tichenese military threat—or was it the Ka Zhir threat?—and decided to invent a miracle weapon that would make Liavek invincible against all foreign enemies. He had been working with glycerine and acid. The accident took two fingers from his left hand, and his left leg below the knee, and the spray of acid left awful scars on his chest and back.

He was still beautiful, Nin thought. There had always been young women around him, and two of them courted him even while the bandages were on; but he had sent them away. He wouldn't even go to the House of Blue Leaves.

She arranged the sheet to cover him properly. She sat down in his chair, said barely over a whisper, ''I have three parts in a play, Kel. I'm to be the irresponsible friend of a lovely young rogue, and a temptress who drives men mad, and the most honest thief that ever was. You'll see, Kel. You'll see people laugh at me, and I won't die of it; you'll see—''

She got up, careful not to make the chair squeak, brushed his fair hair with her small dark hand, snuffed the lamp.

Lisel Solenti went cautiously from room to room, calling Pirth's name. He wasn't home. She had a strange energy, something crackling in her bones; she was wide awake despite the hour and vividly aware. She went into the kitchen, nearly dancing, put down the script and began pulling vegetables from the shelves, puffing the fire up brightly. She sliced some bacon thin, spread it into a pan, chopped peppers and mushrooms and vanchace into the hissing grease, then tossed pinches of spice and herb after. As the bacon and vegetables went transparent, she took the membrane from a kidney, sliced it, added it to the pan, and covered it. She stirred together a little mustard and cream—

Pirth was standing in the kitchen doorway, his cloak drawn around him, his face crooked. ''What are you doing?'' he said softly.

She held out her messy hands, giggled. ''What do you think?''

''Then he did not give you—but there were only four of you. Only four. How could he—*not* give you a part?''

''But he did, Pirth! He did, and it's wonderful!''

Pirth's face bent a different way. ''I told you we would go out to dine, once you were successful. You seemed at the time to agree it was a good idea.''

''Oh, it is.'' She took a step toward him, spreading her arms to hug him, then remembered her hands and shrugged. ''I just . . . well . . .'' She paused to lift the lid, stir the kidney.

''Well?''

''Pirth, aren't you happy? I'm so happy I—I don't suppose I know what I'm doing.''

''I'm delighted, Lisel.'' He turned away, spun his

cloak off. "And of course you did not know that arrangements were made for this evening."

"What? You made—oh, but Pirth—this is just a little dinner, I can take it off, change—"

"Smelling of the kitchen. Grease in your hair. No. I shall have to explain the situation later. Somehow."

"I'll write a letter for you."

Pirth winced.

Lisel said, "What do you want me to do?"

"Take the supper off the fire."

She did.

"And come here."

Pirth was a careful and precise man, who always knew just what he was doing. Lisel had needed those qualities when her parents died, leaving her alone and bewildered. "I will know what to do," he'd told her, holding her close, hiding her against himself, "good times or bad, I will always know what to do."

He never struck her where a mark would show outside her clothing. There were never any questions to answer the following day.

She woke face down on her bed, first light coming flat through the window. She could see the playscript on the bedside table. She pushed herself up on an elbow, groped for the script, pulled it to her. The pages were uncreased. Of course. Pirth was superstitious about words on paper.

She ran her fingers into the binding, slipped out the two gold levars. She held them tight. They were cold, but soon they were warm.

Grumbolio the Pirate stamped in from the night, boots flopping, jewelry jingling, beard thick with frost. He turned to the audience, threw his shoulders back and stuck his arms akimbo, bellowed, *"Ho there!* I—"

"Wait," Virshon ola Vivar said. Grumbolio stopped still, then said with Lisel Solenti's voice, "Yes?"

"Too loud. *Much* too loud."

"But I'm supposed to be—"

''The movements are fine. I could practically hear the boots and the slap of your sword. But not the voice. Again, but quietly.''

They were working without costumes or scenery. Wirrel asked why Oten Chitaru didn't simply cast the illusions, and ola Vivar explained that the scenery would be real, painted and carpentered, hung from the ropes and heavy framework, locked to pins in the floor.

They had talked through the entire play during and after lunch, but they weren't playing it through; they did scenes in pieces as ola Vivar stopped, moved, reset them, like a shahplayer studying positions. Every few minutes there would be a collision, of words or bodies, and the Director would chop the air with his hand and start the action over from some new disposition.

Lisel went out again. Grumbolio thundered in, turned, said in an ordinary tone, ''Ho there. I'm from Port Chai.''

Wirrel Skye giggled. Nin il Craith put a hand to her face. Baren Baragon laughed out loud. In a moment, Lisel was laughing too.

Ola Vivar said, ''You're doing more here than getting a fairly earned laugh. You know, but the audience doesn't yet, that Grumbolio isn't a pirate, he's a maritime insurance collector who fancies that he knows all about piracy and ought to be very good at it. So, yes, he swaggers and blusters and shivers his timbers all over the place—but he's not going to forget his manners, and a gentleman doesn't yell in a stranger's house. So, once the audience stops laughing, they should begin to realize that something's wrong. Finally and always, you're staying in character.''

Wirrel said, ''That's a lot for one hello.''

Ola Vivar said, ''Words are valuable. One can only speak so many of them in a minute, one has only so many minutes before the audience's backsides rise in revolt. The words and the minutes all have to carry a terrible load, to persuade the backsides to endure theirs. . . . Now, Lisel, we'll run it through from the beginning once more. Don't laugh at yourself, now, Grumbolio'd rather be keelhauled. You three, feel free, however. No, wait, stop." They did. "Baren, you'll be on stage during this, as Hirander. Would you stand, hmm, *there* . . . and when Grumbolio comes in, you react. Remember, before you became a respectable merchant, you were a *real* pirate."

Baren said, "Suppose, when Lisel speaks, I stand so?" He stood with his feet apart and braced, his arms crossed.

"Quarterdeck stance, that's just right," ola Vivar said, and moved to the edge of the stage. "We'll need to time it properly, so that they see you just as they're recovering from Lisel's laugh—but play it through now, we'll refine it later."

Deep into the afternoon, after a pause for tea and sugar biscuits, ola Vivar stepped offstage and returned with a box. He set it in Nin's lap. "I think you know what to do with these."

She opened the box. Inside was an ornate pistol and kit.

"Go ahead," ola Vivar said, and went to stand by the left wing. "The rest of you, watch her carefully."

Nin poured the powder, rodded and tamped the bullet, primed the pan and cocked the piece. "And shall I—"

"You know what to do," ola Vivar said.

Nin put the case on the floor. She stood up, aimed the gun squarely at ola Vivar's chest, pulled the trigger.

The pan flared. The muzzle blazed. The pistol jerked upward. Ola Vivar's white shirt blossomed red and he was thrown backward into the dark. There was a clatter of cans and wood.

Wirrel stared. Lisel screamed. Baren tilted his head, took a step toward the wing.

Ola Vivar walked back onto the stage. His chest looked like raw ground beef. "Thank you, Nin," he said. "Perfectly done. And by you, Chitaru."

The Tichenese wizard walked on from the right wing.

He snapped his fingers, and the splatter disappeared from ola Vivar's shirt.

Ola Vivar said, "The hit can be done with a bladder of pig's blood, or various other substances, but none of them will launder; easier this than a new shirt every night. Chitaru also does the muzzle flash, because we don't want real powder pointing at anyone. What magic can't do is make the gun kick: that has to be mimed by the player, just as you saw Nin do. We're now going to take a brief respite from lines and entrances, while Nin teaches you all how to convincingly blow each other's brains out."

When they had the motions down to ola Vivar's satisfaction, Chitaru created a breeze to blow the stage clear of pan-smoke and the rehearsal resumed. The players were beginning to tire. Ola Vivar took no notice. They began to sweat. The Director tossed them towels and ordered them to continue. They groped for lines, and he prompted them. "You have to do this perfectly, for an audience, two hundred times," he said. "That means you must do it wrong, for me, at least that many times. Two hundred? Why, we're barely on five!"

Sometime after eight, Nin as Thillius the thief was explaining to Wirrel as Viscusi the doctor/assassin why thievery was the noblest of all professions (the thief being, unlike everyone else in the play, exactly what he claimed to be).

"Money, they say, is the cause of grief, and therefore, they say, those of my pick and slipper bring joy by relieving of grief, as those of your physic and bandage bring joy by relieving of pain. But this is not true, Doctor, this is a loose saying, it has not all its buttons done. For I ask you, does not your kind take away from men of which they have too much a sufficiency, whether in bruise-blood or belly-water or gut-wind, and for this are you not recompensed with money?"

"Aye, Master Nightclimber, gold for the letting of blood," Viscusi said thoughtfully.

"Well then, the money being as—"

Ola Vivar said, "I think that's enough for the evening. You're all looking terribly tired, and it's late; I don't want to sweat you into agues. They're bad for the memory, and hard on a good makeup."

Nin said, "I would like to finish this speech, master."

"I wasn't asking you what you'd like. I was giving instructions."

No one moved for two breaths. Then Nin said, "Give me the cue, Wirrel."

Wirrel looked at Nin, then at ola Vivar. The Director said, "Well, Master Skye? From whom are you going to take direction?"

Wirrel said, "Good night, Nin." He walked away.

Nin was rigid, trembling just slightly. Baren leaned against the stage arch, body relaxed but face hard. Lisel seemed about to weep. Wirrel walked past them all, to the stage steps.

Ola Vivar said, "Baren."

"Yes, Director?"

"I want to try this scene with you as Viscusi. Will you give Nin the cue, please?"

Wirrel stopped cold. Baren moved away from the arch, faced Nin in an easy pose, said, "Aye, Master Nightclimber, gold for the letting of blood."

"Well then," Nin said, letting the tumble of the words cover anything else in her voice, "the money being as unto the grief, do you not then take away the pain, and the sufficiency, and the grief all three, and have the gold for your trouble? But now consider the burglar's lot: he takes from those who have no pain, that which none has a sufficiency of; truly, all he comes away with is the grievous gold, and of that the fence returns not one part in ten for value. Here's two and nine-tenths part shortage, and thus I say the robber is more noble than the healer by thirty times in mathematics."

Viscusi said, "Master Windowdancer, I think you cut logic finer than purses."

"Oh, Master Bonebreak, you speak of skill and I speak of heart's goodness, and those are two things as unlike as specie coin and paper currency: for suppose you could cut a fellow's heart out and spill no blood, would that not be craftily done? But the fellow would be little good done by it."

"You understand my profession very well."

They stopped, turned to ola Vivar. Nin bowed.

"Well spoken, Nin. I trust you won't take that as irony. And, Baren, I think we'll keep the casting as before. Now, good night, thank you all; next rehearsal in two nights."

Nin stepped up the ramp to the back door, held out her key.

There was an explosion from within, a flash at the side windows that lit up the alley like noon. Nin practically threw herself through the door.

Kel looked up. He was wearing a sooty apron, and his face was powder-black, but he himself was intact as he had been this morning. On the table next to him was a twisted and smoldering assemblage of brass and wood.

"Hello, Nin," he said. He was practically giggling. Nin wanted to hit him over the head, wanted to hug him, but instead of either she said, "What in the name of Tracati's ramrod are you *doing*?"

"It's for the railway," he said, pride like a sun shining from him. "It's a firestarter. I went down to the station, to see if they had any hardwood scraps—they've been making benches out of a good maple, you know—and I started talking to one of the crew. She said that when they need to fire an engine quickly, they have to use magic. But their head driver doesn't— Well, you read about him, didn't you? In the *Crier*'s monthly special."

"Yes," she said absently, looking at the wrecked device. He had a name like a metal, Steel or something,

and he told the paper he hated magic, didn't believe in
the gods, only in machines. He was insane, of course.

"Well, you see, then. If I can build an igniter, sell
it to them—why, we could live on that, run the shop as
a hobby." He stopped, looked at her hard, held out his
whole hand. "Or you could act, Nin—you wouldn't
have to worry about what you were paid. Maybe you
could have a theatre of your own. Can you imagine it?"

"Yes, Kel. It would be lovely. Excuse me now, it
was a long day."

"Of course. Good night, Nin."

"Good night, brother." She bent over him; he presented a relatively unsooted ear for her to kiss.

She went to her room. She hadn't lied to Kel: she
could imagine a theatre of her own, and that was the torment of it. The railway man, who had no gods, he was
mad, but was it a pleasant madness?

Her heart was like a balancing top: there was a string
wrapped tight around it, and people kept pulling the
string, spinning the top, to see the marvelous tricks it
could do.

When Wirrel Skye got home, Dijade was dressed for
an evening out; she wanted him to go along, insisted
that he didn't need to change, though she sponged and
powdered his face, combed his hair and tied it back
neatly. He consented; he didn't think. He didn't even
think when the tandem footcab let them off at the City
of Brass, and Dijade swept up the gold-leafed steps,
plumes out, dress trailing, that there was some part of
the thought he was missing.

Then they went in, and he saw the table, and he
could have cut his throat on the spot for being so stupid.
There was wine on the table, fruit and cakes, the City's
best gilded crystal. Around it sat Altaire, and il Umiel,
and the Dayzell; several of the men as well, Spire and
ais Eperray, all dressed magnificently, the ones who
were starring and the ones who hadn't had a good role

in years. And next to each of them was another person, not quite so flash, but neat. Like Wirrel.

He had not been to one of these parties for more than a year, not since Spire's lady Taycee had gotten the role in *Hammer and Anvil*. That had been ola Vivar's, too. Taycee didn't come around anymore. Spire had someone new with him now. For the past year, Wirrel had watched the announcements, made an excuse.

He hadn't even been thinking, tonight.

They poured the wine, and they toasted Wirrel, the famous and the unknowns together. Someone fed him a grape, a sliver of cheese, wine that tasted of lip paint. He reached for another glass of wine, but they all slipped out of his reach. It wasn't fair; they had all been drinking for some time, they were all drunk, he had always been drunk by this point. A slender, long-nailed hand tugged his shirt lacings open, tossed some grapes in; they slid, cold and damp, down his chest, and he felt them pop against his flank, which was already sweaty. He started to reach up, but his wrists were held to his sides. The Dayzell's companion stood up; he was pale as dough, and there were leather bands around his wrists and forehead, tightened into the flesh. He pulled off his silk scarf, held it taut between his fists like a strangler, then threw it around Wirrel's arms and tied him firmly to the chair.

The long nails snagged at Wirrel's shirt, tearing it. Hands were at his boots, his trousers. Someone shook a bottle of sparkling wine and drenched him with the foam. A hand ladled gravy. Another picked up a dish of beets in sauce. The other patrons stared. Some of them came over, and were told to wait their turns. This was a fine old theatrical tradition, Wirrel knew. He understood. He had done it, that was fair. It just wasn't fair that they were drunk and he wasn't.

It was nearly dawn when the last of them staggered away or passed out. Wirrel got his hands free, stood up. He found his boots, what was left of his clothing; there was no one there to see him but the City staff.

And Dijade, sitting at a small corner table, with a brass kaf service in front of her. "Here," she said, and held out a waiter's coat and loose white trousers. "We'll take you home, and put you to bed."

Wirrel nodded, took the clothes from her carefully. He was sticky all over.

"You took it well," Dijade said. "Beautifully."

He didn't ask her what it was for. He'd done that, in the past, once he was sober enough to remember some of what they'd done to that night's victim, and she had never answered him. He didn't ask now for two reasons: because he was afraid she would finally tell him what it was a preparation for, and he was afraid he already knew.

Virshon ola Vivar sat cross-legged on the Red Mask stage, pages of scribbled-on script spread out around him.

"What are the guns for, Vrrshei?" said a voice from the darkened rows of seats.

"I'm relieved to hear from you, Krtsotses," ola Vivar said tiredly. "I thought you might have been hit on the head and lost one of your memories, or arrested for maintaining an overcrowded dwelling."

"The *guns*, Vrrshei. Is that how you mean to kill them?"

"You haven't read the script, of course—you weren't watching during rehearsals? Only one of them is shot to death. The others—well, nine of them die, only two in anything even like the same way."

"Nine . . . ?"

"Yes, two deaths each. Three for Baragon; he's the big fellow. If we're going to talk, Krtsotses, will you come up here? I've been directing all day, and I'm out of voice."

Krtsotses walked to the stage. He was wearing a wig, pulled back and tied much like ola Vivar's hair, sharply penciled eyebrows, makeup darkening his skin to a typical Liavekan shade. "Out of your mind, you mean."

"Hmm? Come up on the stage, man; you're a Drstonan, how can you stand in the pit like that? Must be Krtsotses's influence."

"He has no influence," Mnoreon said, climbing the apron steps. "I am the reason here, I am the effect of your actions. And I see now that you are mad."

Ola Vivar stretched out his arms, rose to his feet, stretched. "Why, what else should I be, Mnoreon? I'm an insane man from an insane country, purveying huge multiple lies to wards full of souls in torment. There will be no happiness in the world until everyone is mad, Mnoreon; there will be no beauty until everyone accepts the lie."

"You killed an entire company of actors, you killed the man whose name you stole—"

Ola Vivar slammed a fist into Mnoreon's flank, doubling him over; he knocked Mnoreon sprawling on the stage, kicked him in the ribs. "Get up."

"You will not kill me, Vrrshei."

"Of course I won't. Get up."

He did, slowly. "I know what it is like to die, Vrrshei. Remember that."

"I shan't make any special effort, Mnoreon. Remind me, should I slip."

"You mock now. But soon you will know what I know."

"*What,*" ola Vivar said, coldly and with no humor at all, "do you think that you know, that I do not? You spent a few minutes in pain, and one moment dying; and then the wizards brought you back and glued you into this puppet body, this *nonentity* cuckolded of a bottle of poison."

The other man's lips trembled. Sweat came through the cake makeup on his temples.

Ola Vivar said, "I wandered the earth for five full years, Mnoreon. Five years of hiding from the stage, scribbling plays I dared not publish, let alone perform, for fear of you, for memory of your death. Can you imagine that exile—either of you, host or parasite? The poorest leper can strike a pose on a streetcorner and declaim verse for thrown coins, but not I. While you, Mnoreon, *actor,* all you've done in that time is—act. Don't tell me your stories of death, player, for I was dead five years, and choked with earth in my living grave, until two better people than a thousand of both of us pulled me out—'' Ola Vivar squeezed his eyes shut. ''Get out of here, Fury. Get out of my house, or I swear one of us *will* die, here and now.''

''I am willing, Vrrshei.''

''No, you're not,'' ola Vivar said, nearly calm. ''You're like the king who killed his wives: you're part of the story now, you're fascinated, you can't end it before it ends. And neither can I.''

The other, smaller, voice said, ''I will not let you kill those people, Vrrshei.''

''You will have your hour on stage, Krtsotses. Mnoreon is fair enough for that.''

Krtsotses stumbled down the steps and went out.

When Jemuel finally found Aritoli ola Silba, the art critic was in the Parkside Market, dressed in gold brocade and white linen, inspecting pomegranates. She waited: they were acquainted, but not well, and a tactful Guardsman, even off duty and out of uniform, does not accost anyone in a public place without being very aware of the effects.

Aritoli looked up. ''Why, good morning, Captain. Looking for some fruit?''

''I'd like to talk to you, master.''

''Police business?''

''Not really.''

''I'm disappointed. I thought perhaps my services might be needed to solve a mystery. Well, it's time for morning kaf: I would be delighted if you would join me.''

''Of course, master.''

''Ari is sufficient—Jemuel?''

''Yes.''

Ola Silba led the way to one of the smaller shops off the Market square, ordered kaf and cakes for two. Pierced screens on the walls made the place a bit brighter than most, and a ceiling fan, driven from belts, stirred the air. Aritoli tossed a copper to the Ombayan boy who sat in the corner, pedaling the fan; the boy caught it between his palms, touched his fingertips to his forehead.

"That's supposed to be lucky," Aritoli said, turning back to Jemuel. "Not that I believe it for a moment."

"I think the boy does."

"True enough." They sat down at a small wooden table, its top inlaid with a shah board. "Now, Jemuel, what did you want to discuss?"

"Virshon ola Vivar."

"That's quite a what."

"You know him better than I do."

"I don't know him well. No one does, I think . . . except perhaps through his plays, and that's dangerous ground."

"How 'dangerous'?"

The server arrived, with potent, grainy, aromatic kaf and a plate of sesame cakes with honey. Aritoli lifted a cup in both hands, inhaled the steam, sipped at it. "I mean dangerous in the sense that quicksand is; a ground that will not bear the weight of argument."

"As a critic, then—"

"Such a terrible word. I am an advisor. And I try not to offer my advice except when it is asked for."

"I'm asking, Aritoli. What do you think of ola Vivar? Does he appear . . ." She struggled with the thought; it was, she knew too well, only vaguely formed in her own mind. ". . . honest, to you?"

Aritoli fiddled elaborately with his clothing. "You say that this is not an official matter?"

"It is not."

"Well then. My area of expertise is primarily in the visual arts, you know, not the lively ones—it is only recently that my opinion has been much asked on the drama.'' She started to speak, but he stopped her with a raised finger. ''And your question is for drama criticism, you understand, whether you meant it in such fashion or not. Do you go to the theatre often, Jemuel?''

''Usually once a month.''

''And have you ever been to one of Virshon's plays?''

''One. The one about the monastery, on the mountaintop.''

''*The Ascent of Delight*. That was his second. Did you like it?''

''Well, I . . .''

''Oh, Jemuel, I'm not trying to compare our critical judgments. Did you *like* the play?''

''Very much.''

''And yet,'' Aritoli said, in a careful, slow voice, ''that play is all about loneliness, and it portrays its subject very well indeed. To anyone who has ever been really lonely—and I daresay that's most of us—it should be unbearable to sit through. Yet crowds of people, yourself among them, did just that, for two hundred performances. Now, how did he do that? Is the play somehow a fraud? Or is loneliness really not so terrible as we think? Or are we responding to other people's pain in a way we might not like to think about?''

''I don't know,'' Jemuel said. She had in fact found the play nearly unendurable, because it was so very true, too much her life. She had not gone to another of ola Vivar's plays, because she did not want her life fingered over like that again.

''Neither do I,'' ola Silba said suddenly, jarring Jemuel so that the cake crumbled between her fingers. ''And I'm a professional at this. I *think* that it's all those, and more, at once—which is my point: analyzing any work of real art brings us to the very edge of what we *can* know.''

''Is ola Vivar somehow different from . . . us, then?''

'' 'Us'?''

"He isn't Liavekan. I do know that. Did you know Risil? Virshon's father?"

"I did not. He was a trader, was he not?"

"Worked his way up from a dockrat. He was always very kind to kids on the docks." A little too carelessly kind, she thought but did not say. "Do you know where Virshon does come from, then?"

"No. Someplace very distant, I think. And he said once . . ."

"Yes?"

"It was said in private, most honorable Captain of the City Guard." He ate a cake, knocked crumbs from a cuff with his gold-painted fingernails, then said, "But it was not said in confidence. Something about 'a place where they hide from one another, behind old verses and dead faces.' I believe that was the substance of it."

Jemuel bit into another cake. After the kaf, it was almost painfully sweet.

Aritoli said, "I am trying to be helpful, but . . . you asked about 'honesty.' Here's a point, a critical point, if you like. There isn't anyone in Liavek who uses illusion—'dramaturgy,' as he calls it—like Virshon. In truth, I can't think of anyone in the history of the Liavekan stage who relies so little on magical spectacle. Others use thunderstorms, appearances of the gods, animated statues—ola Vivar's idea of a major effect is the dinner in *Fogmonth Wine*."

"He had an illusion of a dinner?"

"The food was. Simple enough when you think about it: he wanted a banquet that wouldn't clog the actors' mouths, make their stomachs rumble, or worse yet give them screaming fits after they'd had the same stuff for a hundred performances."

"It must make it easy to find a company wizard."

Ola Silba looked thoughtful, stroked his moustache. "You'd think anyone would do, wouldn't you, but you'd be wrong. As ola Vivar explains it, it's like makeup: when you see, say, Dijade as Camberliona, you aren't supposed to say, 'Oh, what fine makeup,' but 'Look,

there's Camberliona.' The same with acting, really. Any
novice can conjure a talking statue, because our experience of talking statues is rather small . . . but a dozen
lights in a candelabrum, that's difficult, because we all
know how a lamp flickers. Amateurs make them glow
steadily, or blink·them in some kind of pattern, and in
half a scene the audience is watching the candles and
not the action. No, I would guess it's twenty times
harder for Virshon to find someone to do his common-
place food and fires than for the Levar's Company to
wreck a fortress with three tornadoes.''

''You really didn't like *A Tyrant Against the Gods,*
did you, Aritoli?''

''Do you mean *A. Terriot Against the Critics?* No, I
daresay I didn't. But you see, if you want the difference
explained concretely, there it is: Terriot gave us these
wonderful, overwrought frauds conveying a very ordinary truth about stupid, bad people. But in *The Ascent,*
Virshon used the smallest things, sunlight and a few
snowflakes, to light up a story about intelligent, good
people and the terrible things that happen to them.'' He
laughed. '' 'Light up.' Oh, I do delight myself sometimes; excuse me, Jemuel.''

She nodded behind her cup.

''I am not saying that he is the only good playwright
in Liavek, or even the only excellent one. I am saying
that the difference between him and the bad ones is not
one of degree, but of kind. He is not simply better, he
is different. Does that help? Is it at all what you wanted
to know?''

''I promise I'll let you know when I find out.''

''Good enough.'' He tapped his cane, and the server
appeared. ''I'll pay this,'' he said.

''I asked you—''

''And I invited you here. Besides, you have allowed
me to strut my thoughts at an unusual hour of the day,
without its being a business transaction; can't buy a
good audience.'' As they rose to leave, Aritoli looked
up at the wheels and belts that drove the overhead fan.

"Have you noticed," he said wistfully, "how much of the world seems to run by wheels and gears these days? I do believe that someday soon I shall be asked to criticize clockwork."

The upstairs bedroom of the house of Ambassador Oprio was dominated by an enormous canopied bed. Beyond it, a curtained window led to a balcony; moonlight filtered through the drapes. On the other side, between the bed and the hallway door, was a thick pile carpet and an ornately carved wall cabinet. The Ambassador, in his black robes of state, swung the front of the cabinet open, revealing a strongbox with an intricate puzzle-lock.

Oprio fiddled with the lock and the door swung open. He took a long envelope, bearing several enormous seals, from within his robe, stuffed it into the strongbox, shut the door, and scrambled the lock.

"There's downfall for a nation," the Ambassador said. "Now back to my party, and some more private ends for her particular citizens." Oprio went out through the hallway door.

The carpet flapped back, a trapdoor slammed open. A gloved hand emerged from the hole, and dropped a leather bag beside it. Doctor Viscusi the assassin emerged, dusting off his hands. He looked around at the furnishings. "Now here's the room my master's business likes," he said. "There's more death done in bedrooms than in alleys. And why not? A man in a dark alley's thinking on what might come upon him, while a man in a dark bedroom's thinking—well, round about opposite."

Viscusi examined the bed. "I am contracted to murder that fantastic creature Pancrad, who even now dances belowstairs at the Ambassador's ball. . . ." He spread his hands. "Pancrad! Stand him in a contrary wind and he'd choke on his own ruffs and feathers, cinch his stays tighter and he'd die of the gangrene, ravel his brocades and he'd explode of an apoplexy—is this Pancrad material for an artist?'' He shrugged, picked up his bag, and set it on the bed. "Yet this much have I done, in the interest of cunning. At my instigation, he's on to seduce the delightful Honoria—no, instigation's too grand a word for it, the push of a breath was enough to tumble him toward tumbling her.'' Viscusi reached into his bag, produced a handsaw.

"He shall bring her to this room, and once accomplished of his purpose . . . now *here's* instigation for you . . . make his exit from the balcony, as if he were a character in a cheap play.'' Viscusi went to the balcony. "His exit, indeed.'' He stepped through the curtains. There was the sound of sawing. Viscusi reappeared. "It is fortunate,'' he said matter-of-factly, "that city estates are built and gardened as they are; I should not have liked to trust him to less than three floors and a thornbush.''

He gathered his bag and slipped into the trap again. The door dropped shut, and the carpet rolled neatly to cover it.

The door to the hallway swung slowly open, and a woman in a tight black and gold dress backed in. She was tugging at someone's arm. "This one's empty, General,'' the Countess Flara said.

"Are these apartments—safe?'' General Maximenes said as the Countess drew him into the bedroom, toward the enormous bed.

"Why, my dear General,'' Flara said, her voice all butter and honey, "this is the Ambassador's house. Foreign territory. To invade here would be an act of war . . . and I'm certain my General knows all about acts of war.''

"Why, hm, yes, of course,'' the General said. Flara sat down on the bed, twining an arm around a canopy post. "Reminds me, hm, of the time I led the Imperial Hussars to the relief of, hm, yes.''

"Tell me about the . . . relief,'' Flara said, exhaling the last word. She crossed her delicate ankles. The General's knees knocked.

"Well, yes, there I was, at the head of the Impoterial Suthars, charging, horses shot from under me, camels to the right, artillery to the left, elephants in the rear, but on we charged, motto of the Panerial Affars, y'know, artillery to the front of us, camels on top of us—"

"*Ooooooh,*" Flara said. The General dropped to his knees with a thud.

Flara said, "Do you think you could lead . . ." She licked her lips. ". . . one more charge? Just like you did then?"

"Madame . . . an Insperial Huffar is always ready to chound the sarge." He shuffled forward on his knees.

"No, no," Flara said. "From the hall. Burst in, as if you were relieving . . . where was it?"

"I was decorated there, y'know," the General said, and got to his feet, his sword clunking on the floor. He went to the door. "I shall be but a moment, my dove of war."

Flara threw herself backward on the bed. The General clutched his bemedaled chest and staggered through the door, into the hallway.

Flara got up, hurriedly arranged some pillows into roughly a human shape. She pulled long brass pins out of two of the canopy posts. Then she blew out one of the lamps, darkening the room, stepped to the curtained balcony window, walked through.

There was a snap of metal as the balcony supports gave way, and a long fading scream from Flara, ending in a *whump*.

The hallway door burst open. "Never fear, O maiden," Maximenes cried, "I hear your cry, and rush to your rescue!" He sprinted to the bed, leaped full length onto the pillows.

The canopy collapsed on top of him like a cider press on an apple.

"*Right!*" Virshon ola Vivar said. "Well screamed, Flara, well dived, General. Well crunched, bed."

Nin il Craith stepped back through the curtains. Baren

Baragon stuck his head up through the heavy paper of the bed canopy.

"It was good?" Nin said.

Ola Vivar said, "The General's dialogue is either brutally mistimed or hopelessly miswritten, and I've seen greengrocers make their wares more enticing than the Countess." He pressed his palms together. "But yes, it was good."

It was the third tenday of rehearsals: the cast had just begun to work with the newly finished scenery and costumes. They were meeting four days in five; there were still fumbled and forgotten lines, missed cues and marks, costume changes not performed in time—but they were beginning to perform as a unit, to play the parts instead of just carrying them.

"Wirrel, set cue," ola Vivar called, and the bed canopy started to rise again, drawn on a black-painted rope from above. The posts folded back upright. As soon as he had headroom, Baren rolled lightly off the bed. The canopy and posts kept rising, until they disappeared above the audience's line of vision; a new headboard against the back wall of the bedroom set was revealed, making it appear to be a brand-new bed.

Lisel came onstage, wearing the Ambassador's black robes of state. "Chitaru could lift that," she said.

Oten Chitaru bowed his head in acknowledgment.

"And he will," ola Vivar said, "if something should happen so that Wirrel can't work the winch. Should that happen, Chitaru, you will please remember the thing's up there: I can just imagine someone being impaled for real by one of those posts. . . ." He shook his head. "That's something we're going to have to work on, now that the stuff is in place. Ideally, every set and prop cue will have a primary and a backup actor, the backup to make the move if the primary doesn't or can't. That will mean watching, to make certain the primary's doing the job."

Wirrel came through the "balcony" curtains. He had already changed into Bibidiel's ruffled (and padded) ballgown for his next scene. "If you're going to do all this with ropes and muscles, why isn't there a crew to do it? Don't we have enough?"

Ola Vivar looked at him thoughtfully for some time. "Is this something you want me to do?"

"It was only a thought, master."

"I do not mind your thinking," ola Vivar said, and then suddenly, "What's the time?"

Baren looked at the clock hung in the right wing. "Just before ten, Director."

"Ah! You see what happens when you play a good scene? You distract everyone." He snatched a costume cloak from a peg, tossed it over his shoulders. "I have a meeting at ten, and I'm already late. Chitaru has the keys, he'll let you out. I shall see you all tomorrow? Of course. Good night to you all." He dashed offstage; the rear door clanged shut behind him.

Lisel said, "I wonder who he's meeting? At this hour?"

"Backers, probably," Wirrel said. "Wish he'd warned us." He groped at the back of his costume. "Help me with this thing, will you, Baren?"

Baren unfastened the hooks, and Wirrel shuffled off Bibidiel like a snake shedding skin, leaving him in a shirt and tights. "Thanks." Wirrel struck a heroic sort of pose, said in his best heroic voice, "Or perhaps a romantic encounter by moonlight."

They all laughed. Then Lisel said quite seriously, "Do you think he has?"

Wirrel said, "Sure. He goes down to the Street of Trees, and old Granny Carry turns herself into—"

"You weren't born in the city, Wirrel," Lisel said, in a harsh tone none of them had ever heard her use, not even acting. "Don't ever talk about her like that."

"No, he doesn't have a lover," Nin said quickly. "I don't think he's got anything but this stage." Wirrel seemed about to answer, but didn't.

Baren said, "And us. He does have us."

They began helping each other out of costumes and

makeup; Chitaru came out of his work corner, and they racked up the props, shoved the scenery to its storage positions, put out the stage lights. Finally Lisel made some tea (even Chitaru admitted she was best at it) and they sat on the stage, in the glow of the footlights, talking about lines and entrances.

"Chitaru," Lisel said, "I've been wanting to ask you—about the Ambassador."

"Yes, mistress?"

"You must know," she said delicately, "that in Liavek, when people talk about foreign spies . . . that they usually mean . . ."

"I am sadly aware of the private habits of the Tichenese Department of International Understandings," Chitaru said.

"Well . . . do you suppose that if I played Oprio as a Tichenese . . . would that offend you, Oten?"

"Not in the slightest, mistress. And I believe the audience would find it very funny—especially if it was only suggested, so that they believed they were guessing at a concealed truth. If I may assist you with any detail of voice or costume, please ask."

"Thank you, Chitaru. Very much."

Wirrel said, "We could be doing this in public. I'd think we ought to. We *are* ola Vivar's company."

"That and a copper will buy you some ale," Nin said.

"We're chosen, paid professionals," Wirrel said, "in what by any rights should be the best-respected acting company in Liavek—hells and green figs, the best between the Waste and the Sea! Why shouldn't we go out and celebrate it? I know an inn—"

"I couldn't," Lisel said, without any of her earlier confidence. She sounded almost frightened. "I don't go to inns alone."

Wirrel said, "You wouldn't be alone," and then Nin said, more quietly, "No, Lisel. You would not."

"I mean—I'm married, you know. There are times it's right for me to go out, and times when it's not."

"My rooms are very large," Baren said, "if you wish to meet somewhere other than the theatre. No one else is there."

"I think Lisel's right," Nin said. "There *are* times it's right to have a party, but—don't you think—"

"Are you saying," Wirrel said, sounding annoyed, "that we're not ready yet? That, perhaps, the Director will tell us when we're ready?"

"I think both of those are real possibilities."

"Are you an actor? Or a puppet?" Wirrel was angry now. "Isn't this an art? Haven't we been making changes, improvements, that even ola Vivar admits are better than what he wrote for us?"

" 'Even' him?" Baren said quietly.

"He's an arrogant, arbitrary, self-important . . ." Wirrel's voice trailed away. Then he laughed. "And listen to me. Maybe you're right, Nin. But there will come a time, when I dance where I please."

Baren said, "And we'll all sing 'Pot-Boil Blues' in the city square."

Wirrel said, "Fool's Square, more likely. Well, since this is the party for tonight, one more round for everyone?" He took the pot and went around the circle, pouring out the tea ceremonially.

Lisel said, "We will know, won't we? Virshon pushes us, so that we'll learn to be good—but when we are, we'll know."

Chitaru said, "It is so with magic. Praise without achievement is dust in the mouth."

Baren said, "It's so with anything."

Nin said, "Sometimes I think he's keeping something back from us . . . something enormous. And terrifying."

"In twenty-seven nights," Wirrel said softly, "we do this as a whole, before a crowd, no stop-and-start-over, no pause for a breath or a hug to get us through the hard parts."

"But Virshon's seen all that," Nin insisted. "There's

something that scares him, too. I keep wondering what will happen when we meet it.''

''We're actors,'' Wirrel said, bravely but not so firmly. ''We'll improvise.''

They put away the tea service, tidied up and snuffed lights, said good-nights and went out.

The floor trap banged open, and a light shone from below. Virshon ola Vivar pulled himself up to the stage.

'' 'Improvise.' Yes, I do like that.''

On the morning of the tenth day before opening, Nin il Craith was in the Levar's Park, watching a clown at work. He was telling a crowd of mostly children a story of some pirates who went to sea in a bucket (because they had never learned to sail a ship) armed with mops and sponges (because they had played hooky from school during cutlass lessons). They were more successful at the pirate trade than one might have expected, because none of the great treasure captains wanted the reputation of having sunk a bucket, and once aboard, the crews felt so sorry for the Sponge-Mop Pirates that they always took up a collection for the freebooters before sending them on their way. Nin wished that Lisel were here to see the act; Grumbolio could certainly have started as one of this crew.

The clown (should she call him that? He was an actor if anyone was), dressed in green and black motley, broke into a song and dance—well, he was an actor, but as a singer and dancer he left something to be desired. No one in the audience seemed to care, and by the third chorus of:

''The Bucketing Buccaneers, yo ho!
They sink too swift and they sail too slow,
With nothing but water above, below,
The rucketing, bucketing,
Hirating, pirating,
Somewhat historical,

Mopping-the-floorical,
Bucketing Bucket-a-neers, yo ho!''

—he had all the children and most of the adults singing
along.

Finally the Pirates attracted the attention of the King's
Private Privateer and Sea-Dog-Without-Portfolio, Lord
Pifflingham of Greene-Cheese (Piffles to his friends),
who always played the harp between sinking pirate
ships; but he did not play well, having been studying
the cutlass during his harp lessons. The clown mimed
the harp in air, and Nin heard every sour twang. A
confrontation between the two sides was inevitable, and
(to no one's very great surprise, and everyone's delight)
was concluded with no more violence than a little fum-
bling sword-and-mop-play. The head Pirate, who had
been a talented harp teacher before going to sea, agreed
to trade music lessons for cutlass instruction, Lord Piffles requiring in turn that the Pirates give up freebooting
for music, becoming (Nin strangled her laughter, not
wanting to spoil the clown's line) the First Pirate Band.

The clown doffed his hat to collect coins. Nin
dropped in a gold levar, said, ''May I talk to you?''

The clown shrugged, pointed at the ground. They sat
down.

Nin said, ''I haven't seen you in the Park before. Are
you new in the city?''

A nod.

''You're very good. I'm an—I'm learning to act, myself.''

The clown bowed, sitting.

''Do I—bother you? Do you not want to talk?''

The clown put his fingertips to the corners of his
pencil-browed eyes and looked around; cupped hands
to his bone-white ears and turned his head left and right.
No one was near. He crooked a finger, beckoned her
closer, then put it to his lips.

He reached into his robes and pulled out a cord of
braided black beads, tiny brass bells knotted into it.

"Oh," Nin said, hearing her voice as a squeak, hoping she did not sound frightened. The beads were a Leper's Cord, a magical device that prevented the wearer from passing his disease (which might be any of several) to others. By the laws of most cities, including Liavek, the Cord was supposed to be worn in view, the bells audible.

The clown held the Cord out, jingled the bells just faintly. Then he held his hand a few feet from the ground, made yanking motions.

"If you show it," Nin said, "people will take their children away."

A slow nod. She could see the traces of lesions, beneath the heavy white makeup.

"How long have you . . . had this?"

Ten fingers; ten years.

"And you were an actor before?"

Hand against chest, hand outstretched; the stock heroic pose.

"But, surely people understand—" The rest of the statement stuck in her throat.

The clown just smiled, pointed to his head, his heart, made a snapping gesture. *Reason does not always rule the heart.*

"But you want to do it," Nin said, "you want to do it so badly that—"

The clown jumped to his feet and ran. Nin started to get up, to follow him.

From a few paces away, Baren Baragon said, "Did I interrupt something?"

"No," she said, "we were just . . . talking. . . ."

"I scare people sometimes. It's being big . . ." He looked at her, with a tight, confused expression. She came up barely to his chest. "You wouldn't know."

"You . . . *scare* people?" She started to laugh, then put her arms around herself to stop it.

Baren said, "We should be starting for the theatre." He looked at the clear sky, the light on the Palace across the canal. "I think it will be a good day."

"It's going to go well," Nin said. "It's all going to go well from now on."

"No," ola Vivar said. "No, no, no. You misunderstand. You are not inviting Hiron to your ship for biscuits and a game of leap-the-camel. You are *angry* at him, and you intend to kill him in the most elaborately awful way the mind of an insurance collector can imagine. You are supposed to be terrifying."

Lisel nodded, tried the line again. "So, man, have ye ever been in the hold of a freebooter?"

Ola Vivar snapped a pencil between his fingers. "You," he said loudly, "are the least convincing unconvincing pirate I have ever seen. Perhaps you *are* from Port Chai."

"I'll try again."

"No. This scene offends my sight; this scene smells so bad I'd vomit if it were played properly. Costume change and we'll do the next."

Nin said quietly to Baren, "What's the matter with him? Things were going so well."

"Perhaps he doesn't know either."

The dockside scenery rose on its ropes, and the panels of Ambassador Oprio's reception hall rotated into place. Lisel, in a white shirt, sash, and black trousers as the Ambassador, came on stage left. She waited.

Something bumped one of the walls from behind, and it shook. Doctor Viscusi the elegant assassin came through a prop door, his hat askew, one boot not quite on. The Ambassador took the cue, spoke: "And where have you been, my fine surgeon? Some hygienic brothel—"

"Oh, *no,*" Ola Vivar said, making a cutting motion. "It's not funny if he *has* just come in from the stews." He turned on Wirrel, who was still struggling with his boot. "Is that where you were, young man? Out for a quick one between costume changes? It's not unheard of."

"I had to change," Wirrel said, "I had to move the scenery and adjust the lights—"

"Actors are notorious for avoiding an ordinary day's work, young man, but you haven't the reputation yet to make a career at it."

Wirrel said, "You want me to work hard, I am more than willing to work hard—"

"To you, my lad, 'working hard' means plowing in a straight line, and setting records in the cowchip toss."

"—but nothing can give you the right to insult me!"

Ola Vivar cracked his knuckles. "Then shall I invite someone who has?"

Silence fell hard.

Nin said, "Is anger the only thing you want us to feel? Is it the only thing you can work with?"

Ola Vivar said, "I can only work with genuine emotions. If you're capable of any others, by all means show them to me."

Lisel sank to her knees, rocked forward. She began whimpering, then to pound her fists on the stage. Baren bent over her, caught her wrists. "No, dear," he said gently. "No. No." Then he looked at her back, at something just visible through her thin shirt. His mouth opened and his face froze, and he traced a red line with his hand.

"Well?" ola Vivar said. "I'm waiting."

Wirrel took a long, sweeping step, then a short, lurching one. His shoulder hit a ladder, and it fell with a crash. "What do you want?" His voice was pitched too high. "For all the gods' sakes, tell me what you want and I'll give it to you, but tell me in something like plain words."

Ola Vivar sat entirely still.

Baren brought Lisel to her feet. He touched her cheek, then moved away from her; she nodded and stood steady.

Baren said, "I think we should go home now. This is not a good day."

"That's the first intelligently delivered line I've

heard,'' ola Vivar said. ''You all have homes to go to, someone waiting for you; go home.''

As they moved off the stage, the Director said, ''I'll see you all tomorrow at this time, or I won't see you again.''

The doors to the lobby swung shut. There was a footstep from the dark.

''If you're going to come back and lecture me, Nin,'' ola Vivar said, ''you'll have to come closer. Your projection's good enough, but at this distance you are a barely discernible dot on the landscape.'' He set the fallen ladder up again, climbed it, and sat on the rungs.

''It won't work anymore, Master Director,'' she said, walking toward him. ''You can't frighten or bully me.''

''Oh,'' he said coolly, *''can't* I now.''

''Why don't you replace me? Replace all of us! Find someone else to read your god-damned words. You said yourself that you could.''

''I also told you that if you didn't want to see me again, you didn't have to. All you need do is stay home tomorrow. And you do have a home, correct, Nin?''

''Why?'' Nin said. ''We've given you everything that you've asked for. Why are you doing this?''

''If you understood,'' ola Vivar said, ''there would be no need to do it.''

''It doesn't make any *sense!''*

''Neither does life,'' ola Vivar said. ''Not like theatre. I long for the simplicity of theatre. I want lessons learned, comeuppances delivered, people sorted out, all before your bladder gets distractingly full. That's what I want. What I *know* is what we all know, whether we'll admit it or not: every attempt to impose the roundness of a well-made play on reality produces a disaster. Life just isn't so, nor will it be made so.''

''How can you talk about disappointment?'' she said. ''All your plays have been great successes, everyone knows your father left you a fortune—''

Ola Vivar said quietly,

"I lie in shadows of your Mercy's power,
    Existing but to share th'unraptured hour;
    I have no voice nor vote. I have no name:
    Yet ice, and fire, and love touch us the same."

Nin said, "What are you saying?"

"I was quoting," he said offhandedly. "From my first play."

"Fogmonth Wine?"

"My *first* play. It closed in one performance. . . . But that was in another country, and besides . . ." He shook his head.

She waited for a moment, but he said no more. She said, "You feel sorry for yourself, so you hurt other people. You brought us here to hurt us." She took three steps toward him. "You chose us because we had no reputations, nothing to fight you with. Just four victims."

"Shall I change my ways? Shall I be transformed, like some black-cloaked villain in a morality pantomime?" He jumped down from the ladder, leaned over her. "Suppose I were, Nin. Suppose I were good and kind and generous. Suppose I could grant heart's desire. What would you like?"

"A little decency is all I want from you. All any of us want. Decent behavior, and just a little bit of respect."

He turned away, shook his head. "No, that's not it. Respect is what people want when they have no hope of anything better." He straightened, snapped his fingers. "Suppose I gave you the theatre."

"What?"

"What higher gift is there? What greater power is there than to be a theatre owner? You rule the lives of players—very perceptive of you to call them victims— while being able to take the stage yourself at any time, for any purpose, without risking anything but a little critical disapproval. And if that happens, you can always hire it out to others with more money than talent.

Bar all else, knock a new door in the front and it'd make a fine stable.''

''I don't want your theatre—what would you do?''

''I would be dead. You don't think I propose to just hand it over to you and walk away? No, it would be willed, and quite properly. Wait there, just a moment. Don't move.'' He walked off into the wing.

Nin waited, listening to sounds of cabinets being opened and papers rustled. Finally ola Vivar returned, carrying a paper scroll and a pen. He held the paper out to her. ''A testament,'' he said. ''Not elaborate, but entirely lawful. I recall a story of a will scrawled in heart's blood on a warrior's shield—or was that just a lawyer bragging? Here, Nin. Sign here.''

''This is absurd.''

''You'll say that with feeling when you see the property taxes. Go ahead, sign.''

''Of course I won't sign that.''

Ola Vivar shrugged. ''It doesn't matter.'' He scratched his name across the bottom of the scroll, handed it to her. ''Well? Take it.''

She did.

''You see, Nin, I know infatuation when I see it. When you're standing here, stripping the flesh from your own actors, you'll look back on this moment and wonder how you ever got along without love in your life.'' He straightened, stretched. ''Now go home . . . or the place you call home. We shall see you here tomorrow.''

Nin stumbled into the house. After the cool night air, the stink of burnt metal made her dizzy. She leaned against the door.

Kel pushed in. His lap was full of tubing and wire. ''What's the matter, Nin?''

She strained to focus on him in the bad light. He turned up the lamp and she blinked, her eyes suddenly wet.

''He gave me the theatre,'' she said.

"He *what?*"

She pulled out the testament, held it at a distance from herself. "He *willed* it to me."

Kel took the paper, unrolled it beneath the lamp. "It's a joke, isn't it? You said he was always—"

"Never mind what I said! I—don't know what it is. He was a—he was awful to us tonight . . . and when I asked him why, he gave me that."

"It has to be some kind of stupid joke—Nin, don't cry."

"I'm not crying."

"Look. I'll just do this, and then it'll all be past." He rolled the paper, stuck it down the lamp chimney. "Solutions by fire. I'll have that painted on the shop sign."

"No!" She grasped his wrist, pulled it from the fire, took the paper from him. "I don't know what this is, but I'm keeping it until I do know. Legal or not."

"All right," Kel said calmly. "Do you want some dinner?"

"I'm going to go to bed," she said, sniffled and coughed. "And in the morning—things will make sense." She picked up the lamp, to light her way to her room.

"Yes," Kel said, as she left him in the dark. "In the morning everything will make sense."

The moon was beginning to descend, and all shadows in Liavek were long and very black. Tonight it would indeed be darkest before dawn.

The alley door of the Red Mask Theatre opened, and a figure in a cloak and a large hat came out into the moonlight. The door closed again, and the figure started up the alley, toward the street.

Halfway along, there was a scuffling sound, like a footstep, and a movement from the darkness, and a small sound of metal rasping, like a clock about to strike. There was thunder, and lightning, and a noise that never had time to be a scream.

* * *

Jemuel of the City Guard was looking at a hat. It had not been a fancy or attractive hat, and it was entirely unwearable now: it was of interest only because it was perforated with buckshot and glued to an alley wall with its wearer's blood and brains. The wearer was spread out below the hat, covered now with a blanket.

It was about two hours before dawn. Half an hour earlier, the regular patrol had heard screams down the alley; they had found a flock of ravens, scavenging and screeching.

Jemuel was on shift when the report reached Guard headquarters. She'd heard that the body was next to the Red Mask, and grabbed her cap and cloak with a terrible feeling inside.

The victim had been a man. The means of death, and the ravens, made a more exact identification difficult. One of the patrol was fairly certain that it wasn't Virshon ola Vivar; a messenger had been sent to ola Vivar's house. Jemuel had inspected the dead man's hands; neither was a brass hook like Master Trice of Gold Harbor had worn.

A Guard said, "Well, at least we know it wasn't magic, Captain."

"Thank you, Ayne, I feel so much better for that." She spanned the rough circle of chipped brick around the hat with her hands. "It was a large bore, and fairly close . . . I'd say from just that side of the alley." She walked to the spot. "Good place to ambush from."

"It wasn't robbery," Ayne said. "His purse has at least sixty levars in it."

"Probably not robbery," Jemuel said. "Seen a couple of cases where the killing scared the thief too badly to finish the job." She looked at the hat on the wall. "This would have been scary enough."

The messenger returned with another person in tow. Lanterns shone on a tall man with long gray hair.

"Virshon ola Vivar?" Jemuel said.

"That's correct."

"Have you ever seen a death by violence, master?"

"Yes."

"Then would you please take a look at the victim, and tell me if you recognize him?"

"Of course."

The sheet was lifted. The lanterns shone down.

Ola Vivar's expression was more curious than repelled. "I don't know him. At least, what's there."

"I understand, master. Thank you."

"Do you have any idea what happened? Besides the obvious, I mean."

"Not yet."

"I'd better go into the theatre, to make certain everything's in order." He paused. "Could you send one of your men in with me? I shouldn't like to bump into a killer in hiding."

"A very good point, master," Jemuel said. "I'll do it. Rusty! Give me a yell when the body cart gets here."

"Right, Captain."

Ola Vivar said, "It's shorter this way," and led her farther down the alley, to a metal door in the brick wall. He unlocked it, stepped in, struck a light.

There were beams and ropes all around them, shelves full of paint buckets and props, sheets of canvas on wooden frames, some white, some painted as walls or doors. There was a creak overhead, and Jemuel looked up: framework extended away into darkness.

"That sound I know," ola Vivar said. "No danger." He was holding a bit of gunmatch in a brass clip, lighting it from the lantern. It reminded her acutely of Master Trice's hook.

Ola Vivar said, "Everything seems in order here. This way." They walked past a rack of swords and pistols.

"Wait," Jemuel said, and sniffed at the gunlocks. "These have had powder fired in them."

"Priming powder only. They're stage guns, can't fire a ball. You may inspect them if you like."

"That's all right," Jemuel said, noting that there

were five spaces in the gunrack, all filled. Anyway, they
were all small-bore pistols, not the sort that had killed
the man in the alley.

Ola Vivar lit a large reflecting lantern with his match,
and the auditorium and stage were illuminated. Jemuel
swept her hand lamp across the draped seats, up toward
the balcony. Nothing was there. They went to the front,
inspected the lobby, which was empty, and the front
door, which was secure.

"I believe it's all right," ola Vivar said.

"Plenty of hiding places left in here," Jemuel said.
She walked to the edge of the stage, looked up. There
was a vast black space above it, with some kind of
scaffolding, lots of ropes. Her lamp shone on wood and
hemp and canvas and iron.

"But none of the doors has been forced. And this
theatre is of different design from all others in Liavek.
A stranger, even an actor, would not know the places
to hide."

"Who would, then?"

"Excuse me?"

"Sorry, I didn't phrase that well. Who is commonly
around this theatre? I'm trying to shorten the list of
possibilities for our dead man."

"And another list as well, I imagine."

"A death like that was someone's doing, master."

"Clearly enough. To answer your question, there's
myself and the members of my company: four actors
and a magician."

"What about this stuff?" She indicated the scenery
and props. "You have carpenters? Painters and crafts-
men?"

"We did, of course, but their work ended several
days ago."

"Who has keys?"

"There is only one set. I keep them, though sometimes Chitaru—our magician—works late; then he locks
up and leaves the keys at my house on his way home."

"And did he do that tonight?"

"No. We finished rehearsals about eleven, and I went home. . . . Your pardon, Captain, but you seem to think that man's death is connected with the theatre."

"I only think that I have to start somewhere, master."

"Yes, of course. I'll certainly help in any way I can."

"I'll need to talk to the members of your company. Not as suspects, you understand."

"Certainly."

She reached into a pocket. "And there's something more personal you might be able to help me with." She held up a pair of black rubber balls, began tossing and catching them one-handed. "Ever see anyone do this?" She palmed one ball, spun the other on her fingertip.

"Yes," ola Vivar said. "I've seen that done."

She tossed him the balls, and he caught them, juggled them; when he tried to spin one, it slipped off, and Jemuel caught it.

"I was never good at the spin," ola Vivar said. "It's just occurred to me, you must be Jem. That was what Risil called you."

"That's right."

"I'm sorry we haven't met before this. Under nicer circumstances."

"I was at Risil's funeral. . . ."

"I'm afraid I didn't notice much at the funeral."

"But he mentioned me?"

"Oh, yes. 'Hardest gem I ever knew—' "

"You did know him," she said, and nearly bit her tongue. Ola Vivar looked at her with a shocked expression. "He was my father," ola Vivar said. "Adopted, but you must have known that. . . ."

"I'm very sorry," she said. "I was thinking of something else. —Where did you meet him? If you don't mind telling me."

"Tourewadeya. On the docks, naturally."

"I hadn't realized that Risil's business extended that far."

"At the time, I didn't think civilization did," ola Vivar said. He turned his face away from her, compressed his lips. Jemuel felt suddenly cool, distant from him: other people's tears always woke disbelief in her. It was not her best or kindest instinct, but it was a useful one, in her work.

"Are you all right, master?" she said.

"Yes. Perfectly. I was just remembering . . . an obligation." He put a hand to his eyes for a moment, said, "Look, would you like to talk—I could make tea—"

"I would like to. But there's a dead man in the street, and we don't even know who he is yet."

A Guard came clattering through the backstage. "The cart's here, Captain. They want you there when they move him."

"Right on cue," ola Vivar said lightly. "Is there anything else I can help you with, Captain?"

"Call me Jem," she said. The Guard tilted his head; Jemuel ignored him. "I still need the names of your company. And we will talk. Soon." She turned to follow Rusty back to the alley. Ola Vivar stood still. Jemuel said, "Are you coming, master?"

"No, I'm quite awake now. We're in rehearsals, and there's always work to do here."

"Rusty, you go on. I'll be right there."

"Captain." The Guard went out.

"Master ola Vivar—"

"I would like for you to call me Virshon, Jem."

"You're certain you were at home tonight? All night?"

"I hope I'm certain."

"Do you have any enemies, Virshon?"

"No more than most men."

"I shouldn't tell you this, since it can't be proven, but I'd bet my commission that the fellow out there wasn't pulled off the street. He was walking toward the street, from this end of the alley. It would have been very dark."

"The alley goes on to Bottlecork Row. And all the

Merchant's Quarter, and by extension to Hrothvek, where it is very dark of nights.''

''You're not listening to me, Virshon. Is that deliberate?''

''I am listening, Jem. And I'm answering you. You'll have to forgive that my answers aren't always direct; it goes with my trade. I certainly have been thinking that whoever it was out there shooting at whomever it was that got shot might have thought the poor devil was me.''

''And—assuming I follow that—what if he did?''

''If that *is* the case, then I should say someone's going to be very embarrassed come morning.''

Baren Baragon was working with a particularly stubborn and noxious weed that had somehow gotten a grip on one of his loveliest plantings. He had a short-bladed knife in one hand, a small trowel in the other, exposing and excising the thing's twisting, groping roots. He had herbicides that could wither it in minutes, but they would poison the soil, blight the whole tray. Surgery was the answer.

He thought as he dug that he might actually prefer the knife to the chemicals for other, older reasons, for the reasons surgeons did. He tugged out the last bit of root, dropped it into a can of spirits, and began elaborately washing his hands, though there was nothing on them but a little potting soil.

There were no really new lives to be had, he supposed. One never did more than spade dirt over the old one, seed some new growth; the roots were in the same place.

But there was more hope in it than that, he thought, looking at his long-fingered hands, thinking of Lisel's slim fingers; sometimes, no matter how twisted and strangled the roots, the new growth would blossom gloriously.

Last night, as they staggered away from the theatre under the weight of ola Vivar's parting words, he had told Lisel the truth: what he felt for her, that she had alternatives, that she had a place to go.

It had been a stupid thing to do. Lisel was married, and marriage always meant something, no matter what went on inside it, outside it.

It was stupid, it was old growth pushing through, there was bound to be pain from it, and it had felt so good, like sunlight in his heart.

Someone knocked. Baren looked up; no one knocked at his door, certainly not in the early morning. There was another knock. He grabbed a towel and wiped his hands as he went to answer.

Two City Guards stood on the stair landing. "Master Baren Baragon?" one of them said. He looked up at Baren, then down, with a strange expression, at the towel in Baren's hands.

"That's correct."

"I've been sent to ask you to come to Guard Headquarters, master. There's someone dead."

"Dead?"

The Guard kept staring at the towel. "Yes, master. Near the Red Mask Theatre, early this morning."

"Can you tell me who?" It came out very offhand, out of old habit: *Oh, good morning, Doctor, we found Bed Five Ward Three dead this morning. Yes, nurse? And who was that?*

The Guard said, "No, master, I can't."

"I suppose I'd better go with you, then."

"If you please."

The two Guards stood in the door, watching, while Baren dried his hands and found a jacket. As he pulled it on, the implications of the Guardsman's *No, I can't* broke through the layers of habit, and Baren caught himself starting to shake; but the Guards were watching, and the actor held entirely still.

Nin il Craith's dream exploded and was gone in light and a touch.

"Nin," Kel was saying from the bedside, "the police are here. They want you to go with them."

"The . . . police? What about?"

"I don't know. It's Rusty Jassil, and Stone, you know them, but they won't tell me until you're there. It's only some questions, I can send them away if you want."

"No. I'll see them. Tell them I'll be right out." She blinked at the windows. "What time is it?"

"Half past eight. There's kaf hot."

"Yes. Definitely some kaf."

She dressed quickly, went into the kitchen, and gulped down the mug of kaf with milk Kel had set out for her. The floor was covered with muddy wheelprints, that she was certain hadn't been there last night; she wondered where Kel had been.

The Guards were in the front of the shop, one examining the merchandise—nothing unusual about that, every Guard who could save the money bought a better sidearm than the ones the city issued—and the other, the red-haired Jassil, examining the record-of-sale book with Kel.

"Hello, Rusty," Nin said. "Excuse me for sleeping late."

"Sorry to wake you, Mistress Nin," the Guard said, "but there's been a killing, down by the Red Mask, and we've got to ask all the theatre company to come in. It isn't an arrest or anything like that."

She felt very cold, slightly sick. "Who is it?" she managed to say rather calmly. "Who was killed?"

"Mistress, we don't know; his head was shot near off, and the body left in the alley. That's another thing: we're supposed to find out who's bought shotguns in the last month."

"You didn't sell one, did you, Nin?" Kel said.

"No. We've only sold some small pistols. Except for the Beyaret."

"That's here," Kel said, pointing to a line in the book. "It has two shot barrels and a rifle, very unusual.

And I sold it to the Margrave of Nicchos. I hope he isn't a suspect.''

"Gods, I do too," Rusty said. "But I have to ask anyway: would you know the gun if you saw it again?"

Kel said, "Absolutely. There can't be more than six of them in Liavek, all with different engraving and stock inlay. Not the kind of thing you'd use to kill a man in an alley.''

"They do, though," the other Guard said, examining an ivory-mounted pocket wheellock.

"The dead man," Nin said, "could it have been Virshon ola Vivar?" Kel looked at her, seemed about to speak, but didn't.

"No, mistress. He's all right. I ought to warn you, they're going to want you to look at the body, and it's a mess. Are you ready to go?"

"Yes, Rusty."

Stone bought a spool of slow-match and a couple of flints, and Nin and the Guardsmen went out. She looked down their alley as they passed; it was clean and dry. She wondered very seriously where all the mud in the kitchen had come from.

Wirrel Skye looked up from his kaf when the knock came, plodded through the house to answer the door. The Guards explained the situation to him, and he poured them each a gratefully received cup, excused himself upstairs to dress.

As he passed Dijade's door, Wirrel opened it just slightly. Dijade was asleep, on her back, hands folded, like a queen in state with her red hair haloing her face. He shut the door again. "Wirrrrll?" he heard, muffled through the door. Without a word, he went on downstairs.

"Have ye ever been in the hold of a freebooter?" Lisel Solenti said as she swept the kitchen. "Have ye ever been in the hold . . ." It was a funny line, of course it was a funny line.

It did not really worry her. After last night, nothing could ever worry her again.

Then the police appeared at the door.

"I don't know," she told them. "My husband is away at work . . . I'd want him to know where I am."

"We'll gladly send the message. Would you like to write a note to him?"

"No, that won't do—" She stopped, collected herself. "If you'll just inform him of where I have gone, that will be splendid," she said, exactly as Ambassador Oprio would have, without the Tichenese accent.

"Certainly, Mistress Solenti," the Guard said, and sent his companion off with the message, then escorted Lisel to a waiting coach.

When they reached the Municipal Building, Wirrel, Nin, Baren, and Chitaru were already there, gathered in a cold stone room around a sheet-draped lump on the table. The Guard Captain carefully explained that the body was in very bad condition, and Lisel did not have to look at it; she replied that she understood and wanted to help.

The Captain nodded and drew back the sheet.

"No," Lisel said, staring at the thing. After the first moment, it was not hard to look at: like meat in the butcher's. "I don't know him." She took a step back. Nin hugged her; Baren squeezed her hand. It was all right.

"Very well," the Captain said, then said to one of the other Guards, "Have Doctor Twist come in." She turned back to the members of the company. "The Doctor's going to try a reconstructive spell. Doesn't always work, and it doesn't always work right, but we need to try it within twelve hours of death or it's no good at all. I'd like to ask you to stay, just in case you might have seen him somewhere, but you certainly don't have to."

They all agreed to stay and take another look. Doctor Twist came in. The magician was wearing a loose silk shirt, leather riding trousers, wool socks and sandals, a long woollen coat over it all. A leather headband held his long white hair, and he carried a carpetbag so worn that the pattern of its material was no longer identifiable.

Twist set the bag on the table next to the body and took out several small glasses. A Guard brought him a pitcher of water, and he sloshed it into the glasses in varying amounts; then he produced a wooden mallet from the bag and began tapping the glasses, humming as he did, taking sips and striking them again.

Captain Jemuel said to a Guard, speaking pleasantly and softly, "Was he *all* you could find?"

"He was home," the Guard said. "I mean, his house was home."

"Of course. This is the only city in the world where the streets go on holiday."

Doctor Twist said, "Now, we proceed." He tossed back the sheet, blinked and clucked over the body, then started to tap the glasses, playing a tune that seemed to have neither melody nor rhythm. The water began to vibrate, bubble, glow in changing colors. The music faded below the range of hearing.

The splattered meat on the table began to fold up, wind itself together into nerves, veins, a skull to hold them. There were gaps, missing bits, and not all the rips quite closed, like a sawn puzzle with lost pieces; still, there was a face.

All the safe doubt that had cushioned Lisel's mind drained away like water from a pricked blister, and she began to scream, and could not stop screaming.

The gunshop was closed when Nin got home. She went into the house through the back, and found Kel out of his chair, scrubbing the kitchen floor. "Hello, Nin. Mind the wet." He pulled a cane from the table, stood on his leg and the stick; she tended to forget how agile he was out of the chair.

"Did you find out who was killed?" Kel said.

"Pirth Solenti."

"Well," Kel said thoughtfully, and tapped his stick on the floor. It was, Nin saw, his gun cane, a tiny wheellock mechanism built into the handle. "That'll be a good day's gossip at the Merchants' Society."

"That's not how Lisel took it."

"That's *your* Lisel? She was married to *Pirth?*"

"Baren had to give her a sleeping draught—Baren's a healer, it turns out. He never told us." She shook her head. "Everything's upside down this morning. And it was all going to make sense."

Kel said, smiling, "I'm not always right."

"Where were you last night, Kel? After I went to bed?"

"I'm sorry about the mess this morning, Nin. I *did* clean it—"

"Never mind that—I mean, where did the mud come from? Where were you?"

"At the railway station. Their head driver—Copper, you remember I was talking about him—came in with a mail train at two; I wanted to talk to him."

"And did you? Did people see you there?"

"Of course people saw me. And I did talk to Copper—he likes the idea of the igniter, but he's in so much trouble with the magicians just now, he has to go slow. But he's going to talk to the vice president in Hrothvek—who's an inventor too, I guess—and—" He frowned at her. "What's the matter? Usually you're mad at me for *not* being careful."

"I'm sorry, Kel. I think it's wonderful. It's just that sometimes—sometimes you get ideas that—"

"You thought I went out and shot somebody," he said incredulously. "Why would I—it's that stupid will that ola Vivar gave you, isn't it? You thought I went out to kill ola Vivar, so you could get his theatre."

"I didn't. No, that's a lie. I did think it—but I didn't believe it."

"Thank you very much." He spun and dropped into his chair, rolled it out of the kitchen.

"Kel, *wait*. I'm sorry." She ran after him, grabbed

the chair back to stop him, put her arms around his shoulders.

"Nin, I don't know what goes on over there, at your rehearsals—and if you don't want to tell me, that's fine—but does he have you thinking about killing each other?"

"Yeah," she said. "He does."

Seven hours after the body was identified, Nin, Baren, and Wirrel filed onto the stage of the Red Mask. A few panels of scenery were up, part of Hirander the Merchant's office; Virshon ola Vivar, dressed entirely in gray, sat behind Hirander's elaborate desk, leaning back in the chair, feet extended, hands in his lap.

"There are only three of you. Excuse me, four." Oten Chitaru came out of his working corner in the wings. Ola Vivar took a paper from the desk, and a quill. "Nine days left; it's not easy to drill a new principal in that time, but I've done it in less." He dipped the pen, started to stroke it across a line on the paper.

"Don't do that unless you're ready to do it four times," Wirrel said. "We thought you might try to dismiss Lisel, and we agreed that we wouldn't let you."

"No arguments, no pleading," Nin said. "Either you give her some time to recover, or we all leave."

Ola Vivar said, "Will you rehearse without her?"

Wirrel said, "Yes, but not with a substitute."

Ola Vivar tapped the pen on the paper. "No, it won't do. There's never any end to excuses, once they start. A trauma now, and halfway through the run it will be the color of the costumes, or an itch caused by the makeup, or too much scenery to lift and drag."

Baren said slowly, "Her husband was murdered only last night."

"I am certain that she is grieving." Ola Vivar looked directly at Baren, spoke with an absolutely even voice. "I am certain that many are grieving today, for one cause and another. But if you were a farmer with seed to plant, a doctor with patients to treat, a priest with souls to comfort, you would find a way to do it. And whatever was in your heart while you worked, you would find a way to control it, and use it, and be stronger for it—or you *would not be* what you called yourself, farmer or doctor or priest.'' He raised the pen. ''Now. It's time to determine who is an actor, and who isn't. One we know.'' He went *scratch* through a name. ''And the rest of you?''

Nin said, ''Whatever else we are, we're human.'' She looked at Chitaru, said, ''We didn't ask you about this, but—''

Ola Vivar said, ''He's the easiest of all to replace.''

Chitaru said, ''I will gather my materials.'' He went offstage.

Scratch went the pen. *Scratch. Scratch. Scratch.*

Chitaru reappeared with a battered leather rucksack. He and the three players started down the steps, toward the front of the theatre.

Someone stood up from a rear-row bench, walked across the light from the lobby door. ''Thank you,'' Lisel said. ''Thank you all so much.''

''As I told you,'' ola Vivar said, standing up, walking to the edge of the stage with the paper loose in his hands, ''as I told Lisel before the rest of you arrived, an actor finds the strength to act.'' He crumpled the paper, tossed it away. ''That concludes tonight's rehearsal. I will look forward to seeing you all tomorrow. Good night.''

Jemuel came on shift at midnight. Captain Skolny was going off duty; he had a grim look, which was unusual for him, even at the end of shift. Jemuel said, ''So what's the matter? Night more entertaining than usual?''

''Someone's inside to see you. Came in just a little while ago.''

''Who? About what?''

''*Oh*, no. No, she wanted to see you, nobody else. She's all yours.'' Skolny tucked his helmet under his arm, tugged a wool cap on his head, and went down the long, dim corridor, his boots clicking on the floor.

Jemuel frowned and went into the Guard office. Sitting on a chair against the wall, huddled in on herself, sat Lisel Solenti, in a red dress and a green cloak, her yellow hair disarrayed.

"Mistress?" Jemuel said.

Lisel looked up. She had been crying. "I can't stand it anymore, Captain. I have to tell you. I shot my husband."

Wirrel found Dijade standing in the kitchen door, wearing a long silk-sashed robe, her arms folded and her head at a slant. Her hair was caught loosely in coils of green ribbon; the effect was girlish, and, Wirrel found himself thinking, rather silly.

"It must have been a short rehearsal," she said.

"Yes."

"You did it, didn't you. Dared him to let you go."

"We all did. Even the dramaturge."

"So he's got—no company at all? Nine days before opening? What's he going to do?" She came forward and embraced Wirrel. "My poor boy. Can you eat? You must eat, and not brood."

"He has the same company he had this morning," Wirrel said. "We'll open on time."

Her hands went rigid against his back. "Then . . . he forgave you? Of course. Of course, he'd stand to lose so much if he didn't open, he had no choice—"

"He had plenty of choice. But I think—he might have let us go if we *hadn't* stood up for Lisel." He laughed. "Am I beginning to understand him, or am I just going as mad as he is?"

"Don't think about it," Dijade said, and tugged him toward the kitchen. "There's sausage, and greens, and Black Orchid tea. Don't think at all, not tonight."

So she was going to be tigerish tonight. That happened when things had gone either very well or very badly: her needs followed extremity. It was heady stuff to be needed in the bones by a beautiful, famous, powerful woman; it was new wine.

Was the wine going flat now? Losing its bouquet? Or was it his taste that was changing?

It didn't matter. Wirrel was thirsty, wanted to get seriously drunk, and there was plenty of spirit left in the bottle. It didn't matter at all, not tonight, not yet.

Baren Baragon was practicing one of his deaths when the knock came, sometime after midnight.

"Master Baragon," said the armed woman at the door, "I'm Jemuel, captain of the City Guard. We met this morning, at the morgue."

"Yes, of course. What can I do for you?"

"May I come in? I should say that I'm here on business, and you don't have to let me in if you don't wish to."

He held the door wide and she came in. "Were you expecting someone?" she said.

"Not tonight, Captain."

"There are two wineglasses set out."

"I was rehearsing a scene from our play. It requires switching glasses, one of which is poisoned."

"People do tend to die in ola Vivar's plays, don't they?"

"In all plays, I suppose."

"Is anyone shot in this one?"

"Yes, one person. If you don't mind, I'd sooner not explain beyond that—I hope you'll see the play, and I don't want to spoil the joke."

"This murder's a good joke, then?"

Baren smiled, shrugged. "In its place, I think it will make you laugh."

"I could do with that. Do you mind telling me who fires the gun?"

"Mistress il Craith."

"Not Lisel Solenti."

Baren paused a moment. "No."

"You've been working with the widow Solenti for a

while. Do you think she knows how to handle fire-
arms?''

"We were all taught how to load and fire a pistol on
stage. Why are you asking me this?''

"Master Baragon—I'm sorry, it's Healer Baragon,
isn't it?''

"Whichever you like,'' Baren said stiffly.

"Healer, Pirth Solenti was an ingratiating, nicely-
spoken piece of garbage. You know that, I know it, a
number of Liavek's women of pleasure know it very
damned well. But however much the town air is fresh-
ened by his departure, the law says I'm supposed to
find the person who shot him, put her in front of three
judges, and let them sort out the consequences.''

"You said 'her.' ''

"Habit of speech. I had an Ombayan nurse as a
child.''

"I do not think you had any kind of nurse,'' Baren
said. "I think you were a street child, as I was. Lisel
was not. Lisel was taken care of, loved all her life.
Without love she would be very much lost. She would
never hurt the person who loved her, cared for her. She
could not do it.''

"Healer, the first thing a cop learns is that anybody
can do anything. And they do, all the time. Now, maybe
she can convince the judges she was crazy. Maybe you
can help with that. But me, I think they'll figure that
anything she says is one of ola Vivar's actors doing her
stuff, and hang her.''

"You mean to arrest her? Now, tonight?''

"I've nothing better to do.''

"Even though you know that I did it.''

"Now, just when am I supposed to have figured that
out?''

"Whenever you guessed that I love her,'' Baren said,
and moved toward one of the larger planting trays. "You
knew that I would kill for her, but I would not let her
be tried for the crime. Well. I confess. I shot Pirth
Solenti, with forethought and intention. It was a cow-

ardly thing, but I am a coward. Too much of a coward to let myself be hanged.'' He pulled a scalpel from the potting soil, raised it to his throat.

Jemuel moved like a striking snake, kicking up to Baren's wrist, knocking the knife from his hand. It hit the wall and stuck. She took a long step toward him, punched him in the sternum, slapped his face hard. Baren dropped on his rump.

"Feel better now?'' she said. ''I thought you might be clever enough to try that. Thank Kosker that Lisel didn't think of leaving her confession in a suicide note.''

"Lisel confessed? But she didn't kill him—''

"No more than you did. And she confessed for the exact same reason you did: to protect the other one.'' Jemuel went to the door. ''She's downstairs, in the coach. I'll send her up, and you can call each other stupid for the rest of the evening.'' She grinned. ''Or whatever. May I remind the both of you, however, that obstructing justice *is* a crime in Liavek?''

"Captain . . . how did you know I didn't kill Solenti?''

"Because an hour ago, Lisel was downtown confessing to me, and not here with you. If you were the sort who thought murder improved people's lives, you wouldn't have lost any time finishing the repairs in person.'' She adjusted her blue sash of rank, opened the door. ''Good night, Healer Baragon.''

"Thank you, Captain.''

"For this, I get six levars a month, and I haven't earned them until I find the real killer. But you're welcome anyhow.''

"Haul on sail!" Grumbolio shouted at his pirate crew, and put the glass to his eye.

"But—Captain—'' a sailor said, and Grumbolio decked him with a blow. ''I tell ye, make sail! Yon ship's the *Bo'sun's Brother,* out of Fair Harbor, and d'ye know what she carries?''

"No, Captain.''

"In round figures, fifty thousand in fire, stranding, and unspecified loss coverage, wi' no deductible! What are ye waiting for, man? I said, *no deductible!* She'll have no stomach for a fight under terms like that! *Make sail!*"

Sheets ran, and spars hauled canvas; then Grumbolio noticed the coil of line loose around his neck. "Just a moment," he said, too politely to be heard, and he just had time to grab at the rope before it went tight, yanking him off his feet and into the rigging. He disappeared for a moment, and then his boots dangled below the line of the proscenium arch, just in view.

"Aye!" ola Vivar said, and applauded.

Lisel scrambled down a ladder from the scenery tower and came back on stage. Above her, the boots still dangled; Baren cranked a winch and the dummy pirate rose back out of sight.

"Remember," ola Vivar said, "a second too long is better than a second too short. We don't want anyone wondering what two pirates are doing up there."

Nin had come out to help Lisel with her costume; they had undone Grumbolio's frogged coat and unhooked the lifting wires from the leather harness beneath it. The rope around her neck was only for the audience's benefit.

"Well done," ola Vivar said. "Can you all do one scene more?"

They agreed at once.

"Fine. Then we'll stop now, while you've got a drop of juice left. Get cleaned up, and I'll buy you all a cup of tea."

The players finished hanging and folding their costumes, toweling off the last of their makeup, and emerged from the wings to meet the Director onstage around the tea service.

"We open in seven days," ola Vivar said. "I imagine you'd all forgotten that."

They laughed.

"We'll take tomorrow off. I'll be sending the an-

nouncement to the printer tomorrow; the posters will
go up the day after tomorrow. I should say that you can
expect attention, once that happens, so I'll ask now:
do any of you, for any reason, want your names left off
the posters? Or a stage name used?'' He looked at Lisel.
''Your mother's name was very well known in the Liavekan theatre. I'm sure she would not object to your
using it.''

''Thank you, Director. But she made her own name.
I'll leave it to her.''

''As you wish. Anyone else? Very well then, I will
see you on Luckday, for a full technical rehearsal. Good
night.''

When the players had gone, ola Vivar wandered
backstage; he examined the pistols in their rack, the
wooden-bladed cutlasses and carefully blunted rapiers.
He smiled. He rummaged through the cases of old
props: the model flying machine they had used in *Middle Distance*, elaborately bound books (on hollow
wooden cores) from *Fogmonth Wine,* a Leper's Cord
from *The Moon's New Coat,* the sledge from *Hammer
and Anvil*—real steel, nothing else rang true.

He hefted the hammer, swung it at a wooden wig-
stand. The dummy head went flying across the prop-
room, landing in a pile of brocade coats.

''You can't mean to,'' said a man standing in the
stage exit.

Ola Vivar put the sledge down with a ringing thump.
''A knock, and who's without?''

Krtsotses's voice answered, small, trembling slightly.
''Why are you doing this, Vrrshei?''

''Are you impatient with the progress of the drama?''
ola Vivar said. ''These things must be taken in their
time. Only seven more nights, and all questions will be
answered, all problems resolved.'' He pushed past
Krtsotses, walked onto the brightly lit stage.

''Don't kill them, Vrrshei.''

''What's this, a change of character? A plot compli-
cation?''

"Please. Don't kill them." Krtsotses staggered toward ola Vivar, dropped to his knees. "I'll go away. I'll leave you alone, but *please don't kill them.*" He began to sob.

"You simply don't understand, Krtsotses. There is a point, out at the extreme distance of art, beyond which the creation becomes responsible only to itself. Merely human concerns no longer apply." He crouched over Krtsotses, held out his hands. "The players have been stretched, hammered, drawn like metal—and they have not broken; they no longer know what to expect, so they accept everything with equanimity. And on stage, as their roles kill them, they will deny the fact, and play those roles more furiously." His fingers curled; his voice began to break. "Until they have fully denied the bloody, death-rotten reality in favor of the crystalline purity of a laugh. The last thing they hear will be that laughter. No morning after: no cruel notices, no second-night terrors, no gray wandering among a public that does not recognize them without makeup."

Krtsotses said desperately, "Do I have to kill you now?"

"You don't *have to* do a damned thing." Ola Vivar stood up. "And your groveling is disgusting." He scuffed a boot on the stage near Krtsotses's knee, then turned away. "O gods of rope and scrim, Krtsotses, depart from me awhile. Mnoreon may be an inflated god's-mask delusionary, but at least he's interesting company. You, my dear fellow, are a low-comedy bore inflicted on me through a stock-melodrama sin, and I'm thoroughly ill of you and your bumbling, stumbling attempts to make your farce into tragedy. Now get out of Mnoreon's light."

Krtsotses crumpled. Then he got slowly to his feet, and Mnoreon said, "If there's a loss of patience here, Vrrshei, it's mutual."

"I've told you. Seven more nights."

"The weapons back there, Vrrshei. Are all of them false? A gun fires quickly, a sword thrusts and is done in an instant. And your traps? Your ropes? What's the secret you're holding over your wizard?''

Ola Vivar said, ''You must know—and this is not idle, it is *necessary* that you know this—I will do what I mean to do, Mnoreon.''

''As will I, Vrrshei.''

''I'm counting on that.''

Mnoreon looked puzzled.

Ola Vivar said, ''Let yourself out by the alley door, will you? It locks itself—but then, you know that.'' He turned away again, paused, looked back. ''Before I leave you all alone with yourself, tell me, Mnoreon: what did Pirth Solenti want, the other night?''

''What do you mean?''

''Oh, Mnoreon, I'm certain you didn't kill him. But he wouldn't have been in the alley unless he'd gone out that way; he wouldn't have known of the door otherwise. Now, I didn't let him in. And Chitaru didn't. So you must have. And you wouldn't have done it without pretending to be me.''

''Do you think I'm such a good actor as that?'' Mnoreon said with dry venom.

''Of course you're a good actor. I hired you once, remember? Besides, for a Drstonan to turn down an offered role would be . . . unnatural.'' Mnoreon inclined his head. Ola Vivar said, ''Before you take your success too much to heart, I'd never met Solenti.''

''He let that slip early on.''

''An admission, finally! So what did he *want?*''

''He asked that the opening date for the play be postponed by at least a tenday, preferably longer.''

''Why?''

''He didn't think his wife was ready. He was afraid her career would be wrecked if she appeared without enough training. He had quite a lot of gold with him. . . .''

''Which you refused, naturally. Excuse me, which *I* refused.''

''Of course you did. Then he became abusive, threat-ened you with violence. You were cool and sarcastically unimpressed.''

"Thank you.''

Mnoreon made a dismissive gesture. "He was not the sort to fight a man who might beat him.''

"You do have an actor's perception, Mnoreon. And so he went away unsatisfied.''

"Yes. I heard the shot. When I went out—''

"After a dramatic hesitation.''

"—there was nothing I could do for him.''

"No faulting that.'' Ola Vivar walked to the right wing of the stage, examined the edge of a scenery flat. "Of course, you thought it had been me. Shooting at what I thought was you.''

"I thought—''

"It's all right, Mnoreon. You too, Krtsotses. I can hear you starting to bubble to the surface. All but the trashiest melodrama requires some ambiguity of motives.''

"You should know that I have done things, Vrrshei,'' Mnoreon said, and took a few steps across the stage. "I have set things in motion—''

Ola Vivar reached to the wall, pulled a lever. A rope whistled through a pulley, and a sandbag hit the stage inches in front of Mnoreon, who staggered back. Ola Vivar pulled another lever, and a stage trap dropped open just behind the other man. Mnoreon pivoted, leaped over the trap, and fled.

"That's what I like so much about professionals,'' ola Vivar said. "They always hit their marks.''

Fog Way was not actually foggy at all times of day, just most of them. The buildings rose high to either side, sometimes leaning out far enough to bridge the street, holding in shadow and mist and smoke. The doors did not have numbers, and the shops did not have signs.

A raven-headed cane knocked at one of those doors;

a little light showed through an iron grill, and a smooth, polite voice said, ''May I help you?''

''I am Aritoli ola Silba. I am expected.''

The door opened, and a butler in silk and velvet, carrying a black rod of office, bowed to Aritoli. ''Of course, master. This way, please; do follow me closely.'' He led the way into clean, narrow, mazy corridors.

The inn was called Brodny's Intercession, partly because it was located near the Pardoner-priests' hostel, and partly because Brodny the proprietor specialized in arranging discreet meetings. No one was quite certain how many entrances, or rooms, or even floors the place had (some said not even Brodny), but it was entirely proof against eavesdrop or intrusion, and it was generally believed that no one had ever actually been murdered there, just because it would have seemed such an obvious place for it.

Aritoli was taken to a carved door, behind which were a table and two benches. On the table sat a lamp, a bottle of Dragonsmoke, and two glasses; on one of the benches sat Virshon ola Vivar.

''Was this really necessary, Virshon?''

Ola Vivar poured two drinks. ''What I have to ask you must not be overheard. Nothing to do with your discretion, I assure you. And of course you know that I'm—you'll pardon the expression—incurably theatrical.''

Ola Silba accepted a glass, sipped slightly at it. It was real Dragonsmoke from the Silverspine Mountains, which meant that drinking it was like having a well-drilled herd of desert palominos gallop down one's throat, not camels as with the cheap imitation. When his voice came back, Aritoli said, ''Well. Ask.''

''I want your advice on a professional basis, Aritoli. Shall we say . . .'' Ola Vivar put a stack of coins in the center of the table.

Aritoli said, ''You have me at a loss, Virshon. Which

is, as you doubtless know, a considerable admission for
me.''

Ola Vivar nodded.

Ola Silba said, ''As long as I'm making dangerous
admissions, I should add that most of those who . . .
consult with me want my artistic taste to stand in for
theirs, if any. That can't possibly be the case with you.''

''No?''

''Virshon. This isn't appropriate among friends. We
are friends, are we not?''

''We are friends. Exactly why I want this as a business transaction.''

''Very well.'' Aritoli hooked the coins with the raven
head of his cane, pulled them into his palm. ''Value
received. It's business, and may I congratulate you on
your taste in advisors?'' He stroked his upper lip.
''Now, what do you want my advice on? Portraits?
Murals?''

''Theatrical investments.''

Ola Silba dragged his gilded fingernails across his
neat little moustache, doing neither any good at all.

''So where was the note left?'' Jemuel said.

''On one of the benches in the Entry Hall,'' said
Eban the desk serjeant. ''Addressed to 'The Commander of the Guards.' ''

''Not the Captain-General.''

''Commander was the word, Captain. The script is
odd, too—not like Liavekan, or Tichenese. You see, the
connectors—''

Jemuel listened patiently while Eban indulged his
specialty. Then she said, ''So what we have is either
someone not Liavekan, or who wants us to think he or
she isn't Liavekan.''

Eban spread his hands.

Jemuel read the note once more. It was unsigned,
naturally; it had been done (according to Eban) on
cheap paper with a cheap quill, nothing at all distinctive
about it.

It read: IF YOU WOULD TAKE A MURDERER,
BE AT THE RED MASK THEATRE TONIGHT AT
TEN EXACTLY.

It was a few minutes before ten. Under a single
downlight on the Red Mask stage, Virshon ola Vivar
was examining the newly printed broadsheets for the
premiere six days away. Across the dark auditorium was
a square of light: the door to the lobby, propped open.

Someone stepped into the light, began moving toward the stage. Ola Vivar looked up.

"Master Director?" Nin il Craith said.

"Nin?" Ola Vivar walked quickly to the edge of the
stage as Nin climbed the stairs with a purposeful step.
"We weren't meeting today."

She took a rolled paper from her bag, started to put
it on one of the stacks of posters. The blocky type, her
name, held her eyes for a moment, then she set the
paper down. "I wanted to give that back to you. It's
the testament you made out."

"Testament? Oh. That. It wasn't much of a joke, was
it?"

"I didn't take it as a joke," she said. "It was a while
before I knew just what to make of it—but I never
thought it was a joke."

"I still haven't taught you very well, I see. As an
actor, you should consider all the possibilities in every
text. Especially the possibilities of humor." He picked
up some broadsheets, shuffled them on top of the testament. "But you're right, this one wasn't terribly
funny."

"I couldn't think why you'd write such a thing, why
you'd give me—"

"Acting lessons? It's a form of charity for the ego,
Nin. Now, it's been a long day for me. Do you want a
poster or two? For your wall, perhaps?"

"I won't go until you say it. Until I make you say
it."

"I have, as you and your fellow players know to your

sorrow, a rather large vocabulary. Are you going to make me run through the words one by one until I hit on the correct one, or will I have some prompting?''

''You love me,'' Nin said.

''Black heaven, it *has* been a trying day, hasn't it?''

''Don't play with me, Virshon,'' she said, standing very still. ''Don't play with my heart over this.''

''Say good night, Nin, and go home. Go away, before I find the right words to make you leave.'' His voice was dry as the Great Waste, and as empty. ''You know I have the vocabulary.''

''It's too late for that, Virshon. You can't make me hate you, no matter what you say or do. Because I'll know that you're lying, that it's all only a performance.''

Ola Vivar's hands whitened on the back of a chair. ''Is that what you tell your brother?''

She stared at him.

''Is that what draws you to human wreckage like us? The idea that it's all just a romantic pretense? Are you infatuated with the strength you think we possess, hidden somewhere under the scar tissue?''

''All right, Virshon,'' she said, trying to control her voice. ''All right, I was too sudden. But I've learned to be patient, not least from you. I will find out why you're doing this, and I will hear you tell the truth.''

She went, slowly, down the steps and through the auditorium, looking back more than once. The street door opened, banged shut. Ola Vivar breathed deeply, looked into the darkness, at the open door.

There was another thump, another shape in the square of light. A voice, clear across the distance, said, ''Who was that boy, running from here? Something of yours, Virshon?''

Ola Vivar closed his eyes for a moment, sighed. ''Not a boy, and certainly not mine,'' he said. ''That was an actress.'' He pitched his voice up. ''We were rehearsing a bit.''

The figure began walking up the rows. "That would be il Craith? The gunsmith's daughter? That's good."

"I suppose that means you intend to shoot me. Shoot me again, I should say."

The gun came out of a canvas bag. It was plainly ugly, like a piece of drainpipe on a stick. "You understand why it has to be tonight, Virshon?"

"Of course." He tapped the posters. "These go up tomorrow, and then the damage is done. But is it really worth anyone's life, Dijade?"

She came up onto the stage, into the light. She was wearing a low-necked, sleeveless white dress, a blood-red scarf wrapped around her throat and down her bare left arm. It was anything but inconspicuous.

"It's *my* life," she said bitterly. "My death. Do you know what you've done to the dramatic theatre in Liavek? What you've done, in a few arrogant, selfish strokes, to so many of us who've spent our lives building it?"

"The idea that the star actor is lord in the theatre is obsolete—" Ola Vivar shook his head. "No, I suppose you're right. But I'm sure that you're an excellent study, Dijade; why didn't you just open your comedy a tenday ahead of us? Or even two?"

"What would have been the difference? Our audience would begin to thin as soon as your notices went up, and vanish once you opened."

"Pirth didn't think so."

"Who?"

"Oh, come now, Dijade, even if you don't read the sensational murder stories, you must know who your backers were. I'm reliably told that Pirth Solenti put up nearly thirty percent of your production. That was when you thought I'd be staging another tragedy, of course. . . . But Pirth thought that delaying me a bit would be enough. That's what he was trying to do, the night you shot him by mistake."

"But you didn't agree," Dijade said, not entirely as a question.

"No."

She seemed to relax. "Of course not. You will not live in a balance with others. It is time to redress the balance before it shifts any further." She leveled the gun.

Ola Vivar said, without much concern, "Take your second shot carefully. Remember how hasty the first one was."

"Don't patronize me, you bastard!" Her voice rose to just below a shriek. "I heard Wirrel rehearsing—rehearsing *me!*" The heavy pistol wavered a bit. "Am I not quite so funny now, Director?"

"That was an actor's interpretation, not mine. And since we've changed the subject to actors, you don't really intend to let Nin il Craith be blamed for shooting me, do you?"

"She'll distract attention for a while."

"And if they hang her?"

"Why, you silly foreigner. This is Liavek, a city of great sophistication; no one hangs here for a crime of passion. She'll suffer no more than a temporary inconvenience." She laughed. "In truth, we're doing her a service. A bit of notoriety does nothing but good for a young actress's career."

"Well, there's Nin's compensation," ola Vivar said. "I suppose Lisel sees the recovery of her late husband's investment. What are you going to give the rest of my players, in return for taking their opening night away?"

"Pretend that you care." Her voice rose again. "You're not an actor. You order actors around, you stuff words in their mouths and toss them a few coins if they parrot them mindlessly enough to suit your vanity—"

"Stop." Ola Vivar slammed his hands down on the posters. "I've heard this speech any number of times, from any number of actors. As you've probably heard, I am very particular about who I will hear auditions from, so would you just go ahead and kill me now, please? Seeing as you have an adequate light this time."

"Yes," Dijade said, "I will do that, you arrogant—"

The gun buzzed, roared, vomited fire.

Jagged pellets spattered to the floor in an arc just in front of ola Vivar's feet.

Dijade stared. "You're not a wizard—"

"No. But Chitaru, the man just behind you stage left, is a very good one. And Jemuel, out there in the eleventh row, is a Captain of the City Guard. The two sturdy fellows behind her are Guardsmen as well."

"So this is how it ends," Dijade said, not softly but pitched to the last balcony row.

"Maybe not," Jemuel said, coming down to the stage, Rusty and Stone behind her with swords out. "This is a city of great sophistication, after all."

Dijade allowed herself to be led from the stage. "Tell Wirrel . . . I truly did not mean any of this to harm him."

Ola Vivar touched his fingertips to his forehead, inclined his head. He turned to Jemuel, who looked about to speak, put a finger to his lips. "Ssh, Captain. Last word always goes to the star."

When they had gone, Chitaru said, "Do you require me any further tonight, Director?"

"No, Chitaru. Thank you again."

"I only cast the spell, Director. It was you who stood behind it."

They bowed to each other, and Chitaru left the theatre. Ola Vivar wandered about for a few minutes, listening. Quite alone, he stood in the middle of the stage.

"It was a close thing, Nin," he told the empty air. "I thought I'd never get you out of here without an incrimination: but then suddenly you made it too easy for me." He sat down on the stage, clasped his hands around his raised knees. "You shouldn't have made me feel helpless. I was bound to hurt you for that." He sucked in a sharp breath. "Here's this moment . . . oh, Nin, Nin, there are mice in my brain."

He bent forward and hid his face in his arms.

The Red Mask Theatre of Liavek
under the direction of Virshon ola Vivar
presents

MAY THESE EVENTS
An Accidental Comedy

Featured Players

Baren Baragon   Wirrel Skye
Nin il Craith   Lisel Solenti

Oten Chitaru, Dramaturge
Music by Treadmeasures

First Performance: 30 Flowers 3320 at 7 Promptly
Seats ½, 1 and 3 Levars
Proceeds to Benefit the Railway Medical Fund

It was five in the afternoon on the last day of Flowers.

"Last days and first," Virshon ola Vivar said, and
poured Fondness Recalled tea into six porcelain cups.

"Last days and first," the players and the dramaturge
said, and they chimed the cups together and drank. The
tea was strong and smoky, with a hint of sweetness in
the throat.

"Curtain up in two hours exactly," ola Vivar said.
"Chitaru, you will open the door at six. All seats have
been sold; you may have to be firm in reminding people
of that. At a quarter to seven, unclaimed seats are resold at full price, and you may admit up to one hundred
fifty standees for a quarter-levar." He took some cards
from his black velvet tunic. "These are the compli-
mentaries, all three-levar seats *not* to be resold if unclaimed. Aritoli ola Silba; the Margrave of Trieth and
companion; Captain of the Guard Jemuel of Ryo Wharf;
Kel il Craith. Assist Kel with the balcony lift if necessary."

"Could be worse," Wirrel said, smiling but nervous. "You could have mentioned Her Magnificence the Levar."

"She's purchased a seat," ola Vivar said, with supreme indifference. "I repay favors with passes, I don't buy them . . . do keep that in mind when ola Silba arrives?"

"The Levar?" Lisel said.

"She's part of the audience," ola Vivar said, very gently. "That's all. She'll be up in the balcony boxes, at any rate; you won't even be able to see her behind the lights."

"It's all right, Lisel," Baren said. "It really is all right."

Ola Vivar held out his delicate teacup. "As we are all true to our superstitious trade, I will not wish good fortune; but I will say that, in my view of the world, fortune is a thing people make for themselves; and you have prepared . . ." His voice caught, just slightly. "You have prepared very well indeed." He drank off the tea, put the cup down with care. "Let that be our benediction: there are yet marks to hit and words to speak, entrances and deaths to be taken in their turn. Company, to work!"

Baren and Wirrel cleared the table, leaving it in place; Lisel struck the main lights, illuminating the stage as the hall of the Double Deuce Tavern, Act One, Scene One. They fluttered to the corners of the theatre; the dressing cubicles, the makeup trays, the front lobby, the ropes of the fly loft.

Ola Vivar went down a narrow stair to the understage area, a forest of supports and trapwork lit by a few elaborately fireproofed lamps. There were prompt-sheets tacked to some of the uprights, and some props, such as Doctor Viscusi's bag, in place. Above him, he could hear every footstep on the boards, every word spoken.

There was an incorrect creak. Ola Vivar turned, and saw himself: gray hair tied back, black tunic, red trousers. Only the face was wrong—and it was not very wrong at all.

"Opening night, Vrrshei," Mnoreon said, and swung the blacksmith's sledge.

Ola Vivar woke to flashes of light, the taste of blood and leather, and pain across his shoulder and chest. He was on the floor, face down. He inhaled, and felt a stab in his side; a broken rib, probably. There was a strap in his mouth, compressing his tongue; his hands were pulled up tight behind his back and securely tied.

There seemed to be another body next to him. His eyes took another few moments to focus; he saw that it was the dummy pirate Grumbolio from act three.

Someone bent over ola Vivar, put a knee into his back. "Terrible thing, isn't it," Mnoreon said, "the lack of speech? Awful for an actor even to imagine. That's why I knew I'd be unsuspected, you see." He pulled ola Vivar's head up, sending blinding pain through ola Vivar's skull, slipped a noose around ola Vivar's neck. "I thought, 'What will the courts of Drstona never believe? They will never accept that an actor might destroy his own voice.' And so that was what I did."

He put a hand to the gag, showed the blade of a knife. "We'll have a few last words now. Speak above an offstage mutter, and I'll slit your throat; and then you'll miss the play."

Ola Vivar gasped as the leather came out. It hurt. "You weren't . . . supposed . . . to die," he said.

"A miscalculation," Mnoreon said. "It would have been so perfect, at your trial: whatever words you found in your defense countered by my eloquently silent stare of damning accusation. They'd have burnt you alive and protesting on the stage of the Theatre-Royal; what finer exit could you have wanted?" Someone walked overhead; ola Vivar could tell it was Nin by her step. Mnoreon waited, holding the knife to ola Vivar's lips, then continued more quietly: "It would have been . . . the

thing you keep gibbering of . . . a perfect performance.
You were right, the other night, when you were baiting
Krtsotses. It cannot be done with mere intention. It
must come from things stronger than life.''

"Nothing," ola Vivar said, "is stronger than life.
Do you hear that, Krtsotses?''

"Krtsotses no longer exists. He has fulfilled his goal
of destroying you; now he can fade, to the nothing he
so desires.''

"His goal . . . is to destroy the murderer . . . of the
cast of *The Broken Seal*. How did you hide it from him,
all these years?''

"He cannot encroach upon me.''

"Ah. It was ego, then.''

"In truth, Vrrshei, I think he did not care to know.
But you knew. You knew, and you only waited me out.
Why?''

"I was rehearsing a play. I didn't have time for murder.''

"I mean to wait you out, Vrrshei. I mean to kill you
last, after all your players—and you must know that I
will do what I mean to do. But tell me the truth, now,
or you die, now: why did you let me go on?''

Ola Vivar said wearily, "The torturer and the victim
always change places, sooner or later. If you had any
tragic sense you'd know that.''

"Enough commentary from the cheap seats.'' Mnoreon pushed the gag back into place, buckled it tight.
He began adjusting the noose. "Now, pay attention to
what I'm doing. This rope goes—thus—under your collar. And these pins—so, so, hold the collar in place.
Now, the cloth may tear, and the pins may give—and
if you struggle in the least, they will—and you'll fall
till the rope ends you. But as long as you are careful,
stay still, you remain alive.''

Mnoreon pulled a white cloth sack over ola Vivar's
head, plucked at it, cut a slit with his knife just in front
of ola Vivar's eyes.

"Now,'' Mnoreon said, "it must be done quickly,

while they're dressing. Doors open in ten minutes.'' He stood up. ''Good night, Chancellor,'' he said, quoting *The Broken Seal.* ''We'd give thee grand remembrances, bells, chariots, the sun itself for pyre, but that we could. But darkness is by darkness swallowed up; and so men say by dark when they depart: Good night, good prince—thou knowest what thou art.''

He disappeared. A moment later, ola Vivar heard his steps, light on the stage, heard and felt the trap open above him. The rope pulled at his neck, lifted him to his knees, his feet—he felt his coat stretch—pulled him up through the trap, past the stage set, the lights—was anyone watching? No, no, they were professionals, they would all be exactly where they were supposed to be—past the arch into the tower.

The slit in the cloth hood gave him an excellent overhead view. He was exactly where the dummy Grumbolio should be, waiting for its cue to drop into view, Act Three, Scene Four.

And if he strangled then, if he kicked, why, he ought to bring the house down.

The Red Mask doors were open. Chitaru was taking tickets, a sparkle of golden light across his fingers as he checked for counterfeits. The musicians had arrived, sufficiently sober, and Nin showed them to their places just before the stage.

Aritoli ola Silba came in. There was a polite gasp from the lobby crowd, and he turned elegantly around—and saw Jemuel, in a long gown of deep lavender and gold; her hair was up and threaded with gold net that trailed around her throat. She took a step. It was a small one. She was clearly unaccustomed to the skirts. Aritoli smiled, tapped his cane once smartly, and extended his hand with a perfect small bow. There was a small brilliant pop, and a white-petaled lotus appeared between his fingers. Jemuel laughed, took the flower with one hand and Aritoli's hand with the other, and they went into the theatre.

The curtain was closed; it was of black fabric, with a crimson mask, two eyeholes and a horizontal slit, in the center. At one end of the stage stood Virshon ola Vivar, also in black and red. He bowed and saluted to the crowd, then slipped offstage without speaking.

Kel arrived in the company of a young couple, well-dressed in the Hrothvekan fashion. The man had the monogram of the Lucksea Coastal & Northerly Railway embroidered on his jacket. Someone pointed, identified them as Korik and Cadie Li, the Railway Vice-President for Hrothvek and his wife. Korik pushed Kel's wheel-chair to their seats, waited for Kel to vault out on his cane, then pulled a few pins on the chair and folded it flat enough to fit beneath the benches. He gave a thumbs-up to Kel, and they shook hands in mutual congratulation before taking their seats.

Her Magnificence Tazli Ifino iv Larwin, Levar of Liavek, appeared, with a perfunctory councilor and a non-perfunctory bodyguard. Chitaru explained the working of the balcony lift to the councilor, a tall, thin, worn-looking fellow, and the Government ascended. At an announcement, all rose in the theatre until Her Magnificence was seated. "If she has to use the lavatory," someone in the lobby said, without moving his lips, "do we get up too?"

Backstage, Lisel was hooking shut Nin's coat, of muslin varnished to resemble boiled leather; Lisel herself wore a long leather coat over a butter-yellow dress. Nin started the play onstage; Lisel came on briefly as a messenger before her appearance in the yellow dress as Honoria.

"Something's wrong," Nin said.

"No, it isn't," Lisel said very firmly. "Nothing at all is wrong."

"Yes, there is. Virshon said that, just before the curtain went up, he'd remind me of something I said. About the suspense, of waiting for him to come on stage. He said it would be funny . . . and it is, but he hasn't come to say it."

"It doesn't mean anything, Nin."

"Yes. It does." She looked through a concealed slit in the stage arch. Chitaru had closed the doors and was selling programs for a ten-copper bit each. The audience was settling itself, rustling papers, adjusting coats, talking softly and not so softly, like the sound and motion of an undulant sea. Then Baren and Lisel turned down the auditorium lights, and they calmed to a rippling in the darkness.

Chitaru went to the back of the house, then down the side passage to his backstage workspace. Nin looked across the stage: ola Vivar was there. He waved, disappeared offstage right. Nin shook herself, stretched and loosened her muscles, walked onto the stage and sat down at the table. Wirrel came out, walking easily as a sailor, sat in the chair opposite. Nin felt herself relax, propped an elbow on the back of her chair, grasped a pewter tankard. Baren, an apron over a gray tunic that further hid Hirander's formal clothing, went behind the bar and began wiping mugs.

Lisel uncatched a lever, pulled it, and sandbags drew ropes through well-oiled pulleys; the curtain glided open.

Two young idlers sat in an inn, one with a book in his lap, the other toying with rum and daggers. Outside, a sign of two dice, showing two spots each, flapped in the breeze.

The one with the dagger stabbed it into the tabletop. "So what's your book?"

"Classical verse."

"You mean poetry, I think."

"Poetry, I think, is what poets write. Whatever this fellow may be, he's no poet."

There was a small, almost embarrassed, laugh from the audience.

"Well, read me some verse, then."

" 'To unconceal the mysteries below, and carry milk and honey in a spoon,

" 'Pin the pivot of the calipers, and measure by hand the distance of the moon.' . . . This is pretty rude stuff to be classic."

"I've never seen much classic that wasn't some'at rude, my friend. Gold, the most lasting classic I know, is the pimp of the universe. Or take the two of us: are we not the very Sarcus and Sazen of th' tales, brothers in arms against the world's hazards?"

"Surely we're not such rude fellows as that."

"Given the quantity of rum we have drunk and the quality of the house above our heads, I should consider this evening ill spent if it does not end in a very perfection of rudeness."

More laughter, more felt now.

A messenger stamped into the tavern, tugging a long coat about himself. "One glass of rum, or the heat will prostrate me."

The innkeeper started to pour the drink, then stopped. "It's dead winter out there."

"The mails *are* slow."

A good laugh. The messenger paused just until it peaked, then said, "Good rum, gold rum, douse the candles ere I explode. Oh gods, man, you do not know the difficulties of my commission."

One of the two young men turned his head. "What's your complaint?"

"Alas, master, I am commissioned to carry a letter to a rich man's son, who studies at th'university here: 'You will find him in quiet halls,' so runs my charge, 'holding converse with the ancients; or perhaps in chapel chaste.' Now how is a fellow like meself supposed to find anyone in places like that?"

"Indeed," the other drinker said philosophically, "you could wander there for days and meet no one."

The young man with the book said, "Who is this paragon you seek?"

"Hiron, master, son of Hirander the merchant."

"Ah. I'm the man. Give me the letter."

The messenger left on the crest of the laugh.

* * *

The first act rolled on: the characters made their appearances, presented their cases and states—and then were exposed to the audience as something quite different. Anyone who was confused or irritated by the fact that each actor played three major characters (plus an assortment of tapsters, troopers, potboys, pirates, junior clerks, and hangers-on) kept the matter quiet; each time a player appeared in a new costume there was applause, each time a character's villainy was exposed the hisses were of the politest sort.

During a set change, the actors heard something like a small chime in their heads, and Chitaru's voice something like a soft whisper in their ears: "The Levar," he said, "is laughing."

The act spun and meshed like clockwork, and ended on a high rolling chime of laughter and applause. The curtain closed, but the players kept moving, shifting scenery, changing costume and makeup. There would be no interval until after the end of the next act. Ola Vivar appeared for just a moment, as he had flashed through backstage all during the first act. He barely spoke, just a few words and gestures, but his excitement was obvious: he was wound just as high as the rest of the company.

Seconds before the second-act curtain was due to rise, ola Vivar passed close to Nin, and she caught him, lightly by the arm, not wanting to snag Countess Flara's long red false nails on his velvets. "I want you to know, right now," she said, "that I understand."

"That's good," he said, his voice muffled, his face turned slightly away. She could see that he was wearing makeup, no doubt to back them up in some of the walk-on parts.

"All right," Nin said, "maybe I *don't* understand it all yet. But what I don't understand . . . I accept."

Ola Vivar nodded, pointed at the curtain. "Cues," he said, and pulled away from her.

The curtain slid open on a dockside scene. The musicians played drum and pipe and horn. Baren, as General Maximenes, strutted onstage, leading imaginary battalions 'gainst pike and shot. He stopped, stamped, pivoted to face the audience, and began to sing:

> "Oh, I should have been
> A leader of men
> A right dab hand
> With a mercenary band,
> But I lost my way
> When I heard them say,
> 'Here's your left-right-left!' "

The General illustrated with a befuddled, marching dance step his inability to tell one of his feet from the other.

> "Now, I should have gone
> Where the foe leads on
> And faced them all
> With a load of buck and ball
> But you can't attack
> When you can't keep track
> Of your left-right-left!"

A pair of soldiers appeared behind Maximenes, their uniforms much too gaudy to be anything but fantasies. He pointed his sword at a crate, shouted, "To the right flank, *chaaaarge*!" and proceeded to run to the left. The soldiers went on to the crate without him, vaulted it, and kept running offstage. Maximenes listened for a moment. There was a shot, a groan, a thud. The General winced. Bang, oof, thud. Maximenes shook his head in despair. The audience was roaring. The General spread his arms, raised his sword, and pleaded with the gods of war—

> "Yes, I should be there
> In the hollow square

Where the pikes shine bright
At the storming of the height
And I'd win through, too . . .
If my boots rang true . . .
As a left-right-left-right
Take-another-step-right
Military chap might do!''

Baren bowed to the furiously clapping audience,
sheathed his sword, and turned. Ola Vivar was standing
just offstage, motioning vigorously for Baren to stay
put. Baren hesitated. Ola Vivar rolled his hands over.
Finally he rasped, ''Do an encore, you idiot!''

Baren drew his sword, turned back, and repeated the
last verse of the song. They kept on applauding. Baren
turned again; ola Vivar was gone. He made his exit.

He nearly collided with Nin and Wirrel, as Thillius
the thief and Bibidiel the society matron. Wirrel said,
sounding puzzled, a little hurt, ''That was wonderful,
but why did you do the extra verse? Lisel had already
started to move the scene: you nearly ended up singing
it from the Ambassador's hall.''

''Ola Vivar said—'' Baren shrugged.

''I don't *believe* it,'' Wirrel said, and Nin pulled him
past Baren and toward the stage, which was still echo-
ing with applause.

There were no more audience outbursts as great.
Nothing was wrong; ola Vivar had told them this would
happen. The act started with the General's song and
dance, added in the second tenday of rehearsals, to
''bring the crowd back to life, remind them they're still
at the show. After that, you're going to screw down the
suspense, wind them tighter than a Tichenese clock.
They won't laugh so loud; that's all right. By the time
the act ends, they won't know whether to laugh or jump.
And they won't *breathe* during the interval.''

''How will we know if we're doing it right,'' Lisel
had asked, ''if they're not laughing?''

"You'll know," ola Vivar said, "by their not leaving."

And it seemed that he was right. When the curtain closed, with the whole cast of characters marked for death (some of them several times over), there was a long, still pause, as if no one was quite ready to move, to believe the action had paused—then Chitaru struck a gong, clapped his hands, and filled the auditorium with grainy white magelight, and the sea of people rose in waves of cheering.

Chitaru had strong black tea hot in the dressing stalls, and delicate sugar wafers that brought a rush to the head and left nothing to clot the tongue.

"This is how it feels?" Wirrel said, his hands and shoulders trembling as he slid out of costume, toweled the sweat from his chest and back. "This is how it feels every night?"

"There will be bad nights," Baren said. "We've been lucky so far, but we cannot count on this. We cannot count on anything, but that there *will* be bad nights."

Lisel took Baren's wrist, squeezed it hard, looked up at him. "You're wrong," she said. "They may laugh. They may throw garbage. But there will never be any more bad nights. Never, not ever, ever." She buried her face against his sleeve and wept.

The others clustered around her. "Not yet," Nin said. "Hold it in for one more hour. *Use it*, Lisel." Nin looked up. "Where's Virshon? It should be him saying that."

Wirrel said, "It's what you said before, Nin." He controlled his shaking. "He's afraid. But not for himself. The thing's happening now, out of his control. But you know he's watching." Wirrel gestured at the stage, the dark wings and tower above. "You know he cares. Come on," he said, sounding like a leader, if not a Director. "We've only got a quarter-hour interval, and half of that's gone. Fresh makeup, everybody."

* * *

Ola Vivar heard Wirrel order fresh makeup, and he tried to nod, but it made him begin to sway, the stitching around his collar to rip a little more; he tried to relax. If he held himself rigid, he would tremble, and fall, and die. And he couldn't die yet. It would be bad art.

A hand touched him, pulled him to the narrow catwalk, pushed him against the wall. His knees buckled, but a hand shoved his chest, and the pain shocked him upright.

"Wouldn't want to fall from here," Mnoreon's voice said. "You'd come up a few feet short." The rope was uncoiled from ola Vivar's throat. "Now you'd hit but break; wouldn't bother me a bit, but, well . . ."

Mnoreon moved away. Ola Vivar shifted his weight a bit, but if he moved he would fall, and if he fell he would surely break. He tilted his head, to look through the slit in his hood; Mnoreon was hanging the dummy back in place.

"I've changed my plans for you, Vrrshei," Mnoreon said. "I've learned from you: element of suspense, of surprise." He pointed at the stage. "There are nine deaths in the third act, Vrrshei. You know them all, you planned them. The change to the script is that four of them will be real. But you won't know which, not even after they happen. Every time there's a death cue, you'll wonder, *is this one* . . . *?*" He laughed. "I know what you're thinking. Won't they notice the . . . thinning in their ranks? They haven't noticed that *you're* gone. I'm a very—versatile—versa—"

Mnoreon coughed. He wavered, grabbed the catwalk railing. The dummy danced on its rope. Mnoreon pressed his face against ola Vivar's.

"Please," Krtsotses's voice said, tiny and scratching. "Vrrshei . . . please, help me."

Mnoreon shoved his open hands against ola Vivar's flanks, squeezed. Ola Vivar went rigid with the pain; his eyes squeezed out tears, blood trickled from his mouth.

''You think you have some hope,'' Mnoreon said.
''Perhaps I only let you think that. I cannot make you
suffer for long, so it must be severe. Well, think on
this: I've decided how you're going to die. I want you
to know, I want it to *eat* . . . into your brain.''

He pressed his right forefinger against ola Vivar's
chest, raised his thumb, and dropped flint on steel.
''Bang,'' Mnoreon said.

There was only one shooting in the play. Thillius,
surprised in mid-burgle, shoots his erstwhile employer
the Ambassador dead. Nin would fire the gun.

''Should we really kill all these people?'' Wirrel,
dressed as Doctor Viscusi the assassin, said as Chitaru
erased the light from the auditorium, prepared to open
the curtain. ''I think they're even beginning to like Viscusi. I think *I'm* beginning to like him.''

'' 'Death's a remedy no patient complains of,' '' Nin
said.

''Take my life, woman, but leave me my lines,''
Wirrel said, grinning.

The moment of truth was reached midway through
the first scene, when the Countess pulled the pins from
the booby-trapped bed and strolled onto the balcony.
Her scream was punctuated by the crunch of the thornbush below.

There was one instant's silence, and then a young
woman's voice began laughing from the balcony, and
from the belly. Others began to follow, naturally
enough.

''Eight to go,'' Mnoreon whispered in ola Vivar's
ear. They were beneath the stage again, down in the
thicket of beams, the darkness that left all sounds clear.

''The Levar is laughing,'' Baren said to Lisel, his
eyes bright, and then he hurled open the bedroom door,
howled *''Chaaaaarge!''* and flung himself onto the bed.
The crunch barely slowed the laughter down.

''Seven. You don't suppose someone put a bit of steel
in that bed canopy, do you, Vrrshei?''

Nothing stopped the laughter after that. Instead of meeting upstairs as intended, Honoria had convinced Pancrad to meet her in the formal garden. But Grumbolio's pirate crew, sent out on "a night rather dark by even piratical standards" to abduct the lovely Honoria, snatched the plume-dripping fop instead, and nailed him in a crate bound for "the slimy slothful slavers of the lascivious leeward islands."

"Six. Are there air holes in that box?"

Grumbolio himself, his ship loaded with stolen secrets and maidens fair (wrong on both counts), spots a prize at sea and is far too insistent on the finer points of sail handling. The audience gasped as the pirate flew out of sight, then cheered his floppy boots a-dangle.

"Five. But whose boots are they, Vrrshei?"

Doctor Viscusi met Hirander in a quiet room away from the party (which in fact never appeared on stage, being implied by the musicians playing loudly every time a door was opened), for conversation, intrigue, and a sociable drink. There were two identical glasses on the table; everyone knew one of them was poisoned. Every few seconds, something would distract one of the two, and the other would switch the glasses again, or consider and *not* switch the glasses.

Eventually, eyeing one another warily, they drank, at the last moment hooking arms to sip from each other's glasses. Hirander rose slowly, trembled, leaned against the wall.

"You need not have gone to so much trouble, sir," Viscusi said, polishing his nails on his lapel. "Both glasses were in fact poisoned. I took the antidote an hour ago."

Hirander thudded to the floor. Viscusi opened a closet door, shoved Hirander into it, closed it, and dusted his hands. "We'll find out in a day or so how good the maid service is."

"Four. Do you hear anyone leaving the closet? I can't, can you?"

The next scene was virtually a repeat of the last, with

the Ambassador meeting Viscusi this time. The same glasses, same poison, same maneuverings, same gasp of horror by the Ambassador as he pushed away from the table, same nonchalant confession by the Doctor that both glasses had been spiked.

The Ambassador staggered to the table, picked up a glass, drained it. He stood quite firm. "Actually, Doctor, neither glass was poisoned. I had Thillius poison your antidote *two* hours ago."

Viscusi stiffened, toppled from his chair onto his back, knees still bent in a sitting position. The Ambassador tossed back the carpet, opened the trap in the floor, and shoved the Doctor in.

"Three. You can't see what's over there. You can't tell if it's getting up softly to take its next cue, or just lying there, growing cold. And you won't know, Vrrshei. It's your turn now." He wrapped a black gown of office around ola Vivar, put the cap on his head; it was good enough costuming to hide Lisel's sex, it ought to be good enough for this.

The Ambassador tidied the carpet, brushing it with his fingers, went out. Lisel took a slow, deep breath. She saw Nin was adjusting her thief's costume. No one else was in sight; Wirrel should be coming up from below stage, Baren preparing for the next scene shift, Chitaru getting ready to do the gun effects for the next scene.

Lisel said, "Nin . . . look at my hand."

"What happened? Did the dye run on the carpet?"

"It isn't dye, Nin." She ran a finger through the red stain on her palm.

"You've cut yourself! Have Chitaru, or Baren, see to it at once!"

"I haven't cut myself, Nin. There was blood on the carpet. But it isn't mine. Whose is it?"

Nin said, "Find the Director. Quickly."

She nodded, moved away quietly behind the scenery. Nin tossed her thief's tools over her shoulder, reached for her pistol. Her hand came down on the dressing table. She looked: there it was, just not quite where she thought she'd left it. She picked it up and hurried to meet her cue.

Thillius opened the cabinet, looked at the brass puzzle-lock inside. He tapped his foot in annoyance. "Now, these perilous devices," he told the audience, "are a pox and a scurrilation to honest thieving men. For they have no key-holes, as admits your pick, nor any lever-bolts, as admits your jimmy-bar, and they is ineffably lodged in some great mucking furnitures, as does not easily admit being dropped from a high place onto an obliging rock. It is put forward, by their makers and such other villains, that these things is not subject to being opened by thievery at all, but by *cleverness*, a thing which every gentleman knows your journeyman goods-taker possesses not at all."

Thillius spat into his hands, rubbed them together, and rapped a knuckle, very lightly, against the strong-box. The brass slides shuffled themselves around, and the door swung open with a ping. "Of course," he said, "gentlemen are sometimes wrong."

There was a shuffling behind the door. "Here's disturbance, not to be tolerated," the thief said. "It brings prisonings and hands a'cut off, and other little nuisances." He drew his pistol, cocked it. "And has not my employer told me, 'See that thou be not taken alive?' Well, I vowed that I should not—but neither did I vow to be taken any other way. And vows are not of the exclusive inclusive." He paused. "I had that of a lawyer, cost me twelve coppers."

The door opened. The Ambassador stood there, in robe and cap, quite still. Thillius leveled the gun, looked the Ambassador straight in the eye, and fired. The bang was startlingly loud; people jumped in their seats, and pointed at the blossom of red on black. The Ambassador fell like a sack of meal, and the door swung shut.

Thillius stood entirely still for a moment, his hand still in midair from the recoil of the pistol. "I do believe," he said, turning slowly to face the audience, "that I have just obblicated my employer. . . . Murder's a foul thing, my masters; it brings unemployment." He shrugged, put the gun away, stuffed the papers from the strongbox into his kit, and walked around the wrecked bed (eyeing it once again curiously) to the curtained window. "What else but fly where Fortune flows, when Fortune flees from us: I'll take the loot I labored for, and make my exit—thus." He stepped through the curtains. There was a three-story scream and the crunch of an already burdened thornbush.

Lisel came around the back of the set as the gunsmoke was still rising. The Ambassador was dropped in a bloody heap behind the scenery door, and Locarius was walking indifferently away from him, toward the scenery levers. But that was impossible. *She* was the Ambassador, and Nin was Locarius—but Nin as Thillius had just fired the gun.

She bent over the Ambassador, touched the blood, pushed back the cap from the death-gray face.

"Baren," she said, her voice no more than a whisper because she was backstage, and the performance was going, and she *could not* shout out loud—"Baren? Chitaru? Nin? *Anyone, please?*"

She heard a stage trap opening, and Nin giving her exit lines, and Thillius screaming.

Bibidiel confronted Locarius across what had been Hirander the merchant's office, now empty but for a rifled desk, and on the desk a little sphere of red crystal in a wire holder.

"What do you mean," Bibidiel said, with her supremest imperiousness yet, "they're *gone?*"

Locarius leaned against the wall, trimming his fingernails with a long thin dagger. "Transported, madam. Departed, madam. Off contemplating the world's follies, madam. You know, gone."

"And what of Hirander's fortune? I had a lawful claim upon—"

"Hirander's fortune was kept in an extremely portable form," Locarius said. "You have a lawful claim, but Hiron and Honoria have their hands on the loot. . . ." He pointed at the little red crystal. "Except for that trinket."

Bibidiel snatched the sphere from its holder. "*This* is all that's left?"

"It's not such a terrible thing. It's a nice color . . . goes with your eyes . . . keeps papers from blowing away . . ." Locarius picked up a sheet from the desk, read it idly, then with interest. "And if this is correct, it—"

Bibidiel stared furiously at the crystal in her hand, screamed, *"Shit!"*

An eight-foot-wide cowpat appeared above her head, and dropped like, well, an eight-foot cowpat.

"—grants wishes," Locarius finished quietly.

Bibidiel, covered with brown glop, didn't seem to have heard him. Still clutching the crystal, she ran out of the office. Locarius said, "Do be—"

"Blast!" she howled.

"—careful," he said, as the flash and thunder died away.

The crystal came rolling back through the door, fetching up against Locarius's boot. He picked it up, brushed something unpleasant from it, bounced it in his palm.

"Road?" he said.

A light like dawn shone through the far windows of the office. Locarius opened the door, and beyond him stretched a road to the horizon. He stepped through the doorway, paused, held up the redly luminous crystal in his fist, and looked out at the audience.

"Be well," he said, and shut the door behind him.

The curtains slid shut. The applause began. After a moment, Locarius stepped out, alone, in front of the fabric Red Mask, and the applause died down again. "You will all please excuse me," Mnoreon's voice rang

244 John M. Ford

over the rows, "but I seem to be all that's left here to tell you good night. . . ."

The audience roared with laughter.

"You don't understand," Mnoreon shouted, "they're all—"

The laughter kept rising. People were pointing, shaking. Mnoreon looked to the left.

A pistol poked out from the wing, leveled at him. It fired. Mnoreon looked down, at the red hole in his chest. His legs buckled. He fell, hearing the hysterical laughter of the audience as his head hit the boards, seeing from a crazy angle as Nin il Craith stepped out of the wings and blew smoke from the gun muzzle. Hands took hold of his shoulders, and dragged him away under the curtain. The audience was convulsed.

Wirrel Skye, dressed in a clean blue gown, entered from stage right. "If these encompassed follies brought thee mirth," he said, "why then, we have our duty fair discharged."

Nin spun her pistol on "discharged," getting another laugh, and picked up the line: "And if our speeches offer worth for worth, our purses then must surely be enlarged."

Lisel Solenti came onstage. "Have pity on the player's anxious lot, to scent the wind"—she sniffed at Wirrel, bringing another wave of laughs—"now that our round is shot. . . ."

Baren Baragon pushed the curtains aside, came out holding Mnoreon upright with an arm around his back. "So bring the curtains down on laughing doom, and let your hands' opinions ring the room."

The applause was deafening.

"I . . ." Mnoreon said, too softly to be heard by anyone but the other players, "oh, I . . ." He wobbled and started to fall forward; Baren turned it into a bow by the two of them. The others joined in.

Krtsotses's voice said, "And—the Director?"

"Alive," Wirrel said, "at least so far. And you?"

Krtsotses touched his red-splashed chest, brought his fingers to his nose and mouth. "Strawberry jam?"

Oten Chitaru stepped onto the stage, pressed his palms together, and bowed deeply. A flock of white doves fluttered up from behind him, to vanish like soap bubbles above the heads of the audience.

"He's gone," Krtsotses said. "He's gone, and I'm . . . free."

"Join the party," said Baren Baragon, and they took a bow as a company as the audience rose to its feet cheering.

It was just before midnight. The Red Mask auditorium was empty; once the Levar had gone, most everyone else had quickly followed. The company was on the cleared stage, Baren and Chitaru tending to Virshon ola Vivar, who lay on cushions on the stage, heavily bandaged. Krtsotses was there, Kel il Craith in his new folding wheelchair, and Jemuel, sitting with her hands on her gown-draped knees, a white lotus wilting on her shoulder, and a very sour expression.

"You civilians can have no idea," she said, "how completely unnatural it feels for me not to be arresting someone right now." She slapped her knees, stood up. "But since no one seems to want to charge anyone with anything, and I did not personally witness any of what I am morally certain went on up here, I'm going to go home, and put on sensible clothing, and read a trashy book where all the villains die and the heroes live happily ever after." She started down the steps.

"You can use the alley door," Lisel said.

"*No*, thank you." She paused. "And gods help us all if the Levar should get stagestruck." She went out.

Krtsotses was wringing his hands. He knelt by ola Vivar; Nin moved toward Krtsotses, but ola Vivar looked at her, shook his head.

"I'm not entitled to know," Krtsotses said, "but will you tell me why?"

"Which why?" ola Vivar said, not much above a

whisper. "Why did I let Mnoreon go on? Because the only way to stop him . . . was to kill him. Are you glad I killed him, and not you too?"

Krtsotses nodded.

"Why are my players alive? Ask them."

Baren said, "By the time I was supposed to drink the wine, my stomach was turning over so badly I knew I'd throw up if I took one swallow. So I mimed it."

Lisel put a hand to her collar. "I just couldn't bring myself to really wrap that rope around my neck. So I just looped it over my shoulders in front. I *thought* it went up faster than I did, but it was over too quickly to be sure."

Wirrel said, "I don't know. Ask Chitaru."

The wizard bowed and said, "It is an old Tichenese wizard's custom to alter quantities of working materials, very useful for the removal of undesirables without negative social effects. Having once been manipulated into transforming a water commissioner into a sassafras tree, I am constantly concerned with the materials in my spells." He smiled at Krtsotses. "You should not have added *quite* so much ground metal to the lightning bolide. As adulterated, little would have been left of the theatre."

Nin said to Krtsotses, "I'm alive because you caught me just as I stepped into the trap. Thank you."

Krtsotses bowed his head. "It was—what I could do."

Ola Vivar said, "As for why I am here, that is entirely because Nin il Craith—" He moved a hand down to the thick bandage on his left flank. "—missed."

Kel said, "*Missed?* From five paces?"

Nin glared at him, and then chuckled with tears in it.

Ola Vivar said, "Chitaru, will you take five levars from the receipts box and give it to Krtsotses?"

The wizard did so. Krtsotses stared as the coins were counted into his hand. Ola Vivar said, "Understudies receive half wages for the rehearsal period. The other

payment we will consider a gift. Goodbye, Krtsotses.''
He said something in a language none of the players
understood; Krtsotses responded, bowed to everyone,
and left the theatre.

Lisel said "My lord Director—"

"Mnoreon was a fine actor," ola Vivar said,
"Krtsotses is not. No, Lisel, he could not stay with
us.''

"What did you say to him?" Wirrel said.

"A phrase from the country where we were born.
'May you find a role that suits your talents.' "

Nin said, "That's a pretty farewell.''

"Farewell, nothing. It's a curse.'' Ola Vivar
coughed. "I think I should go home now. We have
another performance in a fiveday.''

"*We* do," Baren said. "You're lucky to be alive.''

Nin said to her brother, "Kel, I—"

"I know, Nin," Kel said, his foot pressed hard
against the floor, his fingers tangled in his lap. "I've
known for an awfully long time. I love you very, very
much, but I don't need your help, or money, or anything.''

"I'm taking you at your word.''

He nodded. "The Lis are waiting for me outside.
I'm sure they'll let you use their coach.'' He pushed
his chair toward the door.

"I think I have something to say in this," ola Vivar
said.

"You've done nothing *but* talk," Nin said.

"Get them away from here.''

The others moved back. Ola Vivar said, "I'll make
you hate me. The more I need your help, the harder
I'll try. Words are the one place I'm strong: I'll kill
you with words, Nin.''

"Maybe you will," she said.

"And then who will keep my theatre alive?''

She said to the others, "Will you help me carry him
out?''

"Allow me, mistress," Chitaru said, and closed his

eyes for a moment; ola Vivar rose into the air, hovering at waist height. "It will last for an hour or so." He and Nin moved ola Vivar off the stage, toward the door.

"Baren," Lisel said, "will you take me home, please? With you."

Baren held out his hand. Lisel took it in both of hers, leaned against him. Baren touched her head, tilted it up. "Not like that," he said.

"Yes, of course, you're right," Lisel said, and straightened up. Side by side, just holding hands, they walked out of the theatre.

Chitaru came back in through the alley door, went to his corner, and began packing his equipment, rolling wands and props in colored silks and packing them into his leather rucksack. At the sound of a footstep he looked up, moving his hands, saying, "I warn you, sir or madam, I have some practical powers—oh, Master Wirrel, it is you. I had thought you had gone with the others."

"Not yet, Master Dramaturge."

"Well. I'm glad I saw you. The Director has asked me to start double-locking the rear door; you might have been locked in." He jingled the keys. "Are you ready to leave now? Perhaps we could have the drink you spoke of. Celebrate."

"I was wondering, Chitaru . . . would you let me have those? Let me lock the place up?"

Chitaru said, "Of course, Master Wirrel. You will put out all the lights before you go?"

"I'll be sure to."

Chitaru tossed the keys. They executed a loop in midair, flared with rainbow light, and fluttered down slowly into Wirrel's open palm. Chitaru laughed like a delighted child, clapped his hands, pulled the strings to close his bag. "Good night to you, then, master," he said, and bowed. "Next performance in a fiveday?"

"In a fiveday," Wirrel Skye said, and returned the bow.

Chitaru went out into the alley. The door clanged

shut. Wirrel gave the keys a toss and caught them, then walked onto the stage.

He sat down on the edge of the stage, between the still-glowing footlights, his feet over the edge. He looked into the dark house. No one was there.

He was a star of a play, but the play was over, and there was no one there.

He could find someone, of that there was no doubt at all. Some young woman from the country would see the lights, see him in the lights; that was really all it took.

Beside him, the lamps had burned nearly out. Wirrel swung his legs back and forth, looking out at the empty theatre, wondering what roof he would be under come dawn, knowing a dozen plays by heart and having no idea in the world what his next line might be.

He got to his feet. Moving as quickly as he could, he snuffed the lights, stumbled through the dark back-stage, went through the stage door, and fumbled the keys into its lock; he began sprinting up the alley, the way that Chitaru had gone. If he hurried, he could catch the wizard, and they would find a place with people in it; they would celebrate. If he hurried, there was still time.

BESTSELLING BOOKS FROM TOR

☐	58341-8	ANGEL FIRE by Andrew M. Greeley	$4.95
☐	58342-6		Canada $5.95
☐	58338-8	THE FINAL PLANET by Andrew M. Greeley	$4.95
☐	58339-6		Canada $5.95
☐	58336-1	GOD GAME by Andrew M. Greeley	$4.50
☐	58337-X		Canada $5.50
☐	50105-5	CITADEL RUN by Paul Bishop	$4.95
☐	50106-3		Canada $5.95
☐	58459-7	THE BAREFOOT BRIGADE by Douglas C. Jones	$4.50
☐	58460-0		Canada $5.50
☐	58457-0	ELKHORN TAVERN by Douglas C. Jones	$4.50
☐	58458-9		Canada $5.50
☐	58364-7	BON MARCHE by Chet Hagan	$4.95
☐	58365-5		Canada $5.95
☐	50773-8	THE NIGHT OF FOUR HUNDRED RABBITS	$4.50
☐	50774-6	by Elizabeth Peters	Canada $5.50
☐	55709-3	ARAMINTA STATION by Jack Vance	$4.95
☐	55710-7		Canada $5.95
☐	52126-9	VAMPHYRI! by Brian Lumley (U.S. orders only)	$4.50
☐	52166-8	NECROSCOPE by Brian Lumley (U.S. orders only)	$3.95

Buy them at your local bookstore or use this handy coupon:
Clip and mail this page with your order.

Publishers Book and Audio Mailing Service
P.O. Box 120159, Staten Island, NY 10312-0004

Please send me the book(s) I have checked above. I am enclosing $_____
(please add $1.25 for the first book, and $.25 for each additional book to
cover postage and handling. Send check or money order only—no CODs.)

Name _____

Address _____

City _____ State/Zip _____

Please allow six weeks for delivery. Prices subject to change without notice.

THE BEST IN SCIENCE FICTION

☐	54989-9	STARFIRE by Paul Preuss	$3.95
☐	54990-2		Canada $4.95
☐	54281-9	DIVINE ENDURANCE by Gwyneth Jones	$3.95
☐	54282-7		Canada $4.95
☐	55696-8	THE LANGUAGES OF PAO by Jack Vance	$3.95
☐	55697-6		Canada $4.95
☐	54892-2	THE THIRTEENTH MAJESTRAL by Hayford Peirce	$3.95
☐	54893-0		Canada $4.95
☐	55425-6	THE CRYSTAL EMPIRE by L. Neil Smith	$4.50
☐	55426-4		Canada $5.50
☐	53133-7	THE EDGE OF TOMORROW by Isaac Asimov	$3.95
☐	53134-5		Canada $4.95
☐	55800-6	FIRECHILD by Jack Williamson	$3.95
☐	55801-4		Canada $4.95
☐	54592-3	TERRY'S UNIVERSE ed. by Beth Meacham	$3.50
☐	54593-1		Canada $4.50
☐	53355-0	ENDER'S GAME by Orson Scott Card	$3.95
☐	53356-9		Canada $4.95
☐	55413-2	HERITAGE OF FLIGHT by Susan Shwartz	$3.95
☐	55414-0		Canada $4.95

Buy them at your local bookstore or use this handy coupon:
Clip and mail this page with your order.

Publishers Book and Audio Mailing Service
P.O. Box 120159, Staten Island, NY 10312-0004

Please send me the book(s) I have checked above. I am enclosing $_____
(please add $1.25 for the first book, and $.25 for each additional book to
cover postage and handling. Send check or money order only — no CODs.)

Name _____

Address _____

City _____ State/Zip _____

Please allow six weeks for delivery. Prices subject to change without notice.

THE TOR DOUBLES

Two complete short science fiction novels in one volume!

☐ 53362-3 A MEETING WITH MEDUSA by Arthur C. Clarke and $2.95
  55967-3 GREEN MARS by Kim Stanley Robinson   Canada $3.95

☐ 55971-1 HARDFOUGHT by Greg Bear and $2.95
  55951-7 CASCADE POINT by Timothy Zahn   Canada $3.95

☐ 55952-5 BORN WITH THE DEAD by Robert Silverberg and $2.95
  55953-3 THE SALIVA TREE by Brian W. Aldiss   Canada $3.95

☐ 55956-8 TANGO CHARLIE AND FOXTROT ROMEO $2.95
  55957-6 by John Varley and   Canada $3.95
           THE STAR PIT by Samuel R. Delany

☐ 55958-4 NO TRUCE WITH KINGS by Poul Anderson and $2.95
  55954-1 SHIP OF SHADOWS by Fritz Leiber   Canada $3.95

☐ 55963-0 ENEMY MINE by Barry B. Longyear and $2.95
  54302-5 ANOTHER ORPHAN by John Kessel   Canada $3.95

☐ 54554-0 SCREWTOP by Vonda N. McIntyre and $2.95
  55959-2 THE GIRL WHO WAS PLUGGED IN   Canada $3.95
           by James Tiptree, Jr.

Buy them at your local bookstore or use this handy coupon:
Clip and mail this page with your order.

Publishers Book and Audio Mailing Service
P.O. Box 120159, Staten Island, NY 10312-0004

Please send me the book(s) I have checked above. I am enclosing $_____
(please add $1.25 for the first book, and $.25 for each additional book to
cover postage and handling. Send check or money order only — no CODs.)

Name _____

Address _____

City _____ State/Zip _____

Please allow six weeks for delivery. Prices subject to change without notice.